IF A
TREE
FALLS

SAP'S STORY

Cover and internal design by New Found Books Australia Pty Ltd

New Found Books Australia Pty Ltd
www.newfoundbooks.au

ISBNs as follows:
Paperback — 9781923172340
ebook — 9781923172463
hardback — 9781923172586

Distributed by New Found Books Australia Distribution and Lightning Source Global

A catalogue record for this work is available from the National Library of Australia

More great New Found Books Australia titles can be found at:
www.newfoundbooks.au/our-titles/

JOHN HOWLEY

IF A
TREE
FALLS

SAP'S STORY

To My Sailor Dad,
and Sailor Brother.

CHAPTER 1

At the edge of the forest, in the shadow of a mighty mountain range, grew a remarkable tree. She was the child of a species called Eucalyptus, and her name was Sap.

The deep, dark night was passing, and the early morning mists rose and danced across the clearing, eddying about the moss-covered rocks, and licking at Sap's trunk. The dawn light crept across the glade, washing up against a tall and broad, silver-barked tree, standing where the sapling had stood the night before.

From her new altitude at the crest of the ridge, Sap serenely considered her surroundings, slowly absorbing the events of the night before. The storm, with its thunder and lightning, and her introduction to water. Breeze, which the night before had carried Rain in her arms, now caressed Sap. Her touch caused Sap's leaves to spin this way and that, bowing her limbs, relaxing, then pushing gently again, waving her spectacular array of branches back and forth in a dervish-like dance, at peace in the hub of movement.

The Sun rose vaguely through the mist, glowing softly on the glen and smiling, sweet as treacle on Sap's face and branches, intoxicating her, enticing her to reach up and touch her golden face, to open her arms to her light, spreading branches wide to embrace her, to hold her close.

Sap stretched higher and higher, feeling the raw power flow through her, golden rays of power charging her leaves, sending her roots deeper, feeling the elixir of life, Earth's blood, soak through her thin cellulose legs like dark chocolate, enriching her blood, filling, and expanding the young tree in every dimension. As her senses expanded she shivered, feeling the caress sweep across her bark.

'Dance with me,' whispered the breeze. 'Dance and spin with me. Dance and sing with me. I bring you life, breath, a taste of other skies, other lands.'

As Sap danced, the World danced, and Wind whispered of secret things. Freedom of passage, the power of the oceans, the parched vastness of the deserts, and the cold, majestic magnificence of the mountains. Sap could taste flavours on the air, the salt tang of the oceans, the cool clarity of the mountains, and the gritty desert heat.

She felt the exquisite freedom of Air's ability to be within and without all things, everywhere, and she was not alone.

'We join with you,' sighed the Forest.

'We dance with you,' whispered the Wind.

'We feel you,' swelled the Oceans.

Sap pulsed with the breathing of the earth, She moved with the giants of the forest, the tallest trees joining the dance, weaving, and swaying, passing the chorus across the hills so that the horizons shimmered. Limbs and leaves, rocks and ridges, waves and rainbows played a symphony around the planet.

'Welcome,' called the Wind, 'Welcome to the song, Sap, offspring of Grandis the strong, we wish your singing to be long and joyous.'

'I grow with the strength of my Family' sang Sap, revelling in the oneness she felt with the world.

With the turn of a leaf or the shift of a limb, Sap noticed a rise or a fall in the pitch of the song. As she adjusted the edge of a leaf, the song quivered and sustained a chord, the harmonies weaving through, fascinating her with the shift and hum of the forest. Sap played the breeze, feeling her song join the chorus, rise a little, like a bubble on foam, under some vast waterfall, then float away to be absorbed by the greater song, adding that extra note, by which all knew the choir was swelled by yet another voice.

The song continued through the day and into the evening, joining all of Earth's forests, from the high northern coniferous realms to the ever-moving forests of kelp, deep in the dark fastness of the world's oceans.

The song became one voice, sharing the turning of the planet, and trailing out through the stars as a murmur of life, a sparkling rejoinder with the rest of creation.

'This is the healing/creating song of the universe,' a voice beautifully reverberated within Sap's consciousness.

The voice became a mist which shifted enticingly across the glen, dancing amongst the trees and grasses, always humming softly, sweetly gathering Sap's attention. The soft shape swayed before Sap and gradually took the form of an ancient Antarctic beech tree. Garlanded with mosses and lichen, from crown to root, ornamented and cascading, this tree appeared to be a living relic of those who ruled that primordial continent of Gondwana, five hundred million years ago.

The timbre and tone of the voice softened.

'I am your mother, Sap, and many call me Gaia, I am the heart and spirit of the Earth-planet, I speak for all beings on Earth, and indeed the Earth Herself, for all are my children, and all are part of me.'

'I am the mother who has gathered ice and dust from the heavens, and I have woven them upon my starry loom, into a living fabric that is this world.'

'Nurtured by the warm glow of Sol, My Brother, this world has grown lush and beautiful, enabling countless life forms the opportunity to grow and develop souls.'

Sap, transfixed, listened with each cell and fibre, captivated, as the dripping and draping mosses shifted around the ancient Beech.

Sap witnessed stream upon stream of different life forms arriving and disappearing, rising from the ooze, occupying the land momentarily, then sinking, to rise in another form. All of them briefly populating a spinning planet over which the land masses floated, grinding against each other, and disappearing, across the eons.

Gaia continued, 'We have arrived at a critical time in this planets evolution, Sap.'

'Since creation, We, the Souls and Spirits of the Stars and Planets, have been closely observing the constant growth and genesis of this World. Between growth and renewal there has been balance maintained, until this present era.'

'We are now witnessing the desecration and the potential destruction of all life on this, our beloved Earth.'

Gaia's voice softened, allowing a deep sadness to seep through.

'The damage grinds and destroys, ever onward, over sea, over land and in the air, defeating all efforts to halt it; and so, in response, we must reveal ourselves to the authors of the destruction.'

Sap sensed the hardening of Gaia's sentiment, eclipsing Her sadness.

'Human beings, my own wayward children, believing they are the heirs to this world, continue to dig and delve, not understanding that by removing the very elements that support the structure of the land beneath their feet, they generate Earthquakes, Volcanic eruptions, and rising sea levels.'

'Once the Earths balance factors, these are now often driven by Human interference!'

'They create that, which Humanity fears most.'

'Storms, Cyclones and Typhoons; Tornados, Wildfires, and Tidal Waves, subtle depleting energies, like Drought, Famine, and Bitter Winters.'

The Beech Tree Gaia shook with annoyance, rippling her mosses and lichens. Sap had no experience of Human Beings, but imagined them to be large and powerful like trees, or mountains, especially if they were strong enough to affect this world. She could not understand why a being living, would want to destroy their home.

Gaia shared a vision with Sap, weaving pollen grains and light, creating a galaxy within the glade; within the galaxy, a solar system, then growing and almost filling the clearing, a small, fragile, blue and green planet, floating below a ceiling of white cloud, turning gracefully across a sparkling canvas of stars. Swarming across the surface was the expanding race of human beings.

'This world we all share, is losing the ability to communicate with herself, to contribute experience and insight with those powers that could possibly destroy her; to enable the healing to overcome the hurt.'

'It is time for Humanity to be re-educated. Sap, my beloved tree, you are the world and myself woven into being. Your purpose is to heal all, and once again bind Humanity and Nature, restoring Earth to One World, above and below, within and without.'

Gaia continued ...

'The human universe, every thriving and fading being, walking, crawling, swimming, and flying, above and below the ground recognises that deep in their DNA lies an ancient music. That song will once again ring out across the World to sing it into harmony.'

To Sap's limited experience, The Giant Tree seemed to diminish a little, and Gaia's voice, though ageless and infinite, seemed somehow weary, as She continued narrating the vision.

'The Intelligence that is all existence, all time and space, that which resonates in all existence, of whom I am a small part, has chosen." "It is time!" Gaia's soft voice intoned in the souls of all beings.

'It is time.'

Inuit Eskimos in Alaska heard Her, Indians in the Amazon jungle heard Her, Tuvan herders on the Western Sayan Mountains, beyond the great Himalayas, heard Her. Australian Aboriginal people at Uluru heard Her.

Every being living close to the Earth heard Gaia give the planet notice. Regrettably, Office buildings, busy traffic, satellites, Wi-Fi, radio and television signals interfere with the conversation going on constantly between the planet and its inhabitants, and so, not all people heard Her.

Gaia's words were lost amongst the audience she most needed to reach, the people who seemed to consume the Earth's resources most, and who were blithely unaware of where those resources came from or how finite they were.

Gaia spoke gently to Sap now, knowing the burden She was about to place upon the young tree.

'Throughout the ages, Sap, great beings have roamed the Earth with the purpose of cultivating reverence, or deep respect, among the people; it is beyond time Humans learned the same respect for the other beings sharing this world.'

'Our hopes all rest upon you, Sap. You will approach humanity from nature's perspective, you have been given the deep understanding of mountains, the empathy of oceans, and the compassion of the air.'

'You alone will be able to tell our tale of shared dependence of the Earth.'

'But, be aware, Sap, in exchange for these gifts we require great sacrifice. You will change into forms strange to you, but familiar to humans.'

'You will be held by them and become part of them.'

'You, dear Sap, are this planet's only hope for salvation, for only through this giving of yourself can we enter human society and effect the change we so desperately need.'

'Believe in love ... the great energy that binds all things ... Remember me in dark times'

And with that, the great tree was gone.

CHAPTER 2

Sap's mind filled with visions: she was a spinning green and blue sphere, caught in the light of a fiery sun, on a stage of sparkling stars. The character of cloud became her. As fine mist, she clouded the Earth, caressing the mountain peaks, until the weight overcame her, and she rained from the heavens, saturating the forests and valleys, pooling in gullies and low meadows.

Sap's soul melted into the ground, and in vivid dreams she was the earth herself, the soil, the rocks, clay, and granite. Sap dreamed on, that she spent a billion years as the earth, and the roots of the forest gradually absorbed her, awaiting rebirth as, herself!

Aah ... She recognised the familiar feel of bark on her limbs, the heady sensation of sappy sugars channelling upwards through her body. Her body? Sap's body felt oddly, strangely, different somehow. Slowly she realised she was all trees, all earth, all water, all pieces of the jigsaw puzzle we call life.

The dawn came in a spectacular shower of musical notes, trilled from one of Sap's upper branches. Birds of every imaginable colour, shape and size crowded the limbs of the enormous eucalypt giant, Eucalyptus Grandis, Sap had become.

She felt the weight and presence of herself and opened her heart to the language of the forest dwellers and understood, how, over countless generations, the offspring of the mountains become the rocks, the children of the rocks become the soil, and how they depended on each other. Our tree was flooded with waves of information, emotion, and experience. Sap felt what the forest felt, knew what the forest knew, and remembered what the forest remembered.

The scene before her was dusted with fading stars and washed by an eastern glow. Reds and golds flooded across the deep blue curtain, dissolving the display of diamonds, as vast streaks of bright pink cloud swept across the sky.

'In the beginning, the stars were all that existed,' Gaia's voice said, close to Sap. 'They existed as one star. This star then shared Herself with the emptiness. Expanding in every dimension, she reached out to embrace all of space and sparkled colours beyond the range of rainbows, the children that sprang from her numbered in their billions, from one side of heaven to the other.'

'The stars are light, Sap, many stars you believe you see each evening simply do not exist, yet their light continues to shine, light which trickles down through the ages, continuing to sustain life in all its forms.'

'You also, are light, Sap. You have the sun in your eyes and the moon and stars in your blood. Your trunk, the body you inhabit, is earth and water consisting of a phenomenal crowd of energies, working, and playing in harmony, to create the tune we call Sap.

'This tune plays out its existence in the time and space allotted to it, as all the players come and go, contributing to the song that is the Universe.'

CHAPTER 3

The day began badly for Fernyvale farmer, Tom Daily. Looking down at his new Kubota tractor, Tom regretted his decision to cross what normally was a shallow ford, on the track to the back paddock, as muddy water surged across the bright red bonnet, bubbling up and around the motor, revealing blue enamel occasionally visible through the dirty, brown foam,

Cautious of the soft edge of the still bubbling creek , he leaned forward and appraised the damage, beginning to consider contingency plans for rescuing his vehicle. He took a couple of long strides across the sodden, muck-filled tyre tracks to look at his predicament from a different angle.

Perhaps the winch will haul her out, Tom thought. *All I need is a tree or rock, solid enough to take the weight of the tractor, plus the mud and water, for a short time.*

He stood up slowly and considered what had happened. *Odd,* he thought, *how could the creek rise so fast, must have been a flash flood upstream. Maybe a result of that storm last night in the mountains?*

Tom was as still as the air around him. He sensed more than an overnight rainstorm was at play here. He looked for an elusive purpose or reason for the sudden change in the flow of a creek he thought he knew well.

Today his senses were prickling, the 'ken' he inherited from his Romani granny, was buzzing at the back of Tom's head. The water sprites in the creek studied Tom as they gurgled past, and she-oaks along the banks of the swollen water source watched as he considered his course of action.

The breeze stilled, and rested in the little hollow with the man, his machine, and all of nature looking on. *An anchor is what I need, something so solidly part of the hill she won't move when I place stress on her.*

He immediately excluded the mossy, grey boulders strewn across the face of the hill, from the equation; they were far too unstable. Then his vision narrowed and focused on the tall, solid strength of the eucalypt standing at the edge of the forest, fronting the brow of the hill.

Standing taller than every other tree on the ridge, and broader than his tractor at the trunk, Sap dominated her setting in the little valley. All Tom could see was this beautiful creature of wood and leaf, this 'World Tree,' filling his senses, as all other sights and sounds disappeared from his world.

As Tom focused, the bark of the tree faintly began to shift and flow into itself, like eddies in a current of deep, dark water. Bark and surface markings were lost in the whirl and twist of colour running the length of Sap's trunk.

Tom was so immersed in the hypnotic effect of the tree in front of him, he was unaware he had crossed the creek and climbed the face of the ridge to stand directly eye to trunk with the tree.

Sap drew him into her world, a cool green world, of peace and stillness and strength.

'Use me,' she whispered. 'I am strong, I am here, I am yours. I am nature, and I am all around you, human, I have the power to lift your vehicle clear of the water. Use me, work with me, and together, we will change the world.'

Tom Daily stood as still as a statue, his head cocked to one side, listening within: a technique his Gran taught him as a young child.

The surface of the tree shifted again, becoming a mirror, reflecting Tom back on himself, with the hillside, the creek, the tractor, and the rest of the forest as backdrop. Then the colours began to run. As they flowed into each other, Tom became the tractor, the creek ran in the lines of his face, his hair was as wild and expansive as the blue-green forest behind him.

His arms became huge, grey-barked tree limbs, he felt the blood of the earth pump through his veins and throughout his body.

In the core of this cyclone of change, Tom was as still as the tree before him, a man frozen in time, while within, each cell of his body churned and expanded in dimensions uncharted. The cellular structure of the man expanded into the light spectrum and beyond.

Physically nothing changed, but the man touched the rim of the cosmos with his presence. He saw the universe exploding at the dawn of time, countless galaxies wheeling through the vastness of space. He witnessed the effects of every action, creating ripples in the fabric of the universe, spiralling outwards in every direction to affect beings and destinies far beyond the wildest of Tom's dreams.

With this vision seeded by Sap and Gaia, taking root in his fertile mind, Tom became fully aware of what was occurring. In this state, Tom Daily had the perspective of a God.

He had a part to play in this drama, to save a planet and her people, and walked with a new sense of purpose back to the tractor to weave his destiny into the new pattern of life on planet Earth.

The stink of diesel fumes filled the gully with its blue haze and acrid tang, while the scream of the winch at the front of the tractor reverberated around the clearing.

The steel cable, wrapped about Sap's trunk, tightened slowly, cutting deeply, tearing at the bark. Splintering the softer timber beneath, the vicious metal strands dug deep into the flesh of the tree and gripped, crushing the wood under its tightening bonds. The tractor roared and dug its huge, black-patterned wheels into the soft mud and sand of the creek bed.

Shuddering her protest, the cap of the exhaust, was a manic percussionist, snapping and barking its blue breath, while the juddering and lurching bonnet of the tractor, red paint looking like a bubble of blood, rose under the litter of debris from her trauma, and lumbered up from the creek bed.

Like a red whale breaching in some great ocean, the tractor breasted the muddy water, cascades of foam, sticks, and leaves spilling from her bonnet. With the symphony of metal against metal, screaming and venting its angst against wood, the beast collided with the steep, rocky bank.

Boulders and earth tumbled in a landslide down into the water, crushed and churning in mucky slurry beneath the front wheels of the slowly rising machine. Now the entire weight of the tractor, plus several tonnes of earth and water, were hauling violently against the trunk of the tree.

Small pebbles crumbled beneath Sap's toes, the tightly packed soil between her roots cracked and collapsed upon itself, and at last the hillside began to shift.

As she buckled and teetered at the edge of endurance, Sap regarded the two clouds hovering above her, in a pristine, blue sky. Her roots heaved upwards in an explosion of soil and grass showering the hillside with shrapnel.

Tom gazed in awe as the giant eucalypt whipped backwards, then teetered forward, dangerously, precariously. Seeking cover behind the steering column of the tractor, and striving to avoid the rain of debris already hammering the red bonnet, he heard a screeching, ear splitting wailing, rise from the direction of the hillside. As he watched, the great tree parted from the earth, twisting, and cracking limbs, sending half the hillside spinning wildly into the sky.

Broken branches, twigs, bark, and leaves rained down around the lonely looking figure, seated high upon the now resurrected vehicle, but Tom had ceased to seek shelter, overwhelmed with the spectacle before him.

He had felt every bite and tug of the cable; every splintering branch was a limb Tom had known as an extension of his own body, the body that was now careering towards the ground with one long, last, submissive groan.

Sap hit the ground with a shudder that quivered her entire length, bounced twice, billowing clouds of dust and fragments, then settled, still as a painting, sprawled across the grassy knoll she'd once commanded with such nobility.

Tom was already out of his seat and racing through the slowly settling haze of destruction, to halt at the first branches, trailing their wreath of leaves in wild abandon across the site. He stood, hands dangling at his sides, helpless, looking down on the wreckage at his feet.

'It is not over,' a voice whispered in Tom's mind. 'This story is just beginning. I am yours, and you are mine, Tom Daily, we are now one story. We are begun.'

Tom's intuition washed over him like a shower of windblown blossoms in a spring storm. He felt the breeze stroke his cheek like a reassuring hand, felt the solid earth beneath his feet. In touch, again with the elements, Tom was washed clean, newly baptised, refreshed, restored, and ready to set out on the new adventure.

With a farmer's pragmatism, he set to work, mentally measuring the weight of the tree, accessing for vehicles to haul her out, considering the extent of trimming he had before him, when his cell phone interrupted the task.

'Tom Daily,' Tom responded, swinging the phone earwards.

'Tommy, It's Trev. Trevor Manning, from the mill, G'day!'

'G'day Trev, what's up?' Tom felt the hairs on the back of his neck stand on end, he knew what was up, and was pretty much aware of why Trevor had called.

'Tommy, I hear you've dropped a fair-sized tree, and I figured you might need some help. With the removal and clean up, I mean. It would be to both our advantages,' Trevor hastily added. 'I'll go you 50/50 with the timber, and I'll mill you up any size you want.'

'Trev, look, ah, thanks for the call. Can you tell me how you heard about the tree?'

'I can't exactly say, Tom,' Trevor replied, 'I was out in the yard stocktaking, when I heard this thunder in the distance, up the valley towards your place, and then, well, then, I sort of saw the tree fall.'

'I guess. I imagined I saw you and a fallen giant flooded gum, up the back of the range, and I just knew. You know what they say: "If a tree falls in the Forest, does anybody hear?" Well, I guess they do!'

There was silence from the phone. Only the sound of Tom breathing punctuated the stillness. 'Hey, I know it sounds crazy, but I just knew. Everybody here, they just knew, like they'd been there. I'm right, aren't I? You have a tree that needs milling?'

'Yes, there's a tree here all right,' Tom eventually replied. 'She's a beauty. Flooded gum, I think, over eighty metres. Up in the back forty, over Murphy's creek, and close to the track.'

Trevor Manning had owned the local timber mill for over thirty years. His dad had milled timber for Tom's parents, and for most of the landowners in the area, as far back as anyone could remember. Everyone knew and trusted the man.

As he closed the phone, Tom sat astride the great tree, pondering her future. *What could he use the wood for*? he wondered.

Too good for building, it would have to be something special, he thought. He felt a kinship with the tree, and considered some special feature in a home. *Perhaps some furniture?*

As an image of a beautiful dark wooden desk formed in his mind. Tom could almost feel the presence of the writer at the desk, he could hear the pencil scratching its way across the paper's surface, leaving an almost indiscernible ghost of a story on the wood. Tom shook his head, took off his hat, and wiped his brow with the back of his hand. He breathed deeply, focused once again on the task at hand. 'Come on, Tommy, back to the real world.'

CHAPTER 4

Tom had grown up in the small community of Fernyvale, had gone to school here and knew most of the tradespeople and artisans that called this valley home. As he sat astride the motionless bulk of Sap, considering her purpose, the vision of the desk sprang to mind, complete with the impression of the skill and tools required to make this apparition a reality.

One person came to mind, an extraordinary craftsman and artist, who'd settled in the vale early in the 70s, hoping to heal the scars of war that had haunted him. He practised his trade and lived peacefully with his family on a small farm at the head of the valley.

Jimmy Pringle was the only craftsman Tom knew who could incorporate the living energy of the tree into the vision he had witnessed. There was no finer woodworker, with an intuitive eye for the soul of wood, and perceptive listening skills attuned to timber, not only in the district, but in this country and abroad. James Pringle was an artisan of the highest order.

James was descended from a long, long line of artisans and artists. His Great-Great Grandfather Patrick had arrived from Ireland on the sailing ship *Hesperus* in 1856, to escape the great

Irish famine. His ancestor, long before that, had been the royal carver and throne-maker for the High-King of Eire, as that ancient land had once been called.

The art that James Pringle produced, in the guise of everyday furniture, was unique in every sense. They were sculpted creatures, existing as living works of art, a breath away from movement.

These desks, chairs, tables, and even the quiet ruddy/gold slabs of oiled timber that rested in his seasoning racks for up to six years, were alive, hibernating, slower pulse alive, but alive and watching the world go by, waiting for a chance to share with the world this sacred gift they shared with James.

James Pringle's workshop felt and heard Sap fall. The furniture, the craftsman, the leadlight windows high in the alcoves above, resonated with the news, and like the ringing of a wonderful bell, the tolling rang around and within the world, across her many surfaces and down to the core, ringing true in some, though unheard by many.

In James' small office, the telephone rang persistently. Happily unaware of the incessant jingling, James softly sanded a gentle curve along the arm of a seductively comfortable looking armchair.He stood up momentarily to stretch and splayed his arms wide behind him unravelling knots.

The strident tones of the telephone intruded upon his meditative state. James sighed, and moved lightly towards the wood and glass partition that housed his office.

'Yes, James Pringle here,' James answered, sliding comfortably into an ancient leather chair.

He immediately recognised Tom Daily's farmer's drawl. 'G'day James, it's Tom Daily, how's the family?' Tom and James' sixteen-year-old daughters shared the local bus ride to school and both were in Year ten at Fernyvale High School.

'Yeah, the family's fine, thanks, Tom. What's on your mind?'

'Well, I've got a bit of a project for you if you've got the time available. I thought of you as soon as Trevor called me from the mill.'

'It's a little unusual, though I imagine right up your alley.'

Tom knew James well. They had grown up together in the village of Fernyvale, and spent a considerable number of summers together, camping and fishing in the bush.

'I've dropped a tree in the back paddock, Jim. Flooded Gum, I think. I didn't really want to bring her down; I was bogged with the tractor, and I had to use the winch. The rest is history.'

'Look mate, I reckon trees choose their time. Who are we mere mortals to second-guess them? But, I must tell you, we already knew. The dust shook off the rafters here, as she hit the ground at your place. Talk about "When a tree falls in the forest."'

Tom couldn't help but wonder about Trevor's earlier remark. 'Everyone hears, it seems. Trevor said they already knew down at the mill. What do you make of it, Jim?' Tom was fully aware of the double entêndre.

'Well, I'll have to have a listen to her, and see what she feels comfortable in. Flooded gum, you think? Um, hardwood?'

James visualised the rich red heartwood, and the skin tones that shared the grain out to the ghost grey edges of useable timber. 'We might coax out a piece of furniture, or two, if she's as big as I sense she is. By the way, get Trev to hold on to the bark and chip the cut-offs, Mai's got her own industry happening out in the shed, uses every bit of waste I produce. Between herself and the kids, she has set up this great little papermaking business, shredding and pulping whatever timber leavings they can find. Beautiful paper it is too, no bleach involved, no nasty chemicals, and you can really feel the tree in it, see the colours of the bark.'

'It seems there's quite a market for what they call "boutique" stationery. What with cards and specialist art and letter kits, the girls are doing quite well, thank you.'

Tom smiled at James' enthusiasm for his wife's industry and creativity. Mai-Li was the apple of James' eyes.

Different now from the frightened waif that arrived with James when he returned from the war in Vietnam in 75. Confident, beautiful, and clever. James was a lucky man, and blessed with two beautiful daughters.

'All right, my friend, we'll save what we can so your lady can keep you in luxury. Meanwhile, I'll work out with Trevor what we can comfortably mill up.'

Sap had spent the night discovering a new perspective. From where she lay, on the side of the hill, the sky filled her dreams.

The two clouds she remembered seeing when she fell were still there, hovering above her amongst her glimpses of the stars. A breath of cloud spiralled down towards the supine tree and touched her already sagging branches.

'We are your link to the stars, and to your mother, the earth.'

The trees around Sap whispered, 'Our hopes and dreams go with you, sister. Earth to wood, as wood draws water, as water becomes air, as air breathes spirit.'

The forest surrounding the prostrate tree began to hum, chanting these words: 'Earth to wood, as wood draws water, water becomes air, as air breathes spirit.'

Then the trees began to dance. Forming a circle about Sap and moving sideways, in a rhythmic, swaying, hypnotic motion. The circle of trees moved faster and faster, their roots never leaving the ground, floating through the soil, leaving no trace of their passing.

'Earth to wood, as wood draws water, as water becomes air, as air breathes spirit.'

As the dance grew wilder and wilder, bark flew from the trunks, leaves floated down through the air, swept up in the ecstasy of the moment, forming miniature whirlwinds, spiralling through the dancing trees in the opposite direction, weaving in and out amongst the grey trunks, looking for all the world like schools of green fish suspended in the air, dashing partners of the dancing trees.

The wind rose in accord with the wild dervish dance, spinning through the forest. Blurring the stars, creation ballet'd across the universe in a tornado of bliss.

Sap felt herself flowing in and out of the other trees, she felt the leaves pass through her, leaving no trace, she dissolved once again to be drawn out amongst the cosmos, to partner stars long gone in a dance never forgotten.

CHAPTER 5

With the dawn came the valley mists that lingered along the creek and haunted the damp hollows among the grassy slopes. Sap lay splayed across the ridge, her fallen leaves already paling on the ground and caught dangling in nests of spears, erupting from tussocks of kangaroo grass.

The rumble of heavy machinery could already be heard, echoing down the track from the valley beyond. A blue, smoky haze rose from amongst the trees defining the road along which the small band of foresters marched, followed by an old yellow D9 Caterpillar, and an articulated Mac truck, both scarred from years of work in the bush.

As they crossed the creek, the scene had an air of quiet reverence. Where Sap rested, a perfect ring of leaves lovingly encircled her horizontal form like a wreath, while Sap's brothers and sisters fashioned a guard of honour at her head.

Amazingly, a path had been cleared from the creek to the tree. Huge, grey boulders now rested to either side of the open space, while saplings and small trees angled down the slope, forming an avenue of approach to the recumbent tree.

Despite the occasional light westerly breeze spinning down the glen, two perfect white clouds hovered above the rise where Sap rested, neither stirring nor dispersing with the wind.

Tom Daily halted the Caterpillar bulldozer at the creek, and climbed down from the cabin, jumping the last metre from the tracks to the ground. He turned and waved a halt to the small convoy slowing behind him.

Striding back up the muddy track to where Trevor stood alongside the heavy Mack truck, purpose-built to haul logs out of hazardous situations, and now rumbling at idle above the creek crossing, he stopped, absorbing the scene before them.

'Looks like we were expected,' Tom half-shouted to Trevor, waving his arm in the general direction of the hill.

'You mean to say you didn't do this?' Trevor said incredulously.

'No way on earth,' Tom replied. 'How could one man do something like this overnight? And, besides, have a look around the rocks and trees, there is not a scuff on the ground, you'd have to levitate or something!'

'I've got to tell you, Trev, there's something very different about this tree, something, well, "mystical" about the whole situation, if you don't mind me using the word.'

'Look, Tom,' Trevor replied, 'we've both been around, and seen a bit of the world, but "Mystical", Tommy? Really?'

Trevor then remembered his experience, knowing the tree had fallen, his "vision", as he termed it. He shaded his eyes and looked up the slope to where the tree rested – her two guardian clouds at escort – and ran his hand back through his hair. 'Well, if a way has been cleared for us, I suppose we had better use it. Mystical or not, we still have a job to do.' Reaching back up into the cabin of the

Mack, he extracted a long blade chainsaw, a can of fuel, some gloves, earmuffs, and a hard hat. He turned to Tom.

'Well, mate, let's do this. You bring your Husky?'

Tom walked back down the slope to the Caterpillar, stepped up and reached behind the seat and hauled out a dusty, faded yellow chainsaw, its contours darkened by exhaust fumes and wood dust, a perfect match for Trevor's, and together the two friends crossed the creek and marched up the slope to trim a tree and shape their destiny.

As the first bite of the chainsaw chewed into Sap's trunk, and the flashing blades spun the air with dust and fragments of her bark, Sap focused on the singing that filled the glen and condensed the mood around her.

The cicadas, that previously had coupled merely boisterously, were now reaching crescendo pitch, drawing all that were near into the vortex of energy they were raising.

The madly screaming chainsaw formed a perfect fifth note below the exuberantly coupling cicadas. The wind in the branches of Sap's brothers and sisters whispered a perfect third above the scale of notes, rising in pitch occasionally with the breath of the world, then dropping below the note, flattening the third tone to create a minor, sombre timbre to the ambience of the scene.

With every millimetre the chains sank into Sap, each atom of cellulose, every molecule of her timbered flesh, raised vibrations to match the song of the forest and the saw.

Harmonising with the spinning steel, Saps flesh flowed around the blades and chain, parting on contact with the machine. Wood as water, no turbulence, no resistance... with the compassion of air leaving above and beyond the blade, a cut, glazed and polished, an almost liquid depth of colour glowing beneath the suspended, still smoking chainsaw.

Barely a third of the way through Sap's trunk, Tom lifted the saw up and out of the cut. Placing it on the ground, he stepped back and looked across at Trevor, who was also stepping back. The men shared the same stunned expression.

Apart from the first chips of bark and dust, there was not a trace of sawdust, no woodchips, no debris of any kind around the smooth, glasslike wounds both chainsaws had inflicted on the tree. Ethereal wisps of blue exhaust smoke disappeared above both men, the only hints of the chainsaw's endeavours.

Both gritted their teeth, nodded to each other, and bent to the task before them, as surreal as it seemed.

Despite three decades of living with timber of every type, shape and species behind him, Trevor Manning was struggling with the reality before him, if reality was what it was. The customary resistance in the wood, the expected dust and peppering of wood chips he was used to, just wasn't happening, and to top it off, the cut he was making wasn't the rough, splintered fibre he usually saw in a slice of green, sappy timber. Instead, it was replaced by a soft, golden amber, as smooth as glass, as deep as crystal, with the age rings of the tree visible below the surface, like galaxies in honey-coloured space.

Undaunted and intrigued, he ploughed on through Sap's trunk, until the strand of wood linking both sides of the cut seemed almost invisible, and the log ready to fall appeared to be suspended in air. The final cut was an anticlimax, for as the saw sliced neatly downward and through, the limb relaxed its hold and floated softly to the ground.

Men and tree changed the moment the limb separated from the

trunk. The energy of a trillion trees flowed from the newly severed stump, sweeping through the two friends, absorbed by every cell of their being. Tom and Trevor remembered lives lived in multiple bodies, down through the millions of years of human existence. They remembered lives in thick cellulose trunks, arms reaching for the sun, when the Earth was much younger, but already ancient.

Sap became aware of hearts, lungs, and brain. She experienced the fragility of the human body, the delicate balances of elements in human blood, and the wonderful creativity of the human mind, and a bond was forged.

All Sap's memories took root in Tom and Trevor's memories, so the two men knew Sap's life as their own, every sun-drenched day on the rocky hillside, every storm-lashed night. The ants and birds, insects, snakes and possums, Sap befriended through her life, became part of Tom and Trevor's life. It was as if they had lived, and spoken, and interacted with all these beings.

Both men understood the language, the nuances, and all the subtle messages every inhabitant of the forest communicated with, as Sap knew humanity. With this Gift, integrated with who they were, both men carried on with the task of sharing the One Tree with the rest of the world.

The slings hanging from the crane on the back of the Mack swung slightly, to and fro, in the afternoon breeze as Trevor guided them over the now stripped and prostrate tree. With great reverence, as if the tree were his only child, he lowered the steel ropes across the vast trunk.

Tom embraced the tree with a cradle of webbing and heavy steel shackles as he bound the trunk lovingly for her journey to the mill, stepped back, and waved up at Trevor in the cabin of the truck.

The roar of the diesel engine, and the plume of blue smoke, like the blare of trumpets and the raising of flags, heralded the beginning of a journey, for Nature and Humanity; a sacred quest, a crusade of the willing to bind the ties that hold the Earth and Her inhabitants together.

The little convoy of people felt the wind change, as they and their vehicles formed a procession through the forest, ant-like against the enormity of the carpet of greenery cloaking the hills. The forest bowed back from their path in deference to the Gift tree and the first human beings to be bestowed the key to one world in over fifty thousand years. The hope of the planet was with them.

CHAPTER 6

Once at the mill, Trevor and his crew set to work. Although usually he would wait until the wood was seasoned and dried, he knew this tree would be entirely different.

The milling of Sap was a repeat of the de-branching in the forest; the enormous blade glided through the timber with not a scream of friction, no smoke, no trauma, no resistance, just the smooth, cauterised, glasslike finish that had amazed Trevor and Tom.

The beams and planks of fine grained, polished wood that peeled from the saw, breathed life. Translucent sap, like blood, glazed the surfaces of the timbers as they piled up, and up, and up. By midday the next day, nearly half the tree was milled. Alongside the saw bench and stacked neatly in front of the warehouse, was a good three tonnes of the finest timber, enough wood to construct two large houses.

Billy Soo-lee, Trevor Manning's foreman at the mill, was intrigued, to say the least.

'This is bloody weird.' He scratched the back of his head and mumbled as he walked around and around the stacks of fresh cut lumber in the yard, while the small crew of mill-hands had smoko under the huge Morton bay fig tree that dominated the corner of the yard, and argued about the phenomenon they had just seen.

At last, he strode over to the intercom on the control platform of the mill and called Trevor.

'Trev, it's Bill. We're. Err ... about halfway through that flooded gum you bought in yesterday. There are some really odd things going on down here, I wondered if you'd like to come over and have a look.'

The answer crackled back in Trevor's unruffled tone, 'Right, Bill. I'll be straight over.'

William Soo-lee, known to his mates as Billy, had his ancestry in Chinese woodworkers and craftsmen as far back as the time of Kublai Khan. Almost a thousand years of heritage and hereditary understanding came to the fore in the way Billy did his job.

Billy intuitively knew the best angle for a cut, the best side of a trunk or log to begin with. He had an eye for detail, great aesthetic taste in timber, and after eighteen years working together at the mill, Trevor Manning trusted his judgement with any project. And this particular project was as close to Trevor's heart as surgery on a member of his family.

'I just can't understand what's going on here, Trev,' Bill said as Trevor strolled over to examine the stacks of beautifully milled timber. 'We've been on the bench all morning with this tree and we haven't had to sharpen the saw. We've had no dust problems, in fact, there has been no sawdust at all. There's no sound when she's cut, only an eerie whistling noise, like wind in the tops of tall trees, and there's the yield; unbelievable. Half a tonne from a big tree is extraordinary, but three tonnes from one trunk, and we're still milling.' Billy then spoke quietly, conspirationally, 'She's not diminishing. The timber comes off, we stack it, we mill, and we stack, and this tree just keeps on giving, and I'll tell you, some of the boys are getting a little snakey about this. Well, it's sort of like a miracle, isn't it? … Like, um, loaves and fishes!'

Trevor looked Billy straight in the eyes. 'I've known you a long time, mate, and, well, it's an interesting story I'd like to share with you, regarding this particular tree. You had better sit down.'

The two men wandered over to the giant Morton Bay fig, where the other workers were finishing their lunch, and sat down on logs Trevor's dad had placed there forty years before, in the shady coolness of the ancient tree.

Trevor, or 'Trev', as he was known by these men in front of him, sitting beneath this fantastic tree, not his employees, more like his brothers. Six honest, hardworking Fathers, Sons, cousins, country folk, feeling folk.

Only 6 Years earlier, these men and their partners, and even their kids, were the glue that held Trevor and Simon together. It was this community that caught the Mannings in a safety net of love as Trevors' wife Annie's cancer was progressing.

He caught his breath, paused, and waited until he had their attention, and carefully watching the men's faces, he began to tell them the whole story.

Friends, mates … We are about to see things we all thought were impossible, probably already have, but we're also about to learn a great deal. This tree we're milling is special.

'Our employer is in fact the Earth Herself, through the agency of an ambassador, I guess you'd call her. She goes by the name of 'Gaia.' Some of you may have heard the name before. It is the name the ancient Greeks gave the Spirit Goddess of the Earth. Now, you'll just have to trust me, I realise this all sounds a little crazy, but it seems this Global Warming, Climate change stuff you hear in the news, and unexplainable weather phenomena all over the planet may or may not be a result of our actions.

'But, when odd things occur in the world, I guess the world has to respond in her own way and sometimes we just have to shelve our disbelief. The tree we are in the process of milling is called a Gift Tree. This is the first Gift Tree ever seen, a tree that has been chosen to give herself to humanity.' The crew of hardened timber workers was silent, watching Trevor.

He surveyed the men he'd worked with over the years, and continued.

'During your lives, you may see others, willing to give a township of timber, but, you will remember this one. Her name is Sap.'

The mill workers, including Billy, knew Trevor as almost a part of their families, certainly an important part of their lives. A 'Down to earth' bloke, a bit fragile since Annie died, sure; but certainly not prone to fanciful stories, not 'greeny, crazy hippy-weirdo' stuff, or giving names to the timber they were milling, so they were all curious about what the boss had to say.

A couple of days ago, I received a call from Tom Daily, out at Fernyvale, to collect this tree. Well, everything seemed pretty straight forward once we got there, but when Tom and I approached the fallen trunk—' Trevor paused, remembering. 'Struth, it almost seems like a dream, now. The trees around this one, had been swept back, or bowed back, evenly around the space she – I mean, it – no, I do mean "she" was prepared for us.'

Trevor looked the men in the eye; he had never been more serious. 'The entire hill had been cleared ready to move her. Five tonne boulders were lined up forming a track, other trees had formed a circle around this one, as if they had been raked up, neat as a hedge. Even stranger still, the circle was woven in and out of the outer ring of trees, all done overnight, on Tom's property without a soul being aware of any activity.'

At the back of the group of men, Sam Accappello, the Timber Workers Union rep, stood up, his dark eyes registering the men's unease.

'If you think you can be working the men with overtime, after wasting our afternoon with fairy tales, you got another thing coming, Boss! We know you been under pressure, but rings of leaves in the bush? Pah! Probably only kids tugging your chain, Mr Trevor.'

'Listen Sam, you will all be paid for this afternoon. It'll be worth it to open your eyes, you may or may not believe me, but I might never have to chop down a tree again.'

Sam raised his eyebrow in a sceptical arch, then looked around the members of his union. A few men nodded, while others shrugged their shoulders. Sam raised his palms in surrender and sat down to hear the rest of the "fairytale."

Trevor recalled Tom Daily saying, 'no-one will believe this.' As they'd attempted to clean up the tree, and limbs would fall off the trunk as soon as the image formed in Trevor and Tom's mind. Not only would the branches fall but they stacked themselves exactly where Trevor was going to stack them: on the truck, ready to drop off at the Pringles.

Trevor started again. 'This is the most amazing thing that has ever happened to me, along with Simon's birth. This tree, communicated with Tom and me. I swear, no word of a lie, as I live and breathe. This tree spoke to both of us in images and words. You've all seen the yield from this tree, don't you think that is impossible? You've all seen the cuts. They're nothing short of miraculous, and the finish is better than a cabinet maker could manage on his best day.'

Sam spoke up from the back, 'And what did the tree say?' He laughed quietly, going along with what he thought was a joke.

'She said, "Earth to wood, as wood draws water, as water becomes air, as air breathes spirit." That is exactly what she said! This tree – "Sap", she called herself – told us she was a gift from nature to the people of Earth. She and other trees around the world, she called them sisters, were chosen by the Earth Spirit, whom she called "Gaia." She said Gaia had chosen Gift trees all around the globe, to end the war between Humanity and Nature, and to heal the planet. She said these trees would supply Humanity with all the timber we required, for eternity, and together we would change our view of the world.'

Trevor glanced across to the mill lying idle, at what would normally be the busiest time of day, saw the whole and complete trunk of Sap lying waiting for the saws and chains; turned back to his team and pointed over in the direction of the mill.

'If anyone still doubts the truth of what Tom and I saw and heard, go over and examine that log on the mill tracks for any cuts or abrasions, and then tell me it's not true.'

The assembly sat immersed in the silence that followed, eyes moving slowly from the mill where the tree waited, to the three small mountains of lumber stacked neatly in front of the warehouse, then fruitlessly searching for answers up into the thousand branches of the giant fig where the sun in her mid-afternoon swing, fractured light into rays of grace, beaming down on the gathered workmen.

'Blessings to all gathered here,' a soft voice said, from among the lofty limbs. The voice rang deep within each man's soul. 'Be at peace, men of wood, hear what I have to say. I am Gaia, the Earth Spirit; I have come to welcome you to OUR world.'

The fig leaned towards the mill. The branches opened their arms and stretched out their leafy fingers in Sap's direction.

'This is my beloved daughter, in whom I am well pleased. Two thousand years ago, similar words were spoken when a saviour appeared. This is not less so, despite the time, and the distance, from what is uttered here today.'

The workmen below the tree became immigrants in the world of the tree, wanderers in a land of sunlight and rain, of growth, of feasting in the Earth's juices. They witnessed the miracle of photosynthesis in action, converting sunlight into sugar and earth-friendly energy, transubstantiation of the highest degree.

Their Humanity was their passport, for the rift between Nature and Humanity for these timber workers was healed, the war was over. These often-vilified workers, discriminated against because they made a living from the flesh of the forest, were amongst the first to live the peace.

Later that evening, Tom Daily's telephone jingled down the farmhouse hallway into the lounge room where Tom had just removed his boots and put his feet up.

'No rest for the wicked, I guess,' he mumbled as he rose from the comfort of the sofa.

'It's okay, Dad, I'll get it,' Susie, Tom's daughter, sixteen and a beautiful replica of her mother, Rosie, jumped up from her royal recline in front of the fire, and dashed out into the hall. Tom could hear her speaking, obviously to someone familiar, as her laugh rang out. 'Thanks, Uncle Trevor, I'll just get him, won't be a minute.' She skipped in and plonked herself back down. 'It's Uncle Trevor, Dad. Could you get him to put Simon on when you're finished? I need some help with my homework, ta.'

'Trev, how did you go?' Tom cut straight to the chase as soon as he picked up the phone.

'It was a pretty interesting day, to say the least,' Trevor replied. 'The boys were a little shaky about the whole thing, especially the yield. Mate, you should have been there. We were under the fig, having a bit of a natter about what was going on, when this light came on in the tree, or the sun got hotter, or something, and these beams of light shone down on every bloke there, and the next thing I know there's this voice...' Trevor Manning's voice went quiet, 'You know what it said, Tom, it said the same to us.'

'Yes, I remember, Trev, it said, "Act Local, Think Global."' Tom had a knack for understanding complex issues and forming them into a simple statement. 'Look, Trevor, we were both at the site, we both heard the voice, we both saw the tree virtually give herself to us.' Tom paused to gather his thoughts. 'And I think we both know what we have to do from here.'

'She's a Gift from Nature, or Gaia, or the planet,' Tom whispered, 'It doesn't matter what terms we use, as long as we use her, and with the finest of our talents, shape her into a mouthpiece for generations to come.'

'I'll give Jimmy a tingle, let him know she's here. He's got the eye for fine timber, he'll know where we turn next, and it'll be good catching up with the family. Oh, and remember, we're saving the world, but we don't have to save it on our own. We'll see you soon mate, thanks for the call. Oh, and could you put Simon on, Susie says she would like to talk homework. Bye Trev.'

Tom handed the phone back to Susie, kissed her cheek, and wandered off to bed, an unlikely looking hero if there ever was one.

CHAPTER 7

The sun was just clearing the trees at the rear of the mill office, shining into his eyes as Trevor bounded up the stairs. He could hear the phone on his desk ringing before he had even placed the key in the lock. Eventually, he managed to open the door just as the ringing died out.

He made himself a coffee, sat down at the desk, when the phone rang again. Trevor picked up on the move.

"Hello, hello," a heavily accented voice said, "This is Salvatore Fiorelli, calling from Italy. I would like to speak with Trevor Manning, please.'

'Mr Fiorelli, this is Trevor Manning speaking, how can I help you?'

'Mr Manning, an old friend of mine whispered to me today that you have some, how we shall say ... "special" wood at your mill, and I would like to purchase some, if I could?'

Trevor considered the logistics of getting Sap all the way to Italy.

'Certainly, Mr Fiorelli. We have a great range of wood for you to choose from here, er, what purpose did you have in mind?' 'Ever since I left Cremona, my home in Italia, you understand? I have searched for this special, magical wood. For longer than you could imagine, Mr Manning, I have sought the raw materials to make my masterpiece; for you see I am a luthier, a co-creator of violins and violas, cellos and basses, and I believe you have my "Holy Grail". I am arriving here in your Australia, today, to see this Tree.'

'I don't know about your Holy Grail, Mr Fiorelli, but you're welcome to come in and see if we have anything that might suit your project. When would you like to drop in?'

Trevor opened his diary and pencilled in: Fiorelli/Instrument maker.

'I could be there una momenta if I wished, but I must be "conventional", eh? I will arrive at three O'clock on tomorrow's train. Do you think you could pick me up, Mr Manning? It would be very much appreciated.'

'Certainly, Mr Fiorelli. Three O'clock then, I'll see you at the station.' Trevor continued his diary entry: Pick up 3pm, Fernyvale station!

Meanwhile, outside the office, hovering ten thousand metres above the grey, corrugated roof of the mill, the two clouds that were Sap's guardians, kept watch.

While in her cradle on the mill deck, on the drying racks in the warehouse, and on the back of Trevor's old Mac truck, Sap waited and learned. The mill told her stories of other trees, trees that had suffered badly by the blade.

The mill saw itself as the whole, and referred to itself as, "we." Made from timber and metal, glass, and earth, We were full of stories of the great mineral mines of the west, and the fiery forges where the giant shining, spinning blades were cast, along with the grand steel girders, supporting the expansive roof.

The mill breathed tales of the extensive forests that provided the masses of timber that supported the huge structure. Some enormous old beams in the roof trusses whispered of previous incarnations as bridges in the big, seaside cities, and the odd creatures they had carried across broad rivers and estuaries, and the even odder spirits they sometimes sheltered.

Each element of the building intermittently rumbled through their musings, audible as structural groans and moans. In the giant glass windows on the northeast and southwest of the building, dreams of beaches drifted, sand dunes against the deep blue sky and the sun.

The Sun, so hot He blended the sand, baptised, and purified the sand and made them the windows they are today, and the views they had seen, both inside and out, they shared with Sap, as she travelled the world and learned of the casting of metals, the manufacture of glass, and the multiple uses Humanity had for the natural World.

How wood, metal and glass had woven themselves into the fabric of the human world so much so, that without them society would collapse.

Later that same day, as heavy grey clouds gathered on the ranges to the west, allowing the setting sun to peek the occasional ray through, the Pringle family, Mai-Li, James' petite Vietnamese wife and their daughters, Rebecca and Sally, were relaxing on the back verandah, enjoying the view that embraced the green checkerboard patterns of the Fernyvale valley.

'Rebecca is in high school, in only two weeks she will be sixteen,' Mai was saying, 'it is time she learning skills, as wife and mother,'

Becky was horrified. 'But that was in the old world, Mum. There's too much to do, too much to see, I want to see the world before I become someone's slave for life; if ever.'

'You very selfish girl, Rebecca Pringle. When I your age I feed my family, myself, I work hard every day, I make—'

'Yeah, yeah, I know, I know,' interrupted Beck. 'But Vietnam in the 60s is nothing like Australia in the 2000s. This is a free country, a country where we can do what we like!'

At that point in the discussion, James emerged from the kitchen with steaming cups of tea, headlong into the mother-daughter dispute. Rather than referee, he often created diversions and new perspectives, just as he would if he struck a particularly tough knot or quandary while working his beloved wood. Peering over the glasses perched at the tip of his nose, James gently corrected his daughter.

'Free? Well, I'm not so sure, try telling that to the refugees in detention centres across the Pacific, who risked their lives coming to Australia seeking freedom. I'm afraid, freedom, young Beckster, is hard to win, difficult to maintain, and vastly unappreciated by those who have it,' he added tactfully, handing the tea to each antagonist. 'So, my love,' he said, cradling Mai-Li under his right arm, 'you'll just have to be satisfied with being the slave driver in the shed, with the card company your decadent capitalist enterprise.'

He bent to kiss his wife on the cheek, and whispered quietly in her ear, 'She's too much like her mother, a will of bamboo. She'll never break, thank God!' He danced out of dangers way, as Mai took a playful swing at his head. 'Okay, You two?' he said. 'We can't have you arguing all afternoon; Tom will be here soon with the off-cuts from this famous tree he's just dismantled.'

'Very good,' said Mai. 'We only got eight pencils left in stock, and we need stacks of chips.' Suddenly she was all businesswoman, calculating requirements for the paper and pencil company she'd established with Rebecca, two years earlier.

They had originally begun as a means of utilising the normally wasted wood chips and twigs left when Trevor Manning made a delivery, or James was involved with a new item of furniture.

Mai and Beck would gather twigs of any type of tree, but mostly eucalypts, measure them carefully, check that they were not too outrageously bent and twisted, and file them away on shelves ranked by length and diameter. After drying for several weeks, the Girls would clamp the small cylinders of wood in one of James' old drill presses and drill out the cores, ready to receive the graphite centres.

The wood and bark pulp the girls collected was further munched in a common garden waste muncher to produce a coarse, powdery pile of sawdust, which they then boiled in an old copper, at the rear of the shed. When the sodden, steaming mess had cooled, Mai would stir in several litres of wood glue, and a couple of handfuls of lime dust, and let it sit for several more days, to allow the lime time to bleach the whole shebang, and the glue to penetrate the pulp.

Beck would then ladle the goo onto frames stretched with fine wire mesh, and stack the trays in homemade drying racks that ran the length of the Eastern wall of the barn; Eastern, because Mai believed the morning sun spirit was gentler and produced finer, and she said, more "tolerant", paper, than the harsh afternoon sun.

She would then run the semi-dried pulp through the ringer of an ancient washing machine, pressing the sheets flat and smooth. The whole enterprise had become quite successful and now lucrative enough to have outlets selling country style paper and pencil sets, in boutique craft stores in several major cities.

CHAPTER 8

Mai and Beck often press-ganged the youngest Pringle, Sally, most afternoons after school, into cutting the large sheets of raw paper into wavy edged and patterned panels. Sally's job then was to dip them quickly into coloured dyes, then hang them out to dry. In return for being such a hard worker she was made a shareholder in the company which they christened, 'Bally Mai' using all their names, with the real reward being all the ice cream Sally could eat, but not before dinner.

It was well after lunch, with the sun a gritty, golden memory of the heat of the day, when Trevor's old truck, with Tom Daily at the wheel, bounced up the driveway to the Pringles home, trailing a small cloud of dust, and chased from the gate by the Pringles crazy, dust demon cattle dogs, diving in and out of the billowing cloud, dodging the spinning wheels, and nipping at the dirt laden air.

Stopping at the house gate, Tom jumped down from the cabin almost stepping on Thunder, the blue heeler, while Lightning, the red kelpie with more than a hint of dingo in her, paced back and forth in front of the gate.

'Bloody dogs!' Tom yelled, 'Get back, Thunder, you mad thing! You'll get squashed one day.'

'Not likely, mate,' came the swiftly barked reply.

'What the—' Tom did a double take. Halfway down from the truck, he looked around to see who had answered him. Suspecting the children, he pretended he had heard nothing, but kept a wary eye out for high jinks and was ready to rumble.

When Tom moved towards the gate where Lightning was wearing a dusty track with his pacing, he heard the unmistakable sound of excitement barely contained, punctuated by short panting. Looking quickly around, Tom saw nothing extraordinary but he heard, 'Come on, come on, let's go, aw struth, come on will ya! I gotta wet, I need to mark, this is my home, truck; mine, I'm the dog, oh yes, I am, who's the dog? Me, Oh, come on!'

Tom Daily could scarcely believe his eyes and ears. The voice he could hear was Lightning! In the back of Tom's mind, he could feel Sap reaching out with her senses, networking with his, analysing this new creature. Her curiosity inspired him, and he walked around to the back of the truck, reached into the bin, and lifted out a half metre long stick of Sap's wood, swung it back over his right shoulder and hurled it down the paddock.

Thunder and Lightning both stopped what they were doing, looked at each other for a full second, then bolted after it.

Thunder reached Sap first, breaking her run with a sideways sliding swing. Using her tail as well as her legs to stop and turn, she opened her jaw and sprang at Sap's branch from below. It bounced off her snout, high up into the air, up to where Lightning, with her wild ancestry, was gliding, halfway through a colossal do-or-die leap, to claim the prize. Lightning won.

Her jaws clamped strongly around Sap, and as they began to descend, Thunder latched on too. Both dogs and stick hit the ground in an explosion of dust.

Now, normally the dogs would wrestle and dispute the ownership of a stick for hours, but today things were different. Today, Thunder and Lightning had bitten off more than they could chew. Sap was in the jaws of both dogs, she smelled their breath on her, felt the sharp teeth rasping and breaking her skin, all the while soaking up the exuberance, the sheer joy of play, the 'dogness' of it all.

Sap was assimilating it into her experience. Soft and gentle as a snowflake, she stretched her senses out to the dogs.

As inviting to a dog as only a tree can be, Sap infiltrated the canine defences, to the souls of both dogs. To Thunder, the stick tasted like cool water on a sweltering day, with a hint of shady riverbanks, and wild ducks. She settled herself down on to her belly, and savoured the sensation.

Lightning was somewhat different. Lightning was descended from the original dog that walked the Australian continent with the first men and women, through time out of mind. To her, Sap tasted of ancient rites, of the Great Spirit, the Rainbow Serpent, and the land. Deeper still, Lightning tasted the music: didgeridoo and bones, the throbbing, humming undercurrent to life lived simply and in tune with the natural world. She too settled quietly.

Tom heard it all, felt every bite, smelled every breath, and tasted every flavour exchanged between Sap and the dogs. A new awareness and respect began to hatch in him, an acknowledgement of other creatures and the depth of their dreaming. Beings we share this world with and have been sadly unaware of, until now.

Tom, being the first human to have contact with Sap, had his mind opened; his higher mind, was already in communion with the dogs and the tree, and the family, now gathering at the gate a little way beyond the quietly idling truck.

James and Mai waved hello from the gate.

Both girls opened it simultaneously and tumbled through. 'Hi, Uncle Tom!' they shouted as they ran past.

'Thunder, Lightning, bad dogs. Where's your manners? It's Uncle Tom.' Realising the dogs were no bother, both girls wandered sheepishly back to give Tom welcoming hugs, and lead him back to the house. Waving them on he said, 'Won't be a moment, dears. I'll just unload this tree, then we can catch up.'

Tom climbed up behind the wheel of the old green Bedford, clutched, and churned the ancient gear stick into reverse, and switched his attention to the open gateway where he could see James waving him in the direction of the bottom shed, below the tank stand. The old truck rumbled and shuddered as she lurched backwards towards the opening.

Tom guided it through with a metre to spare, and turned the wheel hard right to bring the load straight to the shed door.

The shed was an open gated affair, with a rough-hewn, half door and barn gate, and crazily paved with large octagonal concrete slabs with concentric brick circles spreading out from them – mostly Mai's handiwork – and roofed with shingles gleaned from James or his suppliers.

As the truck shook itself to a halt, Tom felt the slightest murmur from the motor.

'Ahh, done! Bon voyage, Sap, my friend,' Morse-coded the Bedford's motor, as the tray of the truck began to rise high in the air, spilling Sap's loose and tangled limbs from the tailgate.

James, Mai, and the girls stood back from the shed to avoid falling limbs and logs. They watched as the first sticks and logs hit the ground, tumbling like dancers, back-flipping up into the air, to land neatly on their ends, roll gently sidewards, and stack themselves tidily by the entrance to the workshop. In seconds, the entire load was off the truck and stacked, ranked by size.

Tom smiled wryly from the other side of the truck. 'I told you this was a very special tree.'

Mai and the children noticed nothing extraordinary. As far as they could see, the wood slid off the truck exactly as it should have, danced across the floor, exactly as it was expected to, rolled, and gymnastically stacked itself precisely as the girls visualised it doing.

Rebecca, Sally, and Mai knew this tree intimately. The trio were long-time sisters to Sap, bonded while caring for Trevor Manning's dying wife, Annie, some years earlier.

CHAPTER 9

Annie had been well known in the small community and vital to the operation of the mill. She'd kept the books, often fed the men, and was a pillar of support to the wives and children of the timber workers.

Without any obvious warning signs, Annie had developed a seriously malignant brain tumour and rapidly deteriorated. The community rallied around her while Trevor continued to operate the mill, care for a dying wife, and raise a ten-year-old Simon.

Recognising that at the time, there seemed little anyone could do for Annie, Toms' wife, Rosie, and daughter Susie, along with Mai, and the girls, had bought her out to the country, as a farewell and 'we love you,' picnic day out by the creek, on the Daily's farm.

The Sydney surgeon, Dr Hordern, advised Trevor to get Annie's affairs in order. As he so tactfully put it: Annie's quality of life would slip away, sooner rather than later.

So, the girls decided to take Annie out and share a glorious spring day in the country. Pale and fragile as she was, Annie's friends knew her love of nature and the presence of her friends, might make the final parting a little softer.

Rosie knew a spot in the 'back forty,' by a bend in the river, below some shady gums. It was accessed by a driveable road, so wouldn't cause too much discomfort for their fragile passenger. Annie had decided, bravely, not to undergo the dangerous and futile surgery. She decided against chemotherapy, radiation, and other interventions, in favour of quality of life, however brief. She acquiesced to pain management, in the form of a small morphine pump she wore on a holster at her hip.

It was this pump she triggered for a couple of seconds before she got out of the Toyota. Annie breathed deeply and closed her eyes, resting her head back against the seat's headrest, appreciating the flood of pain free relief the morphine brought.

She opened her eyes, and there was Rosie, everyone's mum, opening the door of the four-wheel drive, a concerned look wrinkling the otherwise clear brow.

'Are you alright, dear?' she said. 'Are you sure you're up to this? We could easily have a cuppa at home.'

'No, I mean, yes, I'm alright. This is so beautiful, and the creek is so clear, thank you so much for bringing me out here.'

The party had shared their picnic lunch, the girls had exhausted the swimming hole, and by mid-afternoon they were all settled back against the trunk of a beautiful, flooded gum, the sun glancing down through the branches, dappling their clothes and legs. In the distance, the creek could be heard trickling across rocks and bubbling around tree roots, murmuring sedately.

The small group slept, and as they slept, they dreamed.

Rosie dreamed of home. She dreamed all the flowers in her garden bloomed at once. Even the flowers she had only considered planting, found a place, and thrived.

Beck, Sally, and Susie all dreamed of far off exotic places and people. Mai Li dreamed of home in Bien Hua, northeast of Ho Chi Minh City, on the banks of the DongNai River. Small, tangled log rafts of Cedar and Teak floated down the broad waterway, and in Mai's dream each log had a face, turned towards Mai-Li, the lonely, seven-year-old orphan.

Every face floating past her was a friend or a relative, someone she had known. Their heads turned to her, eyes fixed on her own, mouths open, silently moving.

She was suspended above the river, and each limb reached out to her for help, each mouth and knothole crying out, 'Save us. Save us.'

Mai reached out to the logs, crying, 'I will save you. I love you, don't leave me, I love you.'

While Mai was restless in her dream, elsewhere beneath the sheltering branches, Annie was at peace. With her eyes half-closed to take advantage of the light refracting through the leaves, and Sap's strong trunk supporting her, the rippling of the stream in her ears, the breeze across her face, and the hum of the forest singing to her soul, Annie died.

CHAPTER 10

The girls brought her home, laid her out on her bed, and gathered flowers from the garden to place around her. Annie Manning looked as peaceful and lovely in rest, as she had been in life, as friend and mother.

The gathered women knew Annie hadn't really left them. Deep in their hearts, they knew, that a gardener's soul remains in the garden, regardless of where the body has gone. The farm was Annie's garden and she would always be around them, and within their hearts, and amongst her beloved trees.

This was why none of the women were surprised when the limbs sorted themselves. They smiled at each other, and nodded knowingly. Just as Annie would have done, each of them thought.

Meanwhile, James stood, dumbfounded, hands on hips, gaping at the neatly stacked pile of timber. He looked up at the truck, then back to the timber. Looked up at Tom, smiling smugly from the cabin of the Bedford, across to the girls, and back, open-mouthed at the organised stack of branches and twigs.

'Okay, you lazies,' – Mai was all business now, already sorting through the woodpile, measuring stick in hand –'no time for stand around.' Back turned to the group she said, 'James, girls, I sort, you cut. Sally put on rack.' She turned, beaming, back to the truck. 'Thank you, Tom. Would you like a cuppa before you go?'

'Or perhaps you could stay for tea?' James urged his friend. The plea in James' voice was clearly discernible. He missed male company, especially living in the midst of an intense female household. He was sure sometimes he could taste the hormones in the air. His retreat was his workshop, where he poured his passion into the fabulous pieces of furniture he helped create. Today he remained in Mai's service, sorting sticks.

Tom would have liked to have stayed, but he knew how quickly Mai could entangle him in her web of workers and he still had some loads to pick up and deliver.

'Oh, ah, I've really got to get this truck back to Trevor, and pick up the slabs you asked for, James, but, hey, thanks for the offer,' Tom said.

'As I saying, Tom,' Mai's voice cut across his thoughts, 'You bring Rose and Susie for dinner this week, I make famous green curry and noodles, and banana fritter special for you, Friday is good. This wood, special good, many pencil, much paper, many story in this wood... many story,' Mai said, almost to herself. 'We thank you again, for your kindness,' she said with a slight bow to the side of the truck.

'Thanks Mai,' Tom waved through the windscreen to Sally and Bec, and leaned out to catch James' ear. 'I'll bring the slabs over about threeish, okay, Jimmy?'

As the truck rumbled down the hill and through the gate, Thunder and Lightning followed, weaving in and out of the small trees and over clumps of grass, playfulness in nature, floating in spirit, dancing on the planet. The dogs were happy to have the one tree living with what they saw as their pack.

The humans, the farm animals, the machinery, even the sheds and outbuildings, were considered part of the den structure, and the scent of 'home, warmth, food, comfort, love,' permeated the farm they all shared.

Meanwhile, at Fernyvale railway station, Trevor Manning stood reading the local news in the Fernyvale Echo, catching up with all the local stories, and waiting for the arrival of Senor Fiorelli.

Salvatore Fiorelli enjoyed train travel, especially in the country, and in particular on glorious spring days. Farms and villages flashed by, punctuated by broad tracts of fenced pasture, flashes of sunlight reflected from the river below flickered across the walls of his carriage, Salvatore was transported to times long past.

In his former life as Antonius Stradivarius, master violin, and viola maker, he had many friends among the musical fraternity of old Italy. Today he was transported to another sun-drenched afternoon, long ago.

The year was 1798, he and his good friend Lucio Vivaldi, the young composer, were riding in an open carriage, pulled by a pair of frisky geldings, tearing down a tunnel of budding elm trees. It was also spring and Lucio's twentieth birthday. The wind lifted their capes, sunlight flashed through the trees; and Vivaldi, standing unsteadily in the racing vehicle, arms animatedly conducting, gave vent to his song for the four seasons, as he called it. His youthful vitality shone in his strong voice, giving the tune a sprightly air. A ripe recipe for euphoria.

'Ah, but this was in the old days,' Salvatore thought to himself. His eyes misted over with the thought of old friends, other times, and places, long, long, past. He thought, As well I remember, for they are never completely gone. His eyes floated beyond the view of wooded hill and green valley, as his thoughts drifted back to the reason he was on the train.

Salvatore softly breathed a blessing, 'Their spirits live on in many forms, and I hope and pray that today I may liberate one such Spirit, may it be for the greater good.'

The benediction trailed out the window of the train, granting grace to farmers and townsfolk, stock and crops, forest and pasture, creeks, and dams, all along the Richmond River valley.

The blessing skimmed the surface of the river herself, winding like a silver serpent below the brow of the mighty Border Ranges, leaving a barely discernible trail of ripples, disturbing bright red, and blue dragonflies.

As he rested his head on the back of the seat and closed his eyes, he felt the carriage rock forward as the train dropped speed, the whistle signalling their approach to the station. From his window, Senoŕ Fiorelli could see the farms gliding past, ordered into neat parcels of land by wire fences, and long rows of camphor laurel and native myrtle trees. Blue smoke rose lazily behind a large timber mill at the edge of town, and the air smelled heavily of sweet pittosporum and milled pine.

Reminiscent of early spring in alpine orchards, he reflected, remembering the masses of sweetly scented peach and apricot trees with their pink and white blossoms, scattered like occasional quilts across the hills, above his beloved and sorely missed home in Cremona.

The whistle shrieked again and returned Salvatore to the present. The train slowed to a walking pace, and moments later rolled into Fernyvale Station at precisely three fifteen in the afternoon.

Salvatore Fiorelli stepped from the carriage lightly, and arranged himself and his luggage on the platform, preparing for the encounter he had long awaited.

Arrayed in a cape of black satin, lined with scarlet silk, bordered with silver brocade, and an ostentatious hat of obvious European origin that could double as an umbrella, Senor Fiorelli cut an exquisite figure. Even his shadow looked impressive. The gentleman was unmistakeably not from around these parts; a few heads turned, curious, and then quietly continued with the business of their day.

The standard uniform in town was denim jeans and R.M. Williams boots, topped with a flannelette checked shirt (usually a variation on red) and a broadbrim Akubra hat. Trevor, waiting on the platform recognised the flamboyant character immediately.

'Senor Fiorelli, I presume. Welcome to the bush.'

'Ah, Mr Manning, I am pleased to meet with you at last.' Fiorelli had been observing Trevor since he first stepped off the train. With the insight born of four hundred years of travelling and meeting people, Salvatore could read the character of a man by studying the lines on his face, and the calluses on his hands. He concluded Trevor Manning was a deeply thoughtful, hardworking, and sincere man, deeper still he sensed, Manning was a man carrying some heavy burden.

Shaking his hand during the greeting, Senor Fiorelli received many insights into Trevor's character, not the least of which was the grief he still felt after the sudden and tragic loss of his wife, and the stoic face he put on for the world, while being both father and mother to his son, and running a busy mill.

Fiorelli felt empathy engulf him, and immediately warmed to the man.

'I've parked on the main street, Mr Fiorelli, so it's a short walk to the car. Have you eaten? There are a few cafés in town,' Trevor chatted amiably as they strolled along, enquiring about the journey, and the nature of his expertise regarding timber.

'Thank you, Mr Manning, but I have only the one meal in a day; a light supper in the evening I find sustains me quite admirably. I am a simple man, with simple requirements, some bread, cheese and wine, and a comfortable bed in which to sleep, suits me wonderfully. I do have a passion, though, for my work.' Fiorelli admitted. 'I have come a long way to see this, ah, wood you have milled from a special tree, and I would greatly like to examine it, read the grain, and feel the potential within. Oh, and please let us dispense with the formalities, you can call me Sam, if you would and I shall call you Trevor, okay?'

Trevor relaxed visibly, and said, 'Fine by me, Sam.' And the two woodworkers shook hands in agreement.

CHAPTER 11

The drive to the mill, skirted the town along a boundary road, and Sam was relieved to see it was not the mill he had seen burning its waste. Waste, to Salvatore, was indicative of a lack of imagination; there being so many uses for, what he termed "the leavings" after a creative endeavour was completed.

As they slowed to enter the mill yard, Sam could see the ordered mind at work. His respect for Trevor deepened when they drove slowly under the magnificent canopy of the giant Morton Bay Fig tree that dominated the mill grounds. He thought, rare, that tribute is paid to nature, honouring the wood that is milled. But here, in the very heart of where her children are sliced into building materials for humanities sake, the forest is honoured by the presence of the mother. He could physically feel Sap's presence here.

Salvatore Fiorelli, once known long ago as Antonio Stradivarius, late master violin and viola maker, of Cremona, Italy; Good friend of Lucio Vivaldi, and ageless, passionate lover of trees and all their woods and spirits; was as excited as he had ever been in his life.

Salvatore's blood throbbed with the unheard music in the mill yard; his heart beat a complicated tattoo in counterpoint with the waves of vibration buzzing silently through him.

His calm meditative composure belied his excitement. Here was his life's goal, his Shangri-La, his Holy Grail.

His hands trembled, as he reached for the door handle of the car and opened it to the golden light of afternoon, and the hustle and bustle of a mill finalising operations for the day.

He heard men calling to each other, giving direction, the hum of the mills motors, but where was the saw dust? Where was the shrill screech of tortured timber, the ringing of tempered steel stressed to its breaking point?

Senor Fiorelli stepped out of the car into a world where the reverence was tangible. These mill workers had immense respect for the timber that fed and clothed them, but deeper still, they shared a revelation that would change the world. He sensed they all knew Sap.

They knew who she was and why she was here, and were willing participants in the revolution under way to save the planet.

'Well,' he said, stretching his arms wide behind him, as he looked around inquisitively, 'You must excuse me, Trevor, as I'm afraid my curiosity bubbles over, where would we find this element, which I have come so far to see, please?'

'Mr Fiorelli, if you could step this way,' Trevor said, with a faint bow and wave of his hand, then turned and led the way to the mill's timber store.

In the gloom of the warehouse, Sap was reflecting on her life to now and contemplating the large mass of herself, in five separate stacks, suspended centimetres above the cold concrete floor by thick boxwood blocks, and bound with flat steel bands. Above the good-natured grumbling of the boxwood, and the taut humming of the blue steel bands, Sap could feel the presence of Senor Fiorelli.

She could sense his excitement, her cells were aligning already, hinting at the feminine curves and swellings Salvatore dreamed of evoking from her body. Eager to give the world its saviour, Salvatore's senses flowed before him.

A rendezvous about to be consummated between the maker and the subject craving to be shaped, to surrender her definitive form. He savoured the prospect of holding in his hands, at last, what he had searched across four centuries, and the world, to find. Sap reached out to him, soul to soul. Heart of one, to heart of another, unravelling the tangle of language between species, and demystifying the language of nature for the ears of man...

Trevor Manning rolled back the great sliding doors of the warehouse, illuminating the dim interior. The bright shaft of sunlight from the frame of the entrance cast the shadows of the two men across the concrete floor, and over the stacks of new sawn timber.

He could see the faintest glow emanating from the stacks. An aura, a quiet, radiant message of welcome, extended from the deep red ribbons of wood.

Sam Fiorelli crossed the floor in a couple of eager steps, and bent to embrace the mountain of timber, pressing his face close to the polished surface in an embrace akin to lovers meeting after a long absence. He breathed across the surface, fogging the grace-filled wood.

'After all this time, my friend, we meet at last.'

The unmistakable ringing of a great bell resounded across the globe. Ripples formed rings, concentric waves of sub-conscious data flooded out from the source, on the eastern seaboard of Australia, where the continent washes her beaches in the turquoise waters of the great Pacific Ocean.

The energy flowed out and over the planet, like sauce over a pudding, a tsunami of sub-sensory information opening channels of communication between races of humans, between species, weaving a fabric of the Earth herself. The links between minerals, rocks, oceans and plants became highways upon which all could travel.

All that was required now was the instrument. Trevor understood the emotion he was observing, deep sentiments he immediately recognised, surfaced. Feelings for his Annie, six years distant, the pain and separation both he and Simon sorely felt, rose and his eyes filled with tears.

'She is not gone,' Trevor heard a voice in his mind say. 'I know where she is,' Sap whispered to him. 'You can close your eyes, and you will see her everywhere. I will be your link, I will be your bridge.'

Trevor closed his eyes and there she was. As beautiful as he remembered, long auburn hair cascading past her waist, a twinkle in her dark blue eyes, wearing her favourite green dress, with the lace bodice, the one she called her 'Dryad dress.'

Annie seemed to step from the dream into his arms. He felt her press against him, felt her shape fit perfectly on his, and her scent, that sandalwood pool he remembered, bathed his senses once again. And then she was gone. Out of his arms and into his heart. Trevor could still feel that embrace he had thought was gone, could feel the fabric of her dress, could smell the sandalwood, but all on the inside.

It seemed to him that he had absorbed the memory, and was living the experience of holding Annie in his arms again. To Trevor, she was real and living within him.

'Nothing is lost.' Sap spoke softly to Trevor. 'Everything that ever was, still exists, only forms change, if we know, really KNOW the memory, we can create it in our lives.'

The truth, known forever in his mind, now resonated in Trevor's heart. Trevor could only describe it later, as a kind of fulfillment. He was brimming with her presence, he could feel, taste and smell her, and she was all around him. Within him, the missing, empty, longing he had suffered for the last six years dissipated like smoke on the wind.

Momentarily, his senses returned to the warehouse, the softly glowing stacks of timber and ... Salvatorĕ Fiorelli, standing, smiled indulgently and said. 'It is the magic of Love, no?' He continued, 'This tree, this wood is much more than she seems. She carries life, and brings all things together.'

Trevor's eyes were misted when he focused back on the shed and the instrument maker, 'She is here,' he stated, holding his hand over his heart. 'It's like she never left.'

The maestro simply nodded. 'It is so, and so it is the tree which renews life in our hearts, and she will so heal the world. Nothing is lost, all that ever was, still is, all that ever will be is with us now'

The air hummed, and a soft golden aura canopied the companions, still facing each other in the now subtly glowing corner of the large warehouse.

'And now to business,' Salvatore Fiorelli, finally breathed into the sacred space, the craftsman, and soul traveller returning to the here and now, soothing the transition from the where? To the wood.

Salvatore knocked his knuckles lightly against the slab of Sap's heartwood he had selected from the stack, listening intently, his cheek and ear pressed close to the timber. He listened for that magical resonance all objects possess, using his unique imaginative sonar, to map the potential expression within a slab of wood, and occasionally, a living tree.

Salvatore was seeking the minute reverberation surrounding the initial knock, an echo, a response from the 'seat of the form,' as he called it. Like a kernel surrounding a sweet nut of some sort, like rings of water in a pond radiating outwards from a central splash, and Fiorelli's ear was the perimeter of that pond.

What Salvatore heard was the sound of his heart beating. The faint whoosh of blood pumping steadily through his body, the rush of his plasma washing against fleshy beaches, deep within his ribcage.

The internal sighing of his lungs became the breeze cavorting across the globe, caressing oceans of forest, and giving birth to the unmistakable sound of small birds singing, and grasses rasping in waving dances, amongst the whisper and rattle of new growth in lofty treetops.

Spring was forever unfolding deep within the heartwood. He could feel the spreading elasticity of cellulose fibre, as the tree expanded to fulfil her growth, as through her, ripples of water flowed from root to crown, heavy and rich, yellow-golden honey. A salve to Fiorelli's ear.

A concerto resonated around the initial rhythm of the knuckle, rising from the depths of the wood. The Masterpiece was already written, immersed deep inside seasonal rings, her grooves like old wax and vinyl recordings, the wood, requesting a key to release itself.

Salvatore Fiorelli smiled with the knowledge that he, himself, was the key. Sap and the whole world had been waiting patiently through the ages for him to arrive.

CHAPTER 12
Angels in the Rafters

The swallows in the rafters of James Pringle's workshop peered, with craned necks, down over the rim of their mud-spit nests, undisturbed by the commotion caused by the unloading of dozens of sweet-smelling slabs of fresh-milled timber.

It was Friday, only a couple of days since he had delivered the chips and twigs for Mai's paper and pencil enterprise, when Tom, Rose, and Susan arrived in the ancient pickup truck, loaded with slabs of Sap's heartwood, followed by Trevor and Simon, keen to see what plans James had for this particular tree.

Susan Daily and Bec Pringle were best friends, close as sisters and had been since they'd shared basinet space in Lismore Base Hospital, fifteen years earlier. Susan, as an only child, was welcomed into the busy Pringle household, while Mai treated her, as simply another daughter.

The girls often sought sanctuary in the woodshed, cool, quiet, and dark as it was, and so, knew the swallow family quite well, if not by name. Being Friday, the end of the school week, Sally was already home, with some mysterious tummy bug, which miraculously disappeared the moment the Daily's truck turned off the main road.

The end of the week marked a traditional gathering at the Pringles. The magnetic pull of Mai's cooking attracted family and friends alike, and although everyone brought something to the table, it was really the company of the farming community they gathered for.

As welcomes and salutations were exchanged, Susan asked Mai if Sally was still ill. Mai simply inclined her head towards the woodshed.

They could faintly hear Sally singing up in the loft. She loved the way the barn seemed to make her voice reverberate, and spent many happy hours warbling away at the walls and to the swallows who were always an attentive audience.

From the day it was built, the birds had nested in the dim recessed corners of the Pringles shed. When the last sheet of roofing iron was fastened to the roof truss, a family of ruddy breasted, swallows swooped beneath the ladders, in through the open side of the virgin building, and began to build a home, high up in the cradle offered by the truss.

They became the 'Watchers' as Becky called them.

Sally laughingly joked, 'See their little vests, and tuxedos, they'd be better called "The Waiters."'

Today, 'The Watchers and Waiters' twittered amongst themselves as they watched the careful delivery of the one tree to the quiet shelves of James' workshop.

'Two more and we're in business,' James breathed across the surface of the slab he and Tom carried, fogging the polished face of the two-metre sheet of rose/gold wood. The slab was as smooth as glass, and had a depth of unbroken grain that never ceased to amaze him. He wondered how on earth he was going to improve on the miracle of nature.

'There's no weight in these slabs,' Tom remarked as he hefted the other end upon his shoulder. 'The springs on the truck barely moved and the load smoothed the road out to your place. I swear, it was like a magic carpet ride.'

The friends shifted the last sheet of beautiful timber down the length of the shelves at the back of the shed that James used as his drying room. Past the thicknesser under her tent of canvas, past the lathe and the broad workbench where the windows looked out onto the colourful profusion of the garden.

The two men easily hoisted Sap up to the top shelf, where the layers of wood rested in a world of constant controlled humidity, and minimum light. Where strips of mature trees seasoned, and established closer bonds with themselves, rather than with the influences of the outside world. Influences which would incline them to split and splinter, although James suspected the wood he held now would never do that.

One small swallow, among the neck craners in the ceiling, leapt from the rim of the nest and launched herself across the expanse of the shed, wings applauding noisily. Swooping through beams of light and around beams of wood with acrobatic ease, she floated gracefully down to alight delicately on Sap, at eye level, between Tom and James.

Apparently unperturbed by the rocking of the timber, 'Tallow' as she knew herself, rode the plank comfortably, cocking her tiny crest, and watched Tom and James with her garnet jewelled eyes. Just as intently, the two men watched her.

'Oh, Daddy!' a small voice called from the open doors. 'Isn't she beautiful?'

Sally came running in, excited by the advent of the tiny bird. Red hair, haloed by rays of dusty, gilded afternoon sunlight flooding in through the windows behind her, framed a sweet young face. Bright, blue eyes shone with delight.

Ten summers old, and the colour of autumn, Sally skipped to the side of her father. Dancing lithely sideways, she kept pace with the men and the precariously perched swallow. Sally's head inclined a little, chin up and ear leaning attentiveness towards the mutually attracted bird.

Tallow began the greeting he had rehearsed since egglife:

> *'Bless us all, within these walls,*
> *All creatures great, all creatures small,*
> *The tree was called, we heard her fall,*
> *Returned for all, within these halls.*
> *Hair like nest and hair like tree.'*

'I am you and you are me,' sang Sally in response. It was a child's voice, small and clear, perching on unfamiliar musical notes, but timely, in tune, melodic, yet so full of conviction, and ringing with crystal purity.

As strong as a bamboo pillar and as pliable as her mother, Sally was the youngest of James and Mai-li's two children, gifted with a sweet and pleasing singing voice.

Her agility, and gifted dance ability, was already legend in the area, courtesy of her success in every eisteddfod she had entered since she was four years old. A talent nurtured and encouraged by her favourite music teacher at school and attributed to both her Vietnamese Ba-Wai, (Mother's mother) and her Nan in Dublin.

Sally sang as she glided along with the men and the polished bier, carrying its feathered cargo. 'Who are you, little swallow, shall I follow?'

The swallow responded, chattering, and cavorting the length of Sap's surface, trailing riddles. 'You must find your kindest kind, and then, with wings, leave this behind.'

Tallow was as excited as Sally with the breaking of the language barrier, and flew an oblique orbit around the human trio. Again, and again she swept around them, hovering, and changing direction, swooping, and soaring, expressing her joy at Sap's arrival, and the bridge her young human friend and she had just built.

Tom and James glowed with pleasure.

Once Sap was comfortably stowed in the drying racks, the two mates joined Trevor and Simon up at the house. Simon was barely a year older than Bec and Susan, and greatly admired by both. There would be a short period over the coming year, when all three would be the same age, Rebecca and Susan looked forward to that level playing field, that equal status. One year's age difference in school creates a chronological tyranny of distance, especially for the teenage protocols involved.

Out on the verandah, James, Tom, and Trevor settled into some wonderfully carved garden chairs, completed during one of James' rare quiet moments. The man was always busy, always creating. Tom and Trevor both recognised and valued James' art, primarily for its beautiful functionality, flowing form, and, of course, comfort. The chairs were perfect for relaxing and looking over the crazily paved patio, with its Johnny Jump Up pansies, fairy faces colonising corners, and clambering carpets of pennyroyal, creeping towards the feet of giant purple, hydrangeas and blood-orange and gold nasturtiums.

So, being the good son that he was, Simon opened the first bottle and shared a round of James and Mai's delectable homebrewed beer between his extended family.

'Well,' Tom sighed, 'we're rolling.' His eyes met Trevor's, over the three glasses of dark honeyed liquid resting on the table.

'Rolling is the word,' accepted Trevor, taking a deep, appreciative draught of his beer, and setting it down gently.

'I wonder where this wood, this tree, will take us next?'

It all seemed somewhat surreal to Trevor, Starting at the Daily's farm, meeting Salvatore Fiorelli, and especially the experience in the warehouse. Even with the feeling of having Annie close to his heart, healing a gaping wound, Trevor felt he was in some strange movie, watching an actor playing his part.

He took another long draught of the cold, amber fluid, letting it soak through his body before he spoke again. 'It seems to me everyone near the tree is changing, even little Sally, this afternoon.'

'James, mate, she was like a little goddess, dancing and singing to that swallow. I've never seen anything like it.' He paused for a second and leaned forward earnestly. 'And the weirdest part is we understood every word, including the birds.'

James put his beer down on the rainbow mosaic table between them, licked the foam from his upper lip, and sat back in the chair thoughtfully. James spoke and attended to his life, in much the same way he crafted his masterpieces, slowly, with deliberate progress, and patient grace.

'She's always been a little goddess to Mai and I,' he said softly.

Meanwhile, in the drying room, the 'little goddess' was building bridges with her friend, Tallow.

'Just close your eyes,' Tallow was saying, 'And think of warm nests, brothers and sisters huddled together, high in the eaves. Feel your wings growing, a feather at a time.'

Sally and Tallow were enacting a feat, practised from the dawn of time by astute students of nature, the ancient druid blood lineage awakening in Sally, the art, the miracle of transfiguration.

It was a dangerous business, risking your soul, your essence, to interweave your mind with the mind and soul of a wild animal. Anything was possible.

You could lose your mind to the wildness; your soul could become entangled in the soul of a lion or sabre tooth tiger or a wolf. Horror stories still persist today of the terrors of that possession. Tallow's tactic was far more benign, benevolent, and inspired. Tallow's brief came directly from Gaia. Gaia had said, 'Of all the beings on Earth, evolve the children. For the children are open, they have not had years to hone their disbelief. In the children, rests our hope.'

Sally rested on her side, on a length of Sap, at the bottom of the drying racks, her eyes half-lidded as she listened to Tallow. 'Now, spread each feather wide,' Tallow advised. 'You should be able to feel and control over two hundred and twenty-three feathers.'

'I can feel them,' Sally laughed. 'I can really feel them!'

'You must stay focused,' Tallow impressed on her. 'You must remember you and you must remember me. You, little girl, me little bird. You cannot be woven into me, for I have my family to sustain, and you have your people. I will not be woven into your story.'

Sally nodded, with a gravity that said clearly, she had understood the importance of what she had heard. 'How do I fly, Tallow?' Sally asked again, more earnestly this time. 'I promise I'll be careful. Please, tell me how I take off.'

Tallow considered how she felt when she lifted off, and attempted to translate this into something Sally would understand.

'You will remain here in this space, in this body, yet you will feel every breath of air under every feather, you feel the feather spread her plumes. You then catch that air, and breathe it in, making feather light and fat and warm. This is the first secret of flight.' Tallow offered, looking over her beak, deep into Sally's eyes, appearing a little cross-eyed to Sally.

Tallow captured Sally's attention fully, with her beak thrust forward, piercing the young girl's distractions with her glass bead, hypnotic gaze. When she was satisfied that Sally was in the space nothing else shared, Tallow repeated her warning of the dangers of occupying another's body, and shared the second quatrain on the secret of flight.

'Your wings are covered with light, warm, feather plumes, fat with the air they have breathed in. You must now permit your feathers to breathe out, while arching your wings high above your head and bringing your wings down in a swoop, pushing all that expelled warm air below and behind you. You must be your wings; you must breathe the air in and out with the beating of your heart, it is the drum that drives you. This process is natural, the more you are bird, the easier it is, but be warned, the more you are bird the less you are you.'

'I understand,' said Sally, breathing in and out slowly and purposefully. Her eyes were closed with concentration, her forehead furrowed in a sweet little crease as she focused on the task at hand. Tallow gently directed her frowning student.

'If you must try, you will not fly. You must be the wings, be the air.'

Tallow interrupted the nervous atmosphere, to explain to Sally how important it was to relax into her form, to be within what she imagined she was. Sally's face began to lapse into the smile she usually wore, her shoulders rested in their play pose, and her hands began to spread tiny fingers wide, one by one, each arching backwards in exotic dance moves, in a sequence her Vietnamese blood recognised, and her heart synchronised with the rhythm of her breath.

Sally's hands spoke flowing poetry, they sang, and they danced, they breathed. Generations of her ancestors were evoked in the dance of the hands, the ebb and flow of the breath; the tidal pumping of Sally's heart underscored the soft in and out surge of air warming in the child's hands.

'Aah,' breathed Sally, 'I see.'

Her shoulders lifted in response to the attitude, the belief that she was a bird, and swept in a sinuous arc and plunge. Sally could hear the clangs of brass, the weaving spell of Mekong flutes. As her arms arched again she felt the breadth of her outstretched wings. The edge of flesh and feather became blurred, both rising and thrusting, hands stroking up, wings sweeping down, Sally felt her body lift, her tail feathers extend their spread, in a broad fan, swelling with the warm, fat, air, then pushing it out and down, below and behind her. She was so immersed in lift off from the inside, Sally nearly missed the moment her feet left the ground.

Her small claws and legs retracted in the soft down of her tawny underbelly, as effortlessly, Sally pushed, first with the left wing then with the right.

Why, it's just like rollerblading! she thought. Armed with this insight, she pushed hard down with her left wing, inclining her tail almost perpendicular to her torso, spinning her tiny body out of control towards the ground.

Luckily Sally's skating experience, gained over her years of weekly visits to local skating rinks, kept her aware of her little girl body, and the skills that had saved her countless times on the floor of the rink, emerged to rescue the falling bird she was partnered with.

With tail flattened, and wings outstretched, blue eyes searching forward over the protrusion of the beak, Sally broke her fall and transformed it from certain injury to a spectacular swooping power dive through her father's workshop, into the brightness of the waning afternoon light.

Sally was Tallow, and Tallow was Sally, yet both bird and child were still themselves in a kernel of their present reality.

Sally decided to see how high she could fly and pushed in a steep incline towards the two sentinel clouds, overseeing the events below from their ten thousand metre eyrie.

The ground retreated below her as she relaxed into the rhythm of flight, up and up she flew, until the farm buildings became Lego castles on a patchwork quilt of green lucerne and golden canola, with the road to the farm a dusky snake.

The two clouds loomed larger and larger in her vision, until she could see their fluffy, fairy floss edges, and she intensified her efforts to reach them, higher and higher, into the wild white yonder.

In three sweeps of Sally's fully extended wings, she became immersed in mist and swirling white fog. Even though Sally's body was warm and comfortable, resting on Sap's slab in the drying room of the shed ten thousand metres below, she imagined she could feel droplets of moisture gathering on her wings.

Sally could taste the immaculate air at that altitude and wondered at the view the swallow's eyes could see. Deep within the cloud, Sally could make out a soft glow, becoming brighter as she flew closer, and merging until she could make out expansive, radiant, golden wings. A form began to faintly emerge from the mist, materializing between the wings, resembling what she remembered from scripture classes, as an angel.

'Welcome Sally,' the glowing form in front of her said. The voice was a woman's voice, warm and comforting. Sally's swallow floated, motionless, weightless, suspended in the soft glow of the figure in the cloud.

'I am Gaia,' the voice continued, 'I am the mother of the Earth, Sally. Everything you know and all you can see; all of the Earth came from me. And all will, one day, return. I am glad to meet you, Sally Pringle.'

Sally thought she should perhaps curtsy, or bow or something, but was intimately aware of her swallow's body and felt somewhat self-conscious. But she also felt comforted and intuitively knew she could trust this apparent apparition.

Sally was not in the least perturbed, that she was floating in a bird's body, high above the family farm, speaking with an angel, in the centre of a glowing cloud, with her little girl body, half-lidded, meditative, reclining on a slab of wood ten thousand metres below.

'Hi,' she whispered. 'Are you Mother Nature?' Sally enquired softly.

Gaia's glow seemed to amplify; the air warmed palpably. She beamed back at Sally's Floating form. 'Yes,' she said, 'that is who I am.'

Sally continued, innocence and curiosity compelling her on. 'Then'– she hesitated – 'you would be, my mother too, I guess?'

It seemed a logical step, for Sally to arrive at this conclusion, for she had been raised in a family that loved and trusted her, a family that allowed her disbelief to be suspended occasionally as part of her overall education.

'See the dragon in the arm of yonder chair?' James Pringle would ask her. 'How many water sprites can you count in the grain of this mirror?' he would ask. Making mirrors in curves and boles of rich native timbers, was her father's great love, and many times, the deep, pool-like surfaces swallowed Sally, and seeing amazing, semi-ethereal beings was not an uncommon practise for her.

For Sally, to be suspended high in the clouds and speaking to a golden glow was an oddly familiar sensation. Although it must be said, Sally had never been addressed by one. 'Am I dreaming?' she queried. 'Is this really happening?' Sally paused, thoughtful. 'It feels real, except that I'm a bird, that's pretty weird.'

Gaia expanded, until her glow enveloped Sally, and Sally could not see where the swallow she was, left off and the outlines of Gaia began. She felt like a baby again, cradled in mother's arms, suckled and happy for the closeness, the one-beingness, home. Sally's body, semi-asleep, on the warm, oddly soft wood, ten kilometres below, murmured and curled in a foetal position, drifting on the wing, like a swallow's migration trance, breathing lightly and evenly.

'Yes, Sally. I am your mother, and the mother of the world. Like all good mothers, I love my children and wish them all growth in co-operation with each other.' Gaia spoke tenderly, with a trace of sadness. 'But.' She continued, 'Some of my children have grown to become bullies. My own elements have seeded humankind, and yet, they destroy their brothers and sisters, the trees and mountains, The very stuff of which they are made and inevitably will return to.'

Gaia's voice was not dispassionate, nor isolated from her obvious pain. Gaia wept her pain, as fine mist drifting South, by Southwest, toward the mountains and the Sunset.

Sally understood Gaia's sadness. She too, had cried when she first saw a tree felled. Even at her young age, she had sobbed inconsolably, when a small park she often played in with her friends, had been bulldozed, to make way for a sterile concrete car park for apartment buildings, in which she and her friends could never play. They would no longer colonise the dark sticky mango trees, the pirate ships, and fairy castles.

Without the inspiration of the natural world, perhaps their fertile young imaginations would never develop enough to find the cure for hunger, cancer, poverty, or homelessness.

She cried sometimes, when she saw the seven O'clock news, and there were children she never knew, in countries she had never heard of, suffering horribly.

The pictures almost always showed deserts, with no trees in sight, only ochre and grey, windblown, fly-blown, drifting explosions of dust. The news that entered their home usually showed dirty, frightened, and dying families pursued by war, by famine, but most of the time by their neighbours.

'Like fleas fighting over who owns the dog,' Sally's father often said, scorning the foolishness.

Sally's swallow body, wrapped as she was in Gaia's embrace, radiated empathy, a sadness that lifted the weight of sorrow, sharing the burden.

Gaia beamed all around Sally and whispered to her heart. 'You are blessed, Sally, you who I love so very much, you who are so young. You may become the one to save the people of Earth from self-destruction. Sally, would you do something very special for me, and for the Earth you share with your family?'

While Gaia, or "Mother Nature", as Sally saw her, awaited Sally's response, the ten-year-old imagined she was flying over vast forests. Blue Mountains stretched to the horizon, some capped with snow, others with multi-towered fairy castles, and as she swooped low over the glades and clearings, thousands of luminous, colourful, sparkling beings rose from the land to greet her.

Sally was complete enough to realise that all these beings were spirits of the forests and fields, seeking kinship with Humanity so all could share this beautiful jewel we inhabit.

The very existence of everything Sally saw, she knew, relied on her saying 'yes'.

'Yes,' Sally mouthed the word silently. Curled up on Sap, ten kilometres below Sally whispered, 'YES!' Her mouth spoke the word aloud, echoing 'YES!' around the drying racks, raising dust from the sheets of wood all around her.

As Sally returned to her body, she slowly adjusted her eyes to the dim interior of the small wooden shed. The last rays of the afternoon sun emphasized the dust motes swimming in the air, floating and dancing on the multitude of golden roads offered by the treed pattern of the vents that James had cut, North, South, East, and West, following Mai-Li's, intuitive Feng Shue suggestion.

Sally breathed out in a perfectly formed and considered, 'YES.'

'Then follow me.' The diminished, softly glowing, winged form appeared before Sally amongst the swirling crowd of elements. It floated down, landing on the deep, red carpet that was Sap, in front of Sally's nose, and began to sink into the dark wood.

Sally followed the figure with her eyes, down, into the wine dark sea of now shimmering timber. She saw the fairy, Gaia, stretch, and melt into the current-like grain of Sap's bulk. The wood shifted, just as she had with Tom Daily and Trevor. The grain flowed and rearranged itself, like rapids in a fast-flowing river. Gaia merged and submerged amongst the streaming fibre, until she became the strand of the weave that wove the character of Sap. Sally followed. The strands bent and twisted forming a familiar shape that Sally had seen a hundred times before.

The unmistakable shape of a writing desk emerged from the maelstrom of writhing structure. The desk was a masterpiece of the woodcraftsman's art, buried deep within the memory of the slab herself.

Resting on the desk, almost feminine in its curves and graceful sweeps of coppery wood, lay the most beautiful violin Sally had ever seen, glowing deep honey, symbolic of the sweet music she harboured, she seemed to beckon to Sally: 'Play me, Write me.'

Sally noticed there was several of Bally Mai's pencils in a wooden urn, that seemed to grow up from one corner of the desk, as well as a small pile of Sally's unique puckered edged paper, made from the pulp of local eucalypt trees. 'Bally Mai' was the business name Becky, Sally and Mai-li, sold their boutique paper and pencils under, and the combination of elements; the violin, pencils, paper, and desk, asked Sally, like a long-missed friend, 'Play with me.'

The desk merged back into the wood, and the wood merged into the slab Sally was on. The picture was unforgettable, the foundation was laid, and Sally's path to her destiny was illuminated like the runway of an international airport.

Sally slipped from her sprawl across Sap and gathered herself feet first on the dusty floor, brushing imaginary dirt from her jeans and shirt. Tallow was also on the wing, moving with Sally, washing the galaxy of particles into a frenzy, with the sweep of her wings.

The sight of Sally, bursting from the workshop with a swallow looping about her head, greeted James and Trevor as they stood to part ways. Both men and Mai, stepping out the back door, saw Sally loping towards them, obviously excited, and running with a slightly peculiar gait, reminiscent of a small bird, part skip, part step, part launch.

'Daddy, Mum. You won't believe what I did just now.' And not waiting for any real response, Sally excitedly gushed forth the whole story, in a babble of words and hand-motioned pictures.

Tallow, perched on the apex of the garden arch at the edge of the courtyard, almost invisible amongst the climbing roses and wisteria, silently re-lived the experience.

'Come, little one, join us.' Mai-li's voice sang up into the tangled foliage once Sally had eventually paused to take a breath. Standing like a sculpture of a garden nymph, just below the hanging blooms, Mai whistled a haunting little melody, short melismas ending complicated phrases, denoting the tune's origin as Asiatic.

'I once loved a little bird like you,' she sang. 'She was golden as the sun. As silver as the moon, but now she is gone, she is gone.'

Tallow immediately responded with a tune of her own that scaled the lofty altitudes of the biosphere and swooped to earth, ending in a precise trill. Her 'lifesong,' as this signature is known in the avian community.

'And Tallow – that's her name, you know – and I have shared the most amazing dream,' Sally said, as she skipped over to her mother's side. Holding out her hand, she invited Tallow to join the gathering. 'We flew, and we saw clouds from the inside, and we saw you and the farm, and, Mum, it was so wonderful, and we met Mother Nature, and her real name is Gaia – at least, that's what the ancient Greeks called her, and...'

Sally paused to catch her breath, allowing Tallow to settle on her outstretched finger. Securing her grip, she turned to face the adults looking peculiarly at both the swallow and her.

'Daddy, Mother nature has a job for you and me to do together. She showed me, the wood, and the pencils, and ... well, I know! I'll draw you a picture, okay?'

Trevor searched Sally's eyes for a trace of Annie in her story ... any connection he could find ... until a soft voice welled up inside him.

'Yes I am here, in your heart, yet I am also part of this story unfolding, watch closely, my love, and learn ...'

Comforted, as he was, Trevor so wanted to share this experience with Simon. As he looked across at his son, as their eyes met. He knew Simon sensed something, but it was not up to Trevor. Annie would reveal herself to her son when she thought he was ready.

The distant revving of a diesel motor, and the groaning of brakes, interrupted the gathering in the garden, signalling the arrival of the afternoon school bus delivering Rebecca, Sally's older sister, home from high school. Simon felt a thrill jangle across his senses.

Rebecca, or 'Bec' as she was mostly affectionately referred to, was one day short of 15, tomorrow would be her birthday. With the years, Bec had grown into a beautiful young woman, with high, intriguing cheekbones, her mother's golden skin, and sunrise eyes of the most profound green which captivated friends and innocent bystanders alike.

Bec's long bronze legs swung down from the bus, sidestepping away from the departing vehicle. Laughing, she raised her arm in a genial goodbye. Turning towards the farm, her sharp eyes caught sight of the Daily's truck and the Manning's Toyota 4wd.

CHAPTER 13

Her leg had been aching through the afternoon lessons, which occasionally it did when seated for long periods of time. This afternoon, Bec found it difficult to even break into a slow jog towards home, when usually she was a vigorous runner, despite her deceptive disability.

Her pronounced shuffle and rolling gait when walking, betrayed the legacy of her childhood illness. Rebecca Pringle was in the top 300 metre track athletes in Richmond River High School and was ranked highly in the state championships.

Her story could have been different, had James and Mai not noticed she had particular difficulty in standing up and walking when Bec was barely a toddler.

While most of her peers were becoming mobile, Rebecca at two years old stalled putting weight on her legs, and when she did, the effort was often accompanied with her screwing up her face in a grimace, and an occasional whimper of pain. The chief hindrance seemed to be her left leg, which seemed to have a mind of its own. It would skew to the side, or fold under her, refusing even the most basic commands from its owner, like stand, turn, support me in some way.

Her parents were troubled over her lack of mobility, and anguished over Bec's obvious pain, until one evening in the bath, Mai noticed a small lump in her tiny daughter's groin, barely the size of a pea. There it was, a scarcely noticeable rise under the rose-pink baby skin, but a swelling all the same, on the inside of the thigh, pronounced enough to press against the muscle when Mai tentatively touched it, eliciting a tiny cry from her daughter. She called James into the bathroom, and delicately pointed down to the mark on the small body they had believed was perfect.

The Pringles called Dr Aldus DeGabrielle, Fernyvale's favourite, in fact *only*, family doctor, who had attended both Bec and Sally's births. DeGabrielle called for an X-ray, then an ultrasound, then a Magnetic Resonance Image, and within a week Bec was undergoing surgery in Brisbane. All the diagnostics pointed towards a little-known sarcoma, or cancer, named for a Dr Ewing. Ewing's sarcoma occurs in the bones primarily. For Rebecca, the pelvis that seemed to be the issue.

Bec was ironically lucky, firstly in early detection and the fact that the tumour wasn't in her long bones, but, after two years of agony, surgery and radiation, all traces of the disease had disappeared, leaving Bec with a slight rolling sailor-like gait when she walked, which disappeared entirely when she ran.

The tumour had taken a deep piece of Bec's left iliac spine, opening her pelvis somewhat, thereby enabling her to raise her upper leg and knee beyond the range of most other girls of her age. Oddly, her disability gave her a distinct advantage on the track and in yoga classes.

But today she did not run. Tired from a long day in high school, Bec hefted her bulky school bag across her shoulder and headed down the driveway. She unhurriedly strolled the shady avenue of hoop pines and frangipanis, toward the house, with its traditional, broad verandah and overhanging poinciana trees.

Rebecca mused as she made her way beneath the giant trees, I hope Simon is here. I missed him today at school. Although she didn't consciously dwell on the boy, her head and her heart carried a flame. Bec fancied Simon Manning, with his eccentric tastes in music, his seeming indifference to fashion, his unruly hair, and those blue, blue, eyes. Bec conjured several possibilities as she walked.

The approach to the house was carpeted with a vivid red and gold blanket of spent poinciana blossoms, leading up to the broad, open stairs and the cool, sun-dappled verandah. Bec reluctantly returned to the present. As her eyes adjusted to the different light, she could just distinguish several bodies moving about the table and chairs, one of whom she recognised as the object of her affection.

'Hey, Bec,' Simon called out. Embarrassingly oblivious to the adults gathered, he added, 'I missed you at school today. I've been a bit distracted by all this "magic tree business", seems to have dad in a bit of a tizz.'

'Hey, you,' Trevor interjected, 'This "magic tree business," will undoubtedly change all of our lives.'

'Magic tree?' queried Rebecca, suppressing a warm glow rising to a soft blush in response to Simon's warmth. Her self-consciousness dissolved when Sally burst from the kitchen, carrying a jug of fruit juice and a plate of homemade lamingtons.

With the tinkling ice in the glass jug providing music to the story, Sally could not resist this opportunity to tell someone else of her adventure in the clouds, and subsequent conversation with Gaia and Tallow.

Simon stood and pulled a chair out so Bec could cool down and relax a little before someone else would capture her attention. Seeing her evident fatigue troubled him a little. Sometimes he felt so useless around her. If only he could somehow make her better. Even though she denied any disability, Simon simply needed to be needed, and with her immediacy quickening his already loudly beating heart, he hovered.

He wanted to take her in his arms and tell her how he felt every time he saw her, but Sally's amazing story came bubbling to the surface between them.

The incredible flight and meeting, the revelations Sally shared with her extended family, opened so many doors and avenues of thought, and astonishment, the subliminal romance between teens became seriously derailed.

The balmy afternoon air felt palpably close despite, or because of, the intense teenage hormones, and the invisible pheromone tempest. Even on the open verandah, the sense that a storm was building was unmistakable.

The clouds, that through the day had been sparse and occasional, gathered amongst the mountains behind the farm. A breeze lifted branches on the poinciana trees, randomly littering blossoms along the drive. Red and gold parachutes tripped across the open space.

Rising willy willys swirled the dust either side of the drifting shadows on the driveway, churning the blossoms and leaves skywards, blending the gold and reds with a richer and deeper scarlet softly manifesting. The scarlet swirling cape and cane grew from what appeared to be a veil of blossoms and mist.

Stepping into this world from some other parallel universe, was the gradually solidifying, semi-translucent form of Salvatore Fiorelli. The conversation and turbulent undercurrent of emotions came to an abrupt halt as all eyes followed the dramatic appearance of this quixotic figure.

Trevor was the first to gather his manners and suppress his surprise. He was on his feet in a moment with a welcome smile for the man that had witnessed, and he suspected was a catalyst for, his surprising reunion with his dead wife back in the dusty warehouse of the mill.

'Dear Mr Fiorelli, it's so good to see you again.'

'Please, come on up and take a seat, make yourself comfortable.'

Turning to the others, he gathered his thoughts to attempt to explain his odd relationship with this exotic being.

'James, Mai, let me introduce a very remarkable friend.'

'Rebecca, Sally, Simon, this gentleman is Salvatore Fiorelli, come all the way from Italy. He has a very special interest in our friend the tree.'

Salvatore inclined his head slightly, and swept his hat from his head in a small flourish. 'Si, Si ... It is an ultimate pleasure to be meeting with all of you.'

'I have long dreamed of this meeting. We are Conspiracy to change the World, No? Si!'

Sally could not contain herself any longer, 'Mr Fiorelli, do you know Tallow?'

'My friend is a swallow, and she can fly, and she taught me to fly!'

Shuffling her feet, a little and looking around for some support, 'Well, she did!' Sally exclaimed emphatically. 'Even if it was in my mind, I saw what I saw. And it really was from way up there among the clouds.'

She paused, looking up at Salvatore, who smiled back at her.

'Dear Sally. It is Sally, Si? You will find we are all players in this opera. We all believe you. What used to be unusual is not anymore. Why, everybody here is a miracle, everybody here is woven into this story, even the trees and rocks around us know, the Angels in the air, the very air itself and the water. Dear Sally, you show us the way.'

James and Mai, being the hosts of this odd gathering, took this brief respite in proceedings, to welcome Salvatore Fiorelli to their home. Mai immediately took charge, ushering Salvatore up the steps to the verandah and offering him a large woven cane chair, well upholstered with rugs and cushions.

'Your hospitality is greatly appreciated, young lady' he quipped, causing Mai to laugh lightly.

'Why thank you, sir. We do our best.'

Salvatore wasn't finished. Taking Mai's tiny hand in his own, Salvatore peered deep into her eyes, reading her soul, divining her past. A soul journeyer himself, he recognised others along the path and assisted when and where he could. Mai's pain and pleasure, her trials and tribulations came tumbling and bubbling to the forefront of her mind, unbidden.

This profound inquiry by Salvatore took but a second, amongst the circle of friends, but to Mai her life unfolded in this blink of an eye.

The burning, tortured, tormented past life in a fractured Vietnam, swept over her, the tattered remnants of human beings sweeping by on the great river, disappeared. The river was again pure, and her world was renewed. Immense trees greened the landscape and hung over the rushing water, vines and epiphytes cascaded from their branches, mosses, tropical orchids, and many ferns lined the banks of the river, where once Mai had hidden in fear of her life.

The Agent Orange and napalm destruction of her land was gone. No guns fired now, no diving roar of threatening warplanes, no more stealthy, muffled chop, chop, chop of deadly helicopters, leaking even deadlier gases, nor the pervasive stink of decaying bodies assaulting her.

Mai was refreshed. The scent of orchids, frangipani and jasmine wrapped around her like a mantle around a newborn babe. Mai was reborn.

The gentle touch of a loving hand sliding softly around her waist, returned Mai to the present, and the closeness brought with it the scent of rose gum and wattle, James' signature scent. Mai relaxed into the curve of his arm, and focused her eyes to study this man she loved.

As if from another room, she saw him through a veil, or a smokey glass window. He became part of her dream, part of the mighty Mekong jungle. Arms became supporting branches, draped with vein-like vines.

He cradled her there, suspended above the torrent, and she had never felt so new, clean, and loved. The scents of the woods James worked with imbued his skin, and his blood. Sap was the air James breathed, the sweat on his brow, the bones throughout his body ran gold with Sap for marrow. Flowers that fell from his eyes: deep blue clematis, and jasmine tears.

A heart beating deep in the wood, lightly swayed the crimson lady slipper vine decorating its chambers, garlanding the aorta to the left ventricle, and spiralling down the arteries and veins. Mai turned to absorb the immensity of the man, her eyes widened with wonder at this miracle of being, he distorted softly around the edges and as if a giant hand had gathered the canvas, from behind, at a point a little above centre, and had drawn it into itself, the forest shrank back to her own garden.

Trees she and James had both planted, bloomed above her, James' floating smile among them. Mai adjusted her senses to what she saw. While the vision remained deep within her core being, she returned to the group on the verandah.

Salvatore still had her hand. Barely a heartbeat had passed.

'Mister Fiorelli, you have unique and extraordinary talent.' Mai looked a little pensive, momentarily, until she said, 'I thank you, sir, for here,' She gestured towards her chest open-handed, as if cupping a fragile lily. 'And here,' indicating her temples.

James was a little bemused at his wife, on meeting Salvatore. However, he recognised a depth to their exchange, unaware that he'd played a central part in the revelations Mai had just experienced.

'And my husband, Mr Fiorelli, *cảm ơn bạn*, for him, you know? Thank you.' Salvatore swept all thanks aside, with a flourish of his elaborate hat,

'Is what I do,' he said, inclining his head with assurance. 'I see to the heart of things. Be they people, trees, situations,' he continued. 'It is all very simple. We all come out of the earth, we will all return, we are earth, forever potentials, forever recycled, we lose nothing but form, and gain everything. Memory and dream, past and all possible futures.' Stopping for a moment, he scanned the circle of attentive faces before him, before concluding, 'It is my task to see through these fleeting incarnations and free them to fulfil their Purpose.'

James could see that Sal Fiorelli wove a compelling spell embracing the families gathered on his verandah, shaded under the broad spreading limbs of the flowering tree.

'Well, Mr Fiorelli, you may be able to shed some light on the promise ingrained in this wood Trevor bought over this very afternoon.'

'So, it is so! If you are to call me Mr Fiorelli, I must say to you,

Mr Pringle. Is it not easier to call me Sam, while I could say James, yes?' Salvatore inclined his head slightly, eyes gleaming with humour.

'Sam, it is,' confirmed James, and to ratify the welcome, poured Sam a foaming mug of the amber fluid he shared with Tom and Trevor.

'The Tree, we have met.' Sam glanced meaningfully at Trevor.

'I am thinking it is time your son also met this Sap.' His eyes flickered across to Simon, where he sat close to Rebecca. 'You understand, to resolve matters possibly tearing at his heart.'

Simon raised his eyes to consider Salvatore, and his father. There was an obvious familiarity that puzzled him, although he knew that they had met at the mill, earlier in the week, as his dad milled the bulk of Sap.

Simon had noticed that his dad had changed over the week, something subtle had shifted, something only blood could sense, a son would see the father, and recognise a softer side had emerged, perhaps a more unwearied person, as if a weight had been lifted from tired shoulders. Simon carried the same burden.

CHAPTER 14

Boys, at the age of ten, are constructed to deny death. It took Simon years of denial to accept his grief had been disguised as anger over his mother's passing.

It is a country they are not prepared to travel to, or in, or hear of, from anyone. My mother will return; she is not dead. My mother is on holidays, somewhere, perhaps overseas; she cannot get to a phone to call you, to let you know she loves you very much and that she will never leave you, and that she will be back soon.

The soon, continues for years, for some boys, their entire life is consumed with waiting, wanting, poisoning relationships on every level, until the realisation dawns, one sunny day. Never an overcast, rainy, miserable day, always a sunny day, with windblown leaves, and clouds seeking the sun.

Simons 'soon' had lasted over five years, despite his father plumbing the depths of his own grief, reaching down towards a drowning son, while he, himself was barely afloat. After years submerged, the pain began to taper. The waters did not seem so deep, and Simon realised his father was floundering.

One evening, sharing stories of Annie with each other, her laughing eyes, lightning-fast wit, and inability to tell a joke, Simon reached out and grasped his remaining parent's hand, and together they crawled on to shore, holding each other fast, survivors.

The bond that was forged between father and son was potent, and waterproof.

Each surviving day concreted the ties. Trevor and Simon took precious time with the waterproofing, took care of each other, valuing blood and survival, and love. And now the appearance of the tree in their lives had somehow cultivated and enriched the family of two.

Simon knew it was the tree, or something to do with the tree, that had so affected his father. In the week following the felling and milling of Sap, Trevor had connected with Simon on new levels for both father and son. They discussed issues concerning the heart, and women particularly, mostly a mystery to men, which both had skirted as either too close for comfort, too dangerous emotionally, or simply inexpressible.

Issues Annie would have broached confidently with them, had she been there. This recent change in Trevor, evoked rising emotions in Simon, enquiries about his feelings, his loves, and hates, gently prying open the cave where he kept his deepest and darkest thoughts and fears. Exactly as his mother would have done.

Lately it seemed to Simon, that his father would hesitate during conversation and incline his head to one side, as if listening to an unseen voice, after which the subject would take unforeseen directions, directions possibly his mother might have navigated, had she been alive.

Trevor had been unable to fully share with Simon his experience in the warehouse. His restoration with Annie was too fresh, too powerful, too overwhelming to weave words around it, fearing this renewed intimacy would vanish, or be lost or diminished in some way.

Yet he had to try. Possibly now, probably here on the Pringle's porch, but how to broach such a subject?

'Dad? ... Dad,' Simon repeated more urgently. 'Where exactly are you now?'

'Trevor...' Annie's voice called in Trevor's head.

'You need to answer your son, answer *our* son ... don't leave him languishing in the dark.'

'What shall I say?' queried Trevor, deep within his thoughts.

'Tell him the truth about me, about Sap, about the future. He deserves to know the truth, he needs to know I am here ... for heaven's sake, Trevor, he is my son, our son. I love him, and he needs to know that, and that I am accessible anytime through his thoughts and dreams. He needs to meet the Tree, and I believe now is the time.'

Trevor started, startled back to the moment, and looked up to find Simon gazing at him earnestly from across the table.

'Dad ... what exactly are you thinking now? Are you here with us? ... I worry about you, you know. These vacant times, when you disappear from company, from me, where do you go?'

The others: James, Mai, Tom, Salvatore, and Sally, were engaged in their own conversation across the table regarding Sally's adventure, oblivious to Trevor and Simon. Rebecca, on the other hand, sitting next to Simon, was paying great attention to his enquiry. And suspected it was good manners that distanced the others from this intimate and immediate exchange. She reached across, gaining Simon's hand, finger by finger, lending love and support to his plea.

Trevor looked directly into his son's eyes and told the truth.

'I speak with your mother, son. I tell her my fears, how much we miss her, what you are doing, what I'm doing. I tell her our plans and dreams, and listen to what she says, her opinions, her thoughts, what her heart still believes about you and I. And it is all real, your mother lives here,' he said indicating his head and then his heart. When she died, I lost my rudder, my purpose for living. Even with you here, I was simply living from day to day, going through the motions, I guess. It was the tree, that bought us back together. I was lost without her, Simon. Then last week, Sam here introduced me to the tree I was milling, and showed me she was much more than wood and fibre. This tree, Sap is her name, showed me another reality, she essentially bought your mother back to life for me, but, here deep in my heart and head.'

Simon was silent, probing his father's eyes, watching his mouth form the words.

'I speak with her all the time, and she answers me, because she is always with me. And now she says it's time you two were reacquainted.'

Simon felt the world start to spin, he grasped Bec's fingers tightly, an anchor in his current confusion. Bec returned the grip with both hands.

'I knew it, the way you spoke, the words you used, your expressions. I knew it had to be mum, I hoped against all reason, it was her you had in mind when I'd ask something, it was her answering, wasn't it? I need to find her, I need ... to be like you are, you know, with her. Please Dad, can you show me, teach me how?' Simon trembled with the tide of intense feelings pulling at his gut. His disbelief was suspended on a scaffold of hopes and dreams, which he had spent the long years dismantling, only to find them reassembling in this strange moment.

Trevor climbed out of the carved armchair, leaned across the table, placed hands on both Simon and Bec's shoulders softly and beckoned them to follow him. Wrapping his arms around them both, with a brief meaningful glance at Salvatore, he guided the young couple along the shady garden path and around to what Sally called the 'story racks', to meet the One Tree.

The afternoon sun shafted rays across the jungle-like veggie patch, as the three edged past tomato and passionfruit vines clambering to overgrow the wall of the drying shed.

Up the rugged stone steps and out of the light, the feeling of being swallowed by the darkness arose in Simon. Bec sensed his hesitation and fear, and held his hand ever tighter and led the way, almost touching Trevor's trailing hand. Although a father's job has always been to protect and cultivate confidence in his offspring, Trevor was aware Simon was afraid of the dark.

The blackness faded to a dusty dimness. Pencil thin shafts of particled sunlight highlighted racks of sawn wood, stacked from bottom to top under the cob-webbed roof.

Whispers of dust drifted, in an undulating sea of tiny grains, suspended in air across the shelved space. silence dominated the shed.

The breaths of the three visitors was the only sound interrupting the dust settling. Trevor navigated the racks and stacks of timber with the two young people in tow, until he stopped next to a broad slab of deep red lumber resting across two sawhorses. Like a body in repose in some ancient tomb, she lay there.

His fingers absently trailed across the garnet surface, leaving gentle, caressing tracks of care along the waving grain.

In an almost sensual movement, Trevor drew his hand with new intent along the broad panel, until it seemed to Simon and Bec, the wood responded by puckering where Trevor's fingers trailed, rising in a subtle swelling, reaching back towards the man.

Small fingers formed, meshing with his, a wrist, an arm, soft, the colour of varnish, flowed from the slab of wood. In barely seconds, Annie Manning stood in the place of the milled tree, as exquisite as Simon remembered, as attractive and stately as Rebecca recalled her being, before the cancer wasted the body away.

'Simon, my beautiful boy, I have missed you so much.'

The reservoir of tears not shed in six years since his mother died, flooded Simon's eyes, and poured down his cheeks. 'Mum?' he ventured. 'Mum.' He rushed into her arms, 'Oh Mum. I miss you, I love you so much.'

Arms wrapped around him and held him close.

To feel his mother's arms cradle him again, triggered another torrent of tears, this time buried in the scent of her hair, the softness of her, the closeness, warmth, and envelope of love that enfolded him.

Rebecca saw but did not see, felt but could not comprehend, what she had just witnessed. 'I...I was at your bedside,' she gasped. 'I saw you take a last breath, I was at the funeral, I wept for months after you died – passed away – how?' Lost for words, she was also gathered up in those loving arms.

'Bec ... my lovely Bec. It's wonderful to see you again,' Annie breathed against her cheek.

Trevor stepped close again to his past and present wife, took her hand and held it to his lips. 'My love,' was all he could say, saying everything.

'Oh, my dears, don't you see? I never left you. I have been with you all this time. I have been part of Sap, and although I live in a different form, I have always been around you. This tree is changing the world we live in. Miraculously, it seems now, we can live on in many forms, reinventing and reimagining ourselves. My natural essence is now in the wood, but, as you can see, I can reveal myself in any form I choose, although only for short periods. As I understand it, it's about energy.'

Annie smiled indulgently. 'Imagine if all our deceased loved ones returned in their old bodies, what would be the point of leaving their lives?'

'The old must always make way for the new. This is renewal, our souls must learn and grow, and enrich other lives, have fresh experiences, gather as yet undiscovered knowledge, to pass into the material world.' Annie gathered them again to herself, and whispered, 'The love never changes; the love never leaves.'

Simon was reluctant to let his Mother go, holding the waited for embrace as long as he possibly could, memorising again the feel, scent and presence of his own flesh and blood, the first woman he ever loved.

Sap had manipulated, or really, tree-ipulated time, allowing the reunion to occur in a fold of the time continuum, never disrupting the flow, meeting in a momentary backwater she had created for the occasion. Time waits for no man or woman, it leaks around edges, it soaks through the fabric of space, it fritters away.

Trevor gently eased Simon and Bec into his own arms, allowing Annie to sink partially back into the wood, wearing the velvet slab like a draped evening gown. 'I am so proud of who you have become in these past years,' she said particularly to Simon, but also intended for Rebecca as well. 'Your paths are unfolding before your feet as we speak, there are roles you both will play with Sap and I, in the world you see around you, and others you have not yet encountered.'

One final loving look at his mother as the woman and the tree, was all Simon could manage before Annie dissolved back into the wood.

He was at once elated, sad beyond belief, confused, alone, yet, with his father and Rebecca close by. Simon felt the pressure building, his head could not hold everything he'd witnessed, too much, too soon. Information and revelation flooded his mind, with only his humanity to contain it all.

Dizzy with overload headache, he found himself losing control, felt himself spinning out into a space strange and unexplored, and out of his depth.

'All these years, all that time I thought ... I ... I don't know anything anymore!' he shouted at the roof, the walls. His father and Bec, even the swallows chattering among the rafters copped a grief-stricken mouthful from the anguished young man.

'Simon, son...' Trevor tried retrieving his son from the maelstrom of emotions he seemed to be drowning in. 'Simon, we are all here, that's what matters most. Surely, son, you can see we love you. Nothing has changed.'

Rebecca wrapped him in her arms, smothering Simon's cries in her thick coat, her hand gently stroking the back of his head, smoothing his unruly hair, and soothing his unruly heart. He heaved against her.

Could no-one see! She had been taken from him twice: six years ago and just now. She was gone again, after the briefest of reunions, never knowing when they would meet again, he felt his life's deepest wound had been reopened.

CHAPTER 15

Simon broke the embrace, pushing Bec backwards in his effort to free himself. Arms flailing, she crashed against Trevor's chest, throwing him hard against the wall raising a cloud of dust. Simon spun on his heels and stumbled out the door, almost falling down the stone steps, arms akimbo, a dark fugitive, framed in the doorway, escaping.

'Simon!' Trevor and Bec screamed. But they knew he was gone, gone to where he would find sanctuary, somewhere to process this overload. Both Rebecca and Trevor had witnessed this emotional trauma before, the lonely boy, grieving for his lost mum, with few friends...Simon would occasionally boil over. He would find somewhere to be alone, to mull over events that had tipped his balance.

He would chill, retreat, sit for a while, usually somewhere with a view, somewhere he could see things clearly, see events coming, some place he believed he had some control over his life.

Simon came to himself running helter-skelter down the Pringle's drive, shadow and light washed across his face as he ran, tears streaming down, dripping off his chin, images of his mother pouring in and out of his imaginings, trees and flesh, flesh into trees.

He found it impossible to separate the two, until they blurred together, creating an uncomfortable image, of knots, limbs, and face, Chasing him down the road. This time they wouldn't find him, this time he would be far away, God knew where. He wanted no more to do with the world.

The crazy, stupid world, where the dead resurrected and died again, became trees, then slabs of wood speaking to him, holding him. It had felt so real. It was real, wasn't it? Was it? If it was real, where is mum now? Why isn't she here, still with me?

Running with grief, blinded by tears, he didn't even see the limb that tripped him. It snaked out from amongst the poinciana's buttresses, one of hundreds of roots supporting the great avenue of trees. Simon fell, flying forward, arms outstretched to save his face from the rough gravel of the sandstone driveway.

His hurtling body crashed to the ground, sliding across grass littered with red flowers and fallen leaves, towards a deep, gaping crack at the base of one of the giant trees. Slowly the wrinkled wooden lips parted and split open wide enough to swallow his undisciplined entry.

Simons mouth was also wide open, but silence resulted. He roared with defiance and fear, for help, in pain and shock ... but all that issued from his mouth was rasping gasps reducing to pathetic whimpers. The grinding of the gravel and the ripping of his clothing, the swishing, swishing sound of the great limbs retracting, and the almost noiseless inwards drawing of a deep, deep breath, sighed in his ears.

Simon had little time to process his grief over what he thought was the re-disappearance of his mother. Now he felt he was being incorporated into the trees around him as well, and he wasn't going to go peacefully. Dragged, voicelessly towards the twisted, gnarly, hungry base of the huge tree, Simon struggled desperately, rolling back and forth, digging his fingertips in a talon like grasp at the short blades of greasy grass, leaving elongated claw trails where they failed to make purchase.

He eventually realised his efforts were useless as he felt himself being drawn down between the roots, into the dark spaces under the greenery, down among the shadows and the worms.

The light was dimming, the aperture shrinking, and the earth beneath Simon was definitely becoming damper. His desperate fingernails were digging into the soft mosses and humus under and between roots, but still he found no grip solid enough to halt his slippery descent into the bowels of the great tree.

'Help!' a voice cried somewhere, too dark to discern where. Simon thought briefly he had called out, but couldn't recall the exact moment.

His hands grasped at thousands of intertwined tendrils of roots, clutched at soft rotten shafts of old wood, as the walls of his prison slid past.

Sliding, falling, into the darkness, 'Help me!' the voice called again. Simon abandoned any attempt at orientation. Somewhere to the left, maybe? The voice disappearing below him as he descended further.

Sensing a gradual slowing of his plunge, Simon reached out into the soft, tactile, damp darkness, fuelled with a bleak hope of resurrection, waving his arms around in a blind man's search.

The voice called again, 'Here, over here, please help me.' It sounded forlorn in the absolute darkness. He could hear a lonely, echoing sobbing begin, somewhere almost beyond his audible range, fading away in the gloom.

As he gradually ceased to slide, the build-up of dirt and leaves, humus and spongy somethings fell away, off his legs and lower body, into what seemed to Simon a bottomless pit or tunnel that continued below and around him, further than he was prepared to even consider.

He wondered if it had been his own voice he had heard on the way down, and dismissed the idea instantly as absurd. He would have had to think it first, surely? Then, faintly he heard it again, at the far edge of his senses, 'Help me.'

'Where are you? Who are you?' he shouted into the depths.

'Help me, you must ... help me ... please,' an unmistakably female voice rose from the abyss, sounding weak, small, and vulnerable in the darkness.

Like me, Simon thought.

'I can't!' he screamed back. 'I'm sorry, I just can't, I can't even help myself!' he sobbed into the spongy walls of his prison. Hot tears rolled down his cheeks and soaked into the moss cushioning his descent, he was certainly descending again. In a relentless downward spiral, he was ever so slowly being carried on a carpet of soft moss and rotting leaves moving under him, as the wall he hugged, rippled from top to bottom.

Like riding a wave, Simon's body rippled in response and rode the undulation in a break-dancer's motion around and down the dizzy tunnel.

'I'm falling towards you!' he called out to the dark.

Something released within him, the inevitability of his fall and his emotional trauma unravelled like an overwound spring, he let go, trusting in the untrustable unknown. He believed now, the love of his mother, where-ever or whatever she was, his father, who had been with him through everything, Rebecca, and all those he loved, would find him, regardless of where he ended up. He was left with nothing but his belief in love and a deep trust that had developed, and grown within him.

'I have no choice, it seems, so here I come.' He relinquished his grasp of the moss and roots he clung to, and dropped, sliding, tumbling and freefalling into darkness.

As he fell, lights flashed past him. Strings of lights like a passenger train passing, all shooting upwards. No, he realised finally, they weren't going up; he was dropping downwards still, accelerating in free-fall, with no visible sides or bottom, he descended into the bowels of whatever existed far beneath the tree.

Simon heard the clanging of bells, railway or otherwise, he knew them, temple bells, gompa temple bells. Bali, or maybe India, came to mind. Forgetting almost completely his too recent distress and loss, trapped in the moment, immediacy and fascinating engagement in his adventure overrode everything else.

Still the voice cried. 'Help me!'

Still the bells rang out.

'Help me,' they tolled.

On the surface, Trevor and Rebecca were still attempting to process Simon's outburst and explosive exit. Dust was still filtering down from the rafters after the slamming of the door, as the two felt their way out of the woodshed into the tree-fractured light of the setting sun.

'Are you all right, Bec?' Trevor dusted himself off, shaking his head. 'Look, honey, I'm sorry it came to this, all caught up in the family drama.'

Bec was gazing down the driveway in the general direction Simons footfalls had sounded, 'No, I mean, yes, I'm okay. I'm just worried for Simon. 'I feel such a part of your family, Trevor. You must know I have feelings for Simon, and hoped that, maybe … someday. Well, you know what I mean.'

'Me too, little darling. You would be a wonderful daughter to have.' Trevor straightened, brushed off invisible dirt, or hurt, and wrapped his strong arms around her, kissed her on top of the head, and with one arm still draped across her shoulders, guided her back to the group on the verandah.

As they both climbed the stone steps, the first lights along the building flickered on, brightening the table where James, Salvatore, Susan, and Rosie were sitting, waiting for them. A last glance back along the shadowy track, left Trevor wondering where and when he'd see his son again.

While Salvatore watched their return with interest from behind his drink, James rose to greet them. 'Where's Simon?' he asked.

'Simon had a traumatic reunion, I'm afraid,' observed Salvatore. 'This tree, Sap, will evoke strong emotional responses in everyone involved with her, especially those who have loved ones woven into the story. I apologise for not warning you beforehand, but it would have changed nothing, trust me.'

'He saw Annie,' Trevor managed to say, slumping into the nearest seat. 'She rose from the wood,' he said, taking a deep breath and a thankful swig on his now flat beer. 'She lifted from the slab we'd milled, as alive as you or me.'

'Simon cracked it,' Bec spilled over. 'He was there, she was there, we held her, touched her, she was so real. He even spoke with her, she was, is, as awesome as I remember, hasn't changed since … since, she died. Simon cracked it, couldn't handle seeing her there.'

Bec stopped for breath, and quelled the rising emotion threatening to overwhelm her.

'I guess he felt he was losing her twice, when she returned to the wood,' Trevor said softly. sank I understand how he feels, I've been lucky to have had her with me for a couple of weeks now. I've gotten used to having her, with me, inside me, each minute, each day, speaking, sharing my life, as if she had never left.' He sank heavily into the chair, head bowed. 'Have I done the wrong thing?' he asked no-one in particular. 'Has it been too soon? Oh, God, what have I done?'

Salvatore rose slowly, and moved around the table. 'It is not what you have done, Trevor.' 'It is Sap, it is the tree weaving among our lives.' He rested his hand gently on Trevor's' shoulder, as much in blessing as reassurance. 'Such a thing will happen to everyone eventually. The Tree, Sap, she is a mirror to ourselves, you see. Simon is adrift, no anchor, no boat. He floats with no purpose within himself. He must learn to steer by his own nature.'

Salvatore eased himself into the seat alongside Rebecca. 'You know, sometimes our women must steer, must be our ... how you say? Powerhouse, our engine, driving us forward. She will be his strength and guide! We men, ha! We think we are so strong. We are not strong.' He met Rebecca's eyes. 'We are so strong we are brittle, like biscuit, or steel, like giant bridges that carry more than their own weight. When they stress, when they crack, they fall, and everything crumbles to the ground!'

Bec's eyes felt gritty, stinging with salty tears. Mixed sadness and understanding for Simon plumbed her depths. She spread her arms wide hopelessly.

'But what can I do if he won't let me in? How can I even find him?'

Salvatore smiled indulgently at both Trevor and Bec. 'You don't even worry, Sap will find him and bring him back. You must trust; you will learn to trust.'

Mai, behind the kitchen window, was busy at the chopping board desiccating greens and reds, yellow and orange vegetables, blue borage and gold nasturtiums, dandelions, and mint, mixing them in a bowel, weaving her hands over them and softly chanting over their mix, to heal, mend, flavour and sustain, here, love was the primary ingredient.

Sally had picked all these treasures from the garden next to the drying shed, and was on her knees selecting ripe cherry tomatoes, while Simon, Trevor and Bec were meeting Annie. She overheard Simon's outburst and the slamming door, and could but wonder what had occurred that was so troubling for him.

Simon, the big brother, Sally wished for, or the hero, who would sweep her far away and maybe, someday even marry her. She knew it was a dream, but it was her dream, her secret fantasy. Each night before bed she prayed to every god she knew and some she made up, to make it true.

This evening, leaning over the sink washing the tomatoes, she asked, 'Mummy, what happened to Simon this afternoon? Do you think he will be all right?'

Mai looked up at her thoughtfully. 'We will see, dear one. Time will tell.'

CHAPTER 16

Simon had serious doubts about his wellbeing. He felt his fall slowing, but the passing lights did not slow, flashing past at an astonishing pace, a ceaseless elevator rushing up into the dark recesses above him.

As his plunge began to lose speed and eventually stop, he saw that the procession of lights was more than a stream of windows disappearing into the gloom, unless they could be called windows of the soul. As the lights appeared below and disappeared rapidly above him, Simon could now see they were actually in pairs.

Now he was stationary, Simon could see the lights were eyes, shooting upwards like inverted comets, or fireworks, The colour varied, eyes of blue and green, browns, and hazels, violet and indigo. He sensed they were appraising him with a sort of intelligence and a kind of knowing as they passed.

As he watched, Simon discerned subtle variations in colours and, he thought, even expressions, sadness, joy, puzzlement, elation, and despondency. To Simon it seemed individuals were passing, in ceaseless procession upwards.

Closer now, the voice again cried, 'Help me! Do you see me?'

'I don't know what I'm looking for!' yelled Simon in response.

Still the eyes ascended, in a stream of subtle variations.

'Look down,' the voice directed, 'Look deeper.'

As Simon did, he thought he could vaguely discern a ruddy glow, swelling as he watched. A large bubble of what Simon thought looked like lava – or the magma he remembered seeing in National Geographic documentaries – burst below his feet, releasing a rush of hot air around him as he hovered above, suspended there in limbo.

A deep bell tolled, reverberating through, and around Simon. Unable to sense what direction it was coming from, he looked down again. A pair of gompa eyes, incredibly, like those seen on the enormous stupas erected centuries ago across Asia, rose towards him, floating above the seething, red and gold, molten mass below him.

The eyes wept tears that would fill cauldrons, overflowing and pouring down the massive face.

'Help me,' the eyes pleaded, floating between the hot maelstrom and the river of souls. The voice was inside Simon's mind, filling the space of who he was, where he was and how he came to be here.

'I ... I ... don't know, what, or who you are, or where I am, what is *happening* to me?

The eyes became a face, the face became a head, became a dome, was a temple rising from the heaving mantle below.

'You know me,' the voice replied. 'I am your mother, your grandmother, your aunts and your sisters.'

Simon was within himself as he experienced the conversation, in a place of no fear, no distraction, minimal self-consciousness, only awareness of the presence before and the voice within him.

The immense sorrow the figure encapsulated was palpable. Simon felt it radiating in every direction, touching him, cooling the heat he felt from the furnace below.

The bell-like tones in the voice continued, 'I am all you have ever been. I am all you have ever known. I am every soul that ever existed in your ancestry, all beings capable of being human since the beginning of time on this planet pass through me.'

Simon was witness to eternity crossing his consciousness, in a female voice.

'I know you, somehow,' he meekly whispered. 'I feel a closeness, a ... kinship,' he finally offered.

'You are kin to me. You are kin to all, Simon,' the voice intoned. 'You have seen me as Gaia, growing on the surface of this planet as trees, plants, rivers and deserts, mountains and oceans. You now see me as the great mother, recycling all souls through my cauldron boiling below the thin crust beings live upon.

I accept every living object, and there are many more than humans give credit for, living out their existence in the thin envelope of atmosphere on the surface of the Earth. We grind and fold and knead souls between plates, under land masses you are familiar with, and many that have gone before. We subsume and consume great and small civilisations, even continents and oceans, across the countless eons. They all are grist for our ever-turning mill.'

Awestruck, Simon looked on in wonder at the enormity he confronted. There was nothing he could adequately articulate.

'Don't be afraid, Simon, for all have been processed many times over, growing and bringing their experiences with them, the richness of many lives is absorbed and recycled, the infinity of imaginations is also absorbed on other levels. Nothing is lost, nothing is wasted, but lately, over the past two thousand years, a poisonous corruption has entered the blend. Now we need your help. Human ego has become so strong, believing itself so powerful, denying the divine nature of the universe. The stubborn image of separation resists the merging of souls.'

Simon wondered how he could breathe above the glowing maelstrom, and although he felt the intense heat rising from the turbulence, he was not at all uncomfortable, at least not physically.

His thoughts turned to those he had left behind, particularly Rebecca, and his father. They would be wondering where he was, and how, since his emotional explosion had shaken their world, he was coping.

He knew Gaia was aware of his thoughts as they emerged, because before him a panorama opened in the space between him and the magma. In it he saw Rebecca and Trevor, Sally, Salvatore, James, and Mai, settling themselves around the great wooden table on the verandah at the Pringles. Bec's eyes were red from crying. As he watched, a stream began welling below the hazel eyes he loved so much. The lips he had kissed not an hour ago, were quivering with pent up emotion.

He saw his father reach across the table and gather her tiny trembling hands in his massive, weathered ones, cradling them as he had cradled Annie's and Simon's through difficult times.

Deep beneath the surface of the planet, floating above an ocean of boiling magma, Simon could feel the love.

'I have to go back. They'll be worried about me, Bec needs me.'

Before his eyes, Gaia's form began to blur, indistinct, reforming, those eyes still fixated on his, softened, blended green to turquoise, became blue, became Annie, the mother he sought, the one he was escaping from and the salvation he ran towards.

'Bec doesn't need you as much as I need you.' She spoke to his heart. 'Simon, I love you as only a mother can. I know you as part of me, I have, I will *always* love you, whether I am near you or far away, or even in a different form.'

Simon was confused, bewildered. 'Six years ago, you left me ... us. Six long years of missing you, Dad and I. I ... I know it wasn't your choice ... to leave, I knew you were sick, we both saw that each day you were in pain, and we just wanted it to end.'

Annie seemed to become smaller, became more human, and moved closer to the young man still suspended above the cauldron. 'Simon, dear Simon, you knew it could only end with my passing. You and your dad spoke to the doctors every day. It was almost unbearable to leave you and your father behind.'

Her arms were around him, her face close to his. He could feel her pulse and the rising and easing of her breath, as it was when he was watching her die, sitting helplessly by her bedside in the Fernyvale hospital, six years before.

'I understand how you feel, Simon. Leaving you was like another cancer, a loving, longing, parting cancer, slowly eating my heart, tearing apart our family, as my body slowly disintegrated.'

'Oh, son, I love you and your dad so much. I miss you both, beyond telling. But, now I am here, and you are here, in the most unusual of places, deep beneath the surface of the planet. I have a favour to ask of you, actually more of a task I need you to carry out,' she said. 'Simon, your hearts deepest wish was always to be a healer, a doctor, like those who saved Rebecca's life, do you think you can do this for me?'

Simon tilted his head a little, quizzically. 'I still have to finish my higher school certificate. That's in November, only a month away.' As an afterthought, he added, 'If I ever get out of this place.'

This place, he thought, he'd momentarily forgotten where he was. Suspended above the molten interior of the planet, white and golden magma seething below, his mother, six years deceased by his side in conversation with him. Have I gone crazy? The thought crossed his mind, seriously considered, then dismissed as he traced his path here ... all was connected, he couldn't recall any head injuries, but then if he'd had a head injury, would he remember it?

Annie intruded into his thoughts, 'You are not crazy, Simon. What you see and feel is all part of Gaia's plan, for the one tree and for all of us. Miracles are already occurring ... Me and you, here, for example. And above ground Sally is talking to birds, and guiding James and the violin maker from Italy, Salvatore, in creating the vision from the tree. Rebecca has another mission entirely, elsewhere.'

He didn't know how it was possible, but he had almost forgotten about Rebecca, throughout his emotional crisis, and the subsequent escape. Now he felt guilty, and not a little ashamed of his behaviour, and, yes, his selfishness.

'Is Bec okay? I mean, do you know if Bec will be okay? She'll be stressing over me, I know that much.' He shook his head and dropped his gaze. 'And Dad as well.'

His mother moved closer to him, 'They are all fine, Simon. As you saw, they will support each other.' She reached across and gathered both his hands in hers. 'We will let them know where you are and that you're well.'

'Let them know?' breathed Simon, 'How will we let them know? And am I well? Why can't I see them and tell them myself, now?'

Annie held both his hands and his gaze, 'We have an appointment, son.' And with that, the world churned, Simon felt his mother's hands gripping his own, and the spinning dance began again. He watched as the core of fire turned behind the image of his mother holding his outstretched hands.

Immense distances across the internal world sped below and about them, the giant roots of mountains and continents turned above them. The boy and his mother danced together within the globe, a thousand kilometres below the surface.

Molten columns of rock and fire pillared the ballroom, supporting a ceiling flowing with golden rivers, while inverted mountains hung chandeliers of raw diamonds that glittered over them as they turned slowly below.

Deep within the Earth, time slips covertly ahead while distances shrink deceptively. The dance stretched them both along the timeline, until minutes warped into hours, then days and finally six years unravelled as mother and child recovered the years spent apart.

The child was no longer. Simon was now twenty-two years old; issues of separation and anxiety were resolved. Security and maturity took their place, along with a deep sense of purpose to nurture, educate and illuminate the mass of humanity populating the surface.

Annie had not aged a second while the dance continued. To Simon, she seemed ageless and as exquisite as he remembered, even as her blue eyes coloured back to the forest green of Gaia's. Though the image remained the same, he recognised the mother he had always loved; while realising she was a mother beyond that.

Trees, deep-rooted in forests scattered across the Earths' surface, in collusion with the mother reached far down into the Earth's mantle, scooping both beings up in giant gnarly hands and drawing them up, up towards the surface, navigating their way through rifts in the crust, zigzagging along irregular fault lines below continents and oceans.

As they ascended, Annie/Gaia showed Simon how the mechanisms of the Earth's suspension system operated. Continental plates thousands of kilometres across and weighing Trillions of tonnes floated on a suspension of gas mixed with oil and water, and liquefied earth.

She revealed to him the ways this subterranean lubricant allowed the magnificent global plates to slide under and over each other relatively gently, gradually, across millennia, changing and shaping the face of the planet.

They travelled north, below the slow moving and relatively stable Indo-Australian plate, continuing the drawing apart of Gondwana, and dragging the Australian continent towards the equator.

Nestled upon soft mosses in the great knotty hand, Gaia revealed to Simon the fiery rift below Indonesia where streams of magma queued beneath volcanoes about to erupt from Sumatra to the Philippines.

The huge hand changed subtly as they were passed from tree to tree across the subterranean mantle, shielded always from the incredible heat exuding from the magma ocean beneath them. The scent of Eucalyptus was replaced by the richness of equatorial teak and mahogany vessels, even ebony, as the woods of the world passed their precious cargo along.

As they made their way towards the Arabian plate, Annie took her son's hand comfortingly. 'There is something occurring within the Arabian rift, I must show you, Simon. An example of what is occurring all around the world.'

Simon was awestruck by his surroundings, the journey, and the mode of transport. Although he trusted implicitly in his mother, he wondered where this was all heading.

Ahead, he could see what looked like a fine mist, curtaining across their path. It seemed to be raining down in jagged zigzags from high above them, oozing from cracks in the crust of the planet, looking to Simon like the pictures he had seen of auroras washing across the Earth's north and south poles. As the mist touched the boiling, molten rock below, sparks, lightning and smoke billowed upwards.

Simon guessed the clouds rising from this impact had to be thousands of kilometres across, the sparks were explosions that would dwarf an atomic blast.

The giant hand carried them closer to the phenomenon until almost within reach of a human arm it stopped. Simon and Annie could hear the Earth above creaking and groaning as continents wrestled up against each other for space, and below the burp! and exhalation of the magma bubbles venting.

Shrilling above it all, with the deafening hiss of a million angry snakes, a deluge of fine sand was falling through the cracks above and raining over the golden cauldron below.

Over the hiss and bubble, Gaia's double spoke quite clearly to Simon, who was totally absorbed, gazing through the gaps between the great ebony fingers.

'Be careful not to touch; this sand is mostly uranium and thorium. The sparkling silver you see is radioactive and would burn your flesh off the bone if my protection was removed.'

The sand drifted in sparkling drizzles just beyond his nose and he could already feel his skin reddening.

'The active elements of Earth churn above and below, sometimes reaching the surface, occasionally sinking down below the mantle and the crust. What keeps them in circulation in a non-destructive way is the shock absorbing qualities of the gas and oil and water, stored in vast reservoirs beneath the crust.' Gaia's Annie paused and surveyed the scene beyond. 'This fall has been continuous for over one hundred years, it is why there is little water across the Arabian plate, and the deserts encroach ever closer to human settlement. Humans have been draining the oil from this continent and subsequently others around the world, since the turn of the last century to feed their industries and motor vehicles.'

Simon was mesmerised by the glittering downpour and spoke as one in a dream, 'Does anyone else know of this, on the surface, I mean? Surely if they did, someone would act, or at least do something to stop it.' As he gazed on, he murmured softly, 'I guess the middle east has had its share of grief and trouble. Who looks beneath their feet, when they're constantly looking behind them?'

'Simon, dear Simon, people have been told of this for the last hundred years and have done nothing. Oil is the lifeblood of the middle east, and indeed, the world. This is the basis of the economy of hundreds of nations. Consider Egypt, the Sudan, Saudi Arabia, Iran, Iraq, Jordan and Syria without oil. It is the blood that sustains all the Western Nations.

They would have nothing to trade for goods they cannot grow. In fact, the region would see large scale starvation, for the people have forgotten skills that served them well for thousands of years.' Annie and Gaia sighed softly together, an achingly sad harmony.

'This region has been at war for over for over two thousand years, from the early tribes of Abraham and David to the Ottomans, the Sheiks and a thousand different tribes, always scratching to make a living from the most difficult terrain on the planet. And now the changing climate across the globe is causing devastating droughts throughout many lands, forcing farming folk to drift into the cities, where the haves and have-nots fester their anger, and blame each other for the devastation. This must change.'

Gaia's Annie reached down to their son, placing a soft hand on his shoulder, turning him gently around to face them. 'This is the very reason we have bought you here, son. Trust us to guide and help you heal the world. We have considered the rewards and benefits due Earth from humanity and have decided it must be humanity who heals Her.'

The Earth Goddess who happened to be Simon's mother, lightly stroked the enormous black fingers of the ebony hand, and rested her cheek against the first joint. 'Sap the tree will be assisting you in subtle and creative ways. You will simply imagine what you might require, touch wood anywhere, anytime, and she will respond in kind, keep this at the forefront of your mind.

'You always said to me, if you had the chance you would help people, so, we have arranged a time and place where you will receive a degree in medicine, as well as surgical skills well-honed for a warzone, that is where you can do the most good.

'You will be under our protection at all times, and cannot be harmed, but danger appears without warning and affects more than you. You are sorely needed here. So, if you choose to join us in healing the planet, be aware, what you have seen is occurring everywhere. In Texas, Oklahoma, Brazil and Argentina, Alaska to the Ukraine, from Shandong, China to Queensland, Australia, this is but one of the starting junctures. I did say, "If". This is your choice, Simon. If you choose, otherwise you will return to Australia and continue your life as if nothing had happened.' She continued, 'But you can rest assured, despite the one tree, Sap, Myself and the entities of the planet continuing the work, where-ever you are and whatever you do, these Earth changes you have seen will catch up with you and all inhabitants of the planet, until it reaches the inevitable, disastrous conclusion.'

Simon thought unexpectedly of Rebecca. What would she want him to do? He already knew. He recalled the vision of her on the verandah at home, tears welling in her eyes. He thought of his dad, waiting for him to return, and the others in the small community he loved.

He wondered how he could make a difference in the world. He had always wondered how he could make a difference in the world; at least now he knew.

'I'm in,' he said, knowing in his heart this is what Rebecca, and his dad would want him to do, but most of all it was what he had always believed.

Simon smiled at his mother, and echoed his father's oft quoted expression, 'It is better to light a candle, than to curse the darkness.'

He stood, balancing himself on the uneven palm of the great ebony hand, faced his mother and her alter ego, and smiled. 'For years I've wondered about why I'm here, and what is my reason for being alive? Especially after you died, I felt so powerless. It all seemed so unjust; you were still young, you loved dad, and I know dad adored you. I felt abandoned, alone. I was ten years old, and the world seemed so big, and cruel.

'I even asked God to bring you back, and God replied with silence. Deafening silence. I thought I was too small to be heard, too small to change things, and now; now I realise Life unfolds as it should, I guess I just needed some perspective. Now I see we are all doing the work. You, Gaia, me: we all can change the world, given the opportunity, we can all make a difference. I'm yours. Do with me as you will. You can tell the tree I'm ready and willing, and I know together we can do this.'

His mother beamed back at him.

'My Darling, God is not a He, nor a She. The being we refer to as God is a collective of all beings, all energy, in the multi-verses. Light energy, dark energy, black holes and galaxies, ourselves and indeed all the other beings in all the Universes in the Cosmos. It is intelligent, in fact it is intelligence itself, and being all things, it knows all things and all times past, present and future, for all exist in the singularity.'

She propped herself against the ebony thumb, and affectionately wrapped her arm around it, and gave an enigmatic smile. 'As for the Tree, she already knows.'

Tree roots fell from beneath the crust above Simon wrapping him in a cocoon, soft with moss, cushioning the jolt as he was propelled upward towards the surface and through. Simon found himself on a broad stretch of manicured lawn, shaded by towering Cedars, looking up at an imposing entrance arch, with the words: *Primum non nocere, dum valet sentit sapit*, carved above it. *Firstly, do no harm, be healthy, perceptive and wise.*

He immediately recognised the Latin translation, although he could not recall ever studying the language. He knew this was the university his mother and Gaia had chosen, and that the years following would be fuelled by a passionate fire and purpose to bring about real change in the world.

Hefting his bag higher across his shoulder, Simon climbed the ancient stone steps, and walked through the grand oak doors to begin his work.

CHAPTER 17
The Instrument

Salvatore Fiorelli and Sally Pringle were hunched over the soft feminine lines of a honey-coloured, semiconstructed violin, resting on a velvet cloth at the workbench of James Pringle's woodworking shed. Deftly shaving an edge here, measuring and etching, purfling, curving tantalizingly close to the rim of the violin top, not quite completed.

Salvatore mused as he worked, reading the meridians of energy along the grain, how close the lines of force and flow bound to each other. Sally quietly trilled some hedge wren song she'd picked up this morning on her walk along the creek, with vague references to delicious grass seeds, sparkly water, and warm sun. The seemingly aimless melody comforted Sal, and evoked a meditative mood as he called to mind the body this soul had once occupied.

The song transported Salvatore back to late September 1700, a mystical centenary year, the beginning, and the end, Alpha, and Omega. The next year, 1701, would denote a new era, a birthing of a century. Such occasions warranted respect, if only for their age. He was a man who valued and appreciated time, for his craft depended on it. Days, hours, and minutes, his most valuable tools.

It was Autumn, and the days were shortening. Time was an implacable tyrant, and waited for no man.

He, Antonius Stradivarius, 56 years old and beginning to feel his age, was working in a cold, dim workshop whose few redeeming graces were that he could work without interruption, rigorously and painstakingly building his extraordinary instruments, and the fact that the barn doors at the end of the workshop opened on to the mountains and meadows of Northern Lombardy.

The breathtaking view that ranged across flower dotted fields, the red terracotta rooftops of the village of Pontevico, and the sun lit alps floating on the horizon, made this not an unpleasant place to ply one's trade as a master woodcraftsman, in Summer. Winter was a different creature altogether.

The last winter had been severe, as had the last forty. Since 1650 the yearly minimum temperatures had plummeted to consistently below freezing, from early autumn to very late spring, causing some glaciers visible from Antonio's workshop, to advance down the steep mountain valleys.

The soothsayer in the market at the town square had blamed the sun and the fickle planetary cycles as vehemently as the Bishop had blamed the townsfolk's sins. Whichever was true, the cold had been a blessing in disguise for Antonio.

In the long winters and the cool summers, the woods he selected for his violins and cellos (the Norway spruce and sycamore) grew especially slowly and evenly. This meant the grain and growth rings were unique in producing the tones he particularly sought. Antonio also had a theory involving the odd blue fungus stain in the grain, he discovered while sawing violin blanks from this same wood.

He believed the fungus ate a segment deep within the wood, building minute caves through which sound was amplified and gained resonance, the way the caves in the mountains he had explored in his youth had affected his raised voice.

It would take another three hundred years of scientific cellular research to finally validate his discovery. His mind, peering through Salvatore's eyes, saw the same patterns and structures in the ruddy gold form before him now.

Sally's voice was still trilling the same song, and in the time he'd been out of this body, he had barely completed a thumb plane stroke along the inside edge of the violin top, seconds alone had passed.

'So, where did you go to this time?' Sally's blue eyes flashed a smile across the smooth and well-worn handle of a fine woodworking chisel.

'An old man dreams, of times long gone. Ah! But look at what you have fashioned, it is beautiful, no?'

He picked up the finished top, and turned it slowly over and around in his hands. He peered down the slightly pregnant belly of the soundboard, holding it at arm's length, studying the symmetry of the 'F' shaped sound holes either side. He breathed softly across the wood, causing it to rapidly fog and dissipate, highlighting the fine waves of golden grain.

'She is ready, si? We shall try them together.' Salvatore handed the top back to Sally. 'You can do the honours, Senora Sally, this masterpiece is your child, I have only guided you.

He beamed. 'The tree and you together, my young friend, have created beauty, and I expect a voice to swell from this instrument unlike any ever heard.'

Sally carefully ran her long fingers around the ledge that would neatly sit inside and over the blocks and ribbed sides of the finished violin.

As her fingers stroked the wood, she sang a soft incantation learned from a pied butcherbird, and the wood complied. The grain all along the ledge seemed to pucker and rise to the tip of her finger as she deftly ran it over the curves and ridges. It settled softly, smoothly back, perfectly aligned with the body it was wedded to. The magic flowed between human and wood, they were one, and the soft song continued to work its spell.

Each corner block and 'C' rib aligned with every purfled edge with not a hairs thickness between them, it was perfect.

As Sally hummed a deeper descant, cascading down the scale like a currawong at dawn, the violin seemed to stretch and plastically mould itself to its final form.

Salvatore sighed a deep note of satisfaction. Four hundred years of dreams and visions, the culmination of his purpose, fulfilled in seconds.

Sally glowed. Light from this universe, and others, shone from the pores of her skin. Auroras of every colour washed over her body and out across the room, streaming from the doors and windows of the old homestead, and around the world.

The shining colours seeped through gaps around windows, over and under doors, and washed rays of light across the walls of James' finishing room next door, illuminating the other golden glowing entity being constructed from the very same tree. The remarkable desk James was co-creating with the tree herself was a curving, and sinuous solid, on the brink of fluidity, akin to a wooden teardrop with a flat surface of translucent honey. Not heavy as a wooden teardrop might seem, but fine, thinning towards the legs and body, a little feminine in the soft lines the Tree had dictated.

James drew a soft cloth along the edge of this precious timber as the filaments of fibre danced into conformity under his inspired guidance. James, like Sally, took complete artistic direction from the tree; their imaginations linked, and all disbelief suspended. All beliefs sustained. The doors between workshops swung open, as Sally stepped into view, spilling light from the violin next door, onto the desk.

As James looked up from his mesmerisation, the marriage of the violin glow and the desks radiance shone together like a star exploding, catching humans, migrant souls, and magical wood, in a photograph etched upon the walls of the workshop forever. A place the world would revere as a nativity, a birth of a philosophy that would transform the planet with its creative co-operation between inhabitants that had been estranged for ten thousand years.

Sally was ecstatic, and shining herself. 'Oh daddy, it's beginning, I can feel everything coming together.' Throwing her arms about him, her heart beating strong and fast, she gasped next to his ear. 'I love you so much, Dad. Thanks for being here, with me, I mean, and helping me and Uncle Sal, and the tree and everything.' She was almost breathless when she turned to Salvatore.

'It is the light,' he simply said. 'This is the power of love.'

The power of love was strong this night, under the full moon, with the planets Jupiter and Venus almost embracing. So close were they in the western sky, above the small North coast town of Fernyvale, the two planets seemed to be dancing with each other. One could imagine their outstretched arms linking them as they orbited together, though they were a billion kilometres apart.

Far below them in the intensive care ward of Lismore base hospital, Sally's sister, Rebecca, was taking an elderly patient's blood pressure, focused on the swish and rhythm of blood pumping along ancient and weary arteries.

Where Sally, four years younger than Rebecca, was now seventeen and had been recruited by Gaia to sing and play, wedding her gifts to the special magic channelled by Sap; Rebecca, twenty-one, heartbroken and still puzzled over Simon's disappearance, had tirelessly applied herself to nursing studies, attempting to forget the unexplainable, improbable absence of the love she'd never had the chance to realise.

She had chosen nursing as a career to ease her heartache, by easing the pain of others. Rebecca was an exceptional nurse and student. Topping her classes and receiving high distinctions in every aspect of anatomy and physiology.

After graduation as a Registered Nurse, she continued her pursuit of knowledge at various universities and hospitals until she achieved her master's degree as a Nurse Practitioner. Rebecca had decided early on her path, not to become an MD, as she believed it removed her from the personal and time-consuming aspects of practical healing.

This was the reason she was here; her path lay in healing, not necessarily curing, but the holistic mending of human beings, struggling with their mortality. Like her sister, Sally, Rebecca was well acquainted with 'Sap' the saviour tree. Over the six years the tree had lived with the family, every part of their lives had been woven into the story of reunification of humans and nature.

Sally showed Rebecca how to invoke the gods of small things like birds and lizards, spiders, and bees, to look after tiny details in the everyday dealings of life.

Sally had been a natural chronicler of Gaia's message, after meeting "Mother Nature" at the Pringles home, when the newly milled Sap first arrived. She learned to sing with whatever birds were in the vicinity, learn their news, and make peace with nature with one small act of loving kindness after another, regardless of form or feather.

After all, she had been with Gaia, she had flown with the birds, she had scaled altitudes where clouds lived, even been part of Tallow the swallow's identity, all on the first meeting with Sap the tree. Sap and Sally had been inseparable since meeting.

Sally would carry a small stick off Sap wherever she went, or one of the pencils she and her mother, Mai had made from Sap's limbs. Occasionally, she would even secret a tiny splinter under a fingernail; to keep Sap close, a little girl's need for reassuring contact with the loved one.

She did this until one day she realised she had no splinter or shard of wood with her, but the tree still spoke to her as if it was within her mind, a part of who she was. thus Sap, Sally and Salvatore had collaborated to construct the violin. As Salvatore put it 'to sing the Earth well.' This was enough to free her of the need to continually fetch wood.

Rebecca had other talents. Although she could understand well enough the language Sally spoke and communicated with, she had some difficulty shaping her lips to whistle and the nuances some animals and birds used to place finer points on their language.

Sap and Rebecca had a different type of relationship. Rebecca spent time with the tree attempting to understand, from her and Sap's perspective, the psychology of Simon's sudden outburst and hasty escape from the drying shed.

She and Sap explored the human and plant mind, realising that they are not so different. Together, they probed the plant and human body, discovering their similarities and their differences.

Sap could draw Rebecca's imaginative mind deep within any plant, from Grevillea Robusta, the majestic, golden flowered silky oak, down to the heart of a dandelion. She became fascinated to learn that translucent and flexible, a little yellow dandelion out in the field needs to have plasticity so that it can bend, not break, as the wind blows through the field. On the other hand, a fifty-metre tall tree needs a very strong and rigid cell wall, but retain that same plasticity, so that it can grow to its great height and not fall over in the wind.

CHAPTER 18

The unlikely pair travelled on wings of seeds, sometimes a spinning maple seed or a dandelion's delicate parachute, crossing the planets continents and oceans, building and developing knowledge of plant and human anatomy and physiology.

As Rebecca slept in her bed at home on the farm, exhausted after shifts and study through the day, Sap and her astral body would trip the light fantastic. They explored outback Australia, from Uluru to Kakadu, seeking knowledge from fifty thousand years of Indigenous healing. They found evidence in Central Asia of meditative healing methods, going back in time long before Gautama the Buddha walked the land.

Together, the pair floated over the Amazon Basin, as seeds stuck in the wing of a migrating songbird, following this astounding river to its source high in the Andes, where it starts as a spring trickling out of the massive Nevado Mismi, at over five and half thousand metres.

The Amazon was a major objective in their travels. The last unspoiled and unpolluted rainforest remaining on Earth, the Amazon is the lungs of the planet. Rebecca found a university of knowledge amongst the plant, animal, and human life they encountered there.

The educational value to Rebecca through Sap, was immeasurable, instructing her on the structure of plant composition at different altitudes, how different pressures affected growth and eventual size and health. She also instructed Bec on herbs and healing plants yet undiscovered in the wider world: magical fungi and epiphytes only sourced by intrepid healers, shaman, and medicine women from tribes that had never seen a white person, and the surprising catalysts that made them effective.

Bec was awed by the tree climbing ants, who harvested the nectar of some plants, storing it in their nests, preserved with the acid the queen produced to enable its digestion to power the colony, and in the process building an organic Mylar that one day will be used as a cure for various neuronal diseases like Multiple Sclerosis and Motor Neurone disease.

As feather down seeds, they blew across vast continents. Rebecca absorbed knowledge from every font, the information blossoming in her mind's eye, enriched by Sap's presence to embed itself in her memory, ready to be used when the time is right.

Sap's instruction included the importance of having an "intent to heal". this was the stillness of mind and the probing knowledge of the body. Sap termed it, 'Looking without, seeing within.'

Rebecca learned on these nocturnal sojourns to understand the ebb and flow of blood, like sap through cellulose. She knew how cell osmosis occurred, how cell walls in all living objects are subject to flows of nutrients and are obstacles to disease or damaging bacteria and viruses. More importantly, she learned the principle of quantum observation, how simply by observing something, like a disease or symptoms, irregularities in a body, or possibly a mind, we change them at a smaller, sub-atomic, level.

This enlightened view of medicine, accounting for the whole being, physical, mental, and genetic, was a revelation for Rebecca, who absorbed the knowledge like a sponge. Sap illustrated the concept with light. She demonstrated to Rebecca how in the Eastern belief there are energy centres relating to the human body.

The Tree assigned these centres with musical notes and the seven primary colours in a rainbow. Sounds and colours that resonate with organs of the body, exciting or reposing cellular and molecular functions, so, in fact the body heals itself.

Bec would wake up each morning, in her bed on the farm in rural Fernyvale, with the most fabulous and insightful memories of dreams from the night before. Remembered in their entirety, she only once attempted to refer the concepts to one of her professors at university, and was met with such scorn, she never broached the subject with the teaching establishment again.

Despite the pressure of work and university, she began noting her dreams' in a journal, paying attention to the prompts added by Sap regarding her connection with the spirits or devas overseeing the individual plant, mineral, or fungi she sought assistance from. Bec noted in her margins the importance of asking for assistance from the natural world.

The journal grew daily in content and volume. The pages multiplied beneath her pen, as month by month, the chapters rolled out. Beneath the light of a small desk lamp, late each evening, Rebecca would industriously write down the instructions from the night before.

The information required to change our concept of healing and attitude to the natural world grew and grew, page after page, from one journal to several, stacked at the side of Bec's small desk, by her single bed, in her tiny room.

The soundtrack Rebecca composed her journals by, drifted softly out of James' and now Sally's woodworking studio behind the house. Sally had taken to the violin like a duck to water, or more accurately, a bird to the air.

CHAPTER 19

Each evening Salvatore would sit at the amazing teardrop desk with Sally, instructing her in the ancient art of coaxing beautiful music from a magnificent instrument. There were no notes to be studied, no scales to practise, the violin knew, or rather the wood that comprised the violin, sang, told stories, evoked emotions, and soothed souls.

Of course, Sally required instruction on holding the bow at the correct angle, a deviously difficult manoeuvre to sustain for the duration of a piece, but light as feather. The same wood that was kin to the instrument sought the strings as a babe seeks the mother. The bow hair that caressed the strings came from the tail of the Daily's mare, Bucca, the pony Susan Daily rode along the creek that had washed Sap's roots as she grew.

The same mare that massaged her rump against Sap's rough trunk, fertilised the soil she grew in. The fine, pale strands from Susan's Arabian stretched unbroken, strong, and even, for over a metre behind the mare, nourished by the very grass that grew beneath Sap. It was natural they would provide a perfect complement to the bow and violin. Salvatore saw this, so, trusting his four hundred years of intuition and hard-earned knowledge, utilised this exquisite product to hair the bow.

Sally found the unique tone produced by Bucca's hair gave Sap's violin an oddly equine sound, some whinny amongst the whimsy. Salvatore and Sally were also fascinated by the evocative galloping rhythm on some melodies they played, particularly the Celtic reels and jigs that emerged from the instrument.

Whether these emerged from Sap's conjuring up Sally's Irish ancestry or were simply the joy of playing and expression, the violin simply sang, and when she sang, all sorts of reactions occurred. Feet could not stay still. Legs that had never danced, found themselves lifting weightlessly and spinning, stepping, sliding.

Arms reached for bodies to hold close, eyes met eyes over bodies converging under the spell of Tangos from Argentina, Beguines from the Caribbean, Bangras of northern India, Dilan's of Iraq and Iran, all ranks, and classes of dance, both ancient and modern from across the globe. Sap played sadder than dirges and brighter than Bollywood wedding sangeets. Lonely windswept songs from the Kazakhstani steppes, and Zampona Pan Pipes of Peru emerged from the Instrument.

Sap and Sally invoked spirits of dance and song from civilisations long vanished and cultures still in evolution. Words not heard for a thousand years came spilling from Sally's lips, of love and longing, of beauty and sadness, parting songs and songs of welcome.

Not all the songs were in human languages, the melodies and tone spoke of winds in high trees, the mantras of migration chanted by birds on the wing, and the grunting, shambling gait of Bison following ancient tracks across northern tundras. Blue whales echoing in the deep Pacific Ocean and the groaning of glaciers to the whispering melt of ice murmured in the marriage of bow hair, string, wood, and voice.

The music travelled across borders and mountains, knew no boundaries, and took no prisoners.

Every sense vibrating or resonating in response to sound, from reptiles that slithered and crawled and heard with their belly, fish swimming listening with their bladder, mammals lumbering on land, or breaching the ocean's surface recognised their kinship, the recognition that all emerged from the Earth, water, and air of this planet, and were children of Gaias.

This intelligent planet, Earth, brought all beings together with a communication that navigated every type of environment and anatomy. the only obstacle it encountered was the notion of separation.

The Human idea of superiority over others and ego-static is a barrier difficult to break down, particularly when war, with the constant detonation of explosives, and the will to annihilate other beings overrides the same humanity.

So, the chosen few began to develop their strategy.

CHAPTER 20

Trevor Manning missed his son. Each evening he would pour himself a whiskey and watch Simon's distant progress in the company of his deceased wife Annie, on what Trevor called his 'Organic Skype,' a broad, honey-grained, dining table, carved from a slab of Sap, that had become his window on the world.

Gaia and Annie had chosen the Johns Hopkins School of medicine, in Baltimore, Maryland, USA, for Simon to study at the forefront of the healing sciences. Far from his home in Australia, across the wide Pacific Ocean. Together, the mothers had planned a path for him, as part of their grand plan for healing the world.

In the warehouse at the mill, with Salvatore Fiorelli, he had been briefly reunited with Annie, and found he had the capacity to hold and carry his wife within his heart. Whereas when Trevor lead his son to reacquaint with his late mother, to breathe her scent, bereft of morphine and antiseptic, breathing in living cellulose form, Simon had reacted so viscerally.

Simon had also held her, breathed her in, which became the catalyst for his meltdown. He had taken her in and torn himself apart. He basically could not contain her. Annie returned to the wood, retreated to the grainy river within the slab that would become Trevor's dining table, and Simon spilled from the shed.

Trevor never lost Annie, in his heart and in his kitchen. Each evening, after the mill closed, he walked, as he had for over a quarter of a century, down the grassy path behind the warehouse, across the bridge over the creek, and under the trees.

It was here he met Annie each evening, regardless of the time he arrived at the spot, she would meld from the shadows under the jacaranda trees, take his hand and together they would stroll up to the house. He would make his dinner for one and sit at the dining table created for him by Jimmy Pringle, gaze down into the red river of wood, hold the hand of his living wood wife, and together they would observe Simons progress.

He wished the reunion with Simon and his dead mother had gone better, But what had he expected? Six years, over a third of Simon's life, his mum a distant childhood memory.

His son had processed grief, and come from the other side, full circle back to glimpse her briefly, and lose her again. At the time of their reunion, Simon had not realised that fundamental rule of physics, that energy is neither created nor destroyed; it merely changes form. Annie and Gaia had demonstrated this to Simon as they reunited deep below the Earth's crust, in their journey to guide Simon towards his destiny.

Annie had simply changed form. Their relationship, mother to son, still held true, and so it was that Annie turned up on a Wednesday afternoon, at Simon's university, during a chemistry tutorial, via a well-worn plywood desktop, itself buried beneath Simon's pile of notes.

The tutorial had ended, and Simon had gathered his notes under one arm, preparing to leave. He scooped the bulky textbook off the antique desk, and briefly checking all his paraphernalia was collected, glanced down and at once gazed into his mother's eyes. His heart jumped a beat and for the moment, time stopped.

Frozen in situ, Simon stared down at the desk, unaware of the milling crowd of students scraping past, eager to be escape study and begin their evening shift at whatever hospital or emergency room. 'Mum,' he croaked. 'Mum,' he repeated, 'is it really you?' He knew it was.

He leaned in closer to the desk.

'Mum, have you seen Dad?' He paused. 'And Bec?' He had never given up on Rebecca, although the years apart had been anguished. Despite Simons' burden of guilt over his reaction at the Pringles, and his all-consuming mission to save the world, he still dreamed of her nightly. Her image floating to the surface amongst the other dreams that jostled and crowded his thoughts. Simon wondered how she had matured; now she'd be in her twenties.

'Do they know I'm all right? Do you think they know where I am?'

The face and arms floating in the contours of plywood had the soft olive skin and distinctive eyes of his mother in good health. 'We are always with you, son.'

'I show him through Sap; Simon, any wood can channel us. Your Father views us through his "Organic Skype". He is well and wants you to know he misses you awfully. But Gaia and I have convinced him to see the big picture. You need to be given the space to reinforce your lessons, and apply all you have absorbed in the real world of the sick and dying. There is need for your skills and the need grows daily.' Annie addressed Simon's other concern. 'Your Rebecca is a special young woman, gaining skills not unlike your own. Her candle in the darkness is her undiminished love for you, and although her burden is as heavy, it has a different expression. Would you see her at work, you'd see the Tree in her. Sap flows strongly through her, and together their healing ways are exceptional.

'About Bec, Mum. I'd love to see her again, and I swear I will after we change the world. But we're on opposite sides of the globe, and it's difficult to call, you know ... If you see her, tell her I'm sorry.' Simon blushed and fumbled self-consciously with his bag. She has chosen nursing as her career and is documenting her growth and knowledge in a remarkable journal, that someday will be the foundation of all caring professions, including your own.'

'You must complete your studies, and, in time, you may see her again. Sap also flows deeply through Sally and the rest of the family. Sap has continued to grow, although fallen and milled, her body used in a thousand different ways. She has set down roots, grown branches, flowered and sprouted leaves.

Even the simplest of her gifts are changing the world. Rest assured, you do not do this alone.' His mother's face gradually faded back to cracked and ink stained plywood.

CHAPTER 21

Sap's wooden body discovered and delved deep amongst humanity in every country across the globe. Of all her forms, the pencils and paper that Mai and the girls fashioned spread the furthest. The natural forms of the twigs and graphite, and the beautiful paper, engaged people's imagination, and were sent as gifts all around the world. All cultures and all ages were charmed by their simplicity. Cost was no barrier, as they were so cheap to produce, and the pencils refused to write an untruth.

Stories emerged from these pencils that surprised, engaged, and built bridges far greater and with broader spans than could ever have been constructed in the physical world.

Children especially loved them. The gnarly and twisted twigs felt real to them, felt like a day in the woods, an adventure. The sense of connection with the natural world incited the small hands to explore writing. Imagination, with all its fantasy and wonderful creation, was at their fingertips.

The young person with one of these pencils could say on paper what they couldn't express in spoken language. Rebecca wrote in her journals with one of these. With Sap guiding the narrative, the stories unfolded from the heart of each question, each description was vivid, living, expressed from deep in the core of the subject.

Sap's branches spread quickly, reaching China, America, Africa, and Europe. Grandparents and parents sent their children and grandchildren gifts that were considered quaint and unique to the land of origin.

The written word, and the ability to draw pictures and concepts, generates the organic sense of personal expression. Amazing stories began to appear, first in school essays, and letters to local newspapers.

Scientific journals and geographic magazines published articles on climate change, the nature of truth, spirituality. The conversation around dinner tables turned to meaningful discussions about change in the world.

Movements formed, willing to bring about this change. The movements grew into political parties, levering the new model of co-operation to more influential heights. Eventually, countries under pressure from their populations began to exert a political will to weave their economies into the new paradigm.

Leaders around the world realised that societies drove the economies of their countries, and were reliant on clean air, water, and nutritious food. The pencils continued writing. Children and scholars alike wrote inspired articles and essays that swayed millions of readers.

The articles and essays were eventually published in digital form and swept around the world in podcasts and ebooks, and their influence continued to spread.

The old paradigm, of large corporations using a population to extract resources until both the resource and the population were exhausted, was ending. The new story of hope and co-operation spread across the globe and was embraced fundamentally amongst those most affected by the changing climate.

This meant farmers, fishermen and women, populations of low-lying coasts and islands, could see firsthand the continuing droughts on land, the scarcity of fish, and the regular inundation of villages and coastal cities. One farmer who had seen the change approaching was Tom Daily. He had heard Gaia's warning, had been transformed by Sap on the day she yielded to the weight of his tractor and offered herself to the world.

Tom had a new vision of the world, one he shared with his wife Rosie and daughter Susan. The Daily family were transforming their farm in accordance with Gaia's directions.

The first action Tom undertook was to drought-proof his creeks by planting fast-growing acacias or wattles along all the watercourses on his farm. He was rewarded in gold. As the trees matured and flowered, the rivers of gold could be seen flowing across the land, celebrating the richness of water existing where before the collapsing banks and build-up of silt and clay had choked the streams.

Tom's next task with Rosie and Susan involved planting sedges and reeds in the wetter areas of the land to slow down the runoff water, to give frogs and turtles, ducks and cranes, and the myriad of wetland animals and insects freedom to thrive, for which the animals and insects were eternally grateful.

Rosie and her daughter were both avid gardeners and revelled in the work, which they saw as play. They planted black box trees to shade the wetlands and were not at all surprised when only days after their planting they returned to find fully matured trees growing over a thriving ecosystem. The croaking of the wildlife sang in their ears as thanks for providing homes for so many.

Soon, curiosity drew other farmers to visit the Daily's farm, and try to replicate this miracle on their land. A film crew from a Gardening Australia, visited and were amazed at the rapid transformation occurring virtually overnight.

The ABC News segment drew other film producers from all over the world to witness the Daily's, sit by their creeks in quiet contemplation and communicate with what the family termed, "the spirits of the land". the results of this consultation could not be disputed. The proof was evident.

Indigenous custodians and elders began to arrive encouraging and validating the family that understands and talks to the land, corroborating what they had been saying since the first people walked through this country. Confirming their sixty-thousand-year relationship with this land.

Susan Daily would regularly visit the sites they healed, walking Bucca, her mare, who had so graciously given of her tail to hair Sally's violin bow.

Dawdling beneath the flowering wattles, and watching the fallen blossoms drift like tiny golden rafts downstream, Susan hung on the birdsong echoing around her, became a part of the magic flowing through the land and the people.

She knew her father had seen something that had completely changed him. But what, she could not resolve. She was aware that Sally, James, Mai, and Rebecca were devotees of what seemed to her to be almost a religion, a devotion to a tree?

A Goddess of nature? To Susan, with her orthodox upbringing, this seemed pagan, irreligious, and not a little unbelievable. Sure, she had seen the trees mature overnight, had even heard Sally play the most infectious music she had ever heard, even danced ecstatic, and oblivious under its spell. She had held the violin made from the tree her father had felled, and felt the pulse beat within it.

Susan had sat at the desk James Pringle had fashioned from the very same tree, but it was only when she held one of the branch pencils, sitting at the desk, facing a blank sheet of paper, and felt her hand begin to move, then write without her consciously willing it, did she began to comprehend the fantastical implications. What was written that day, was one simple phrase, 'Believe in Love.'

These were the thoughts that, overflowing her mind, spilled out aloud this afternoon by the creek, heard only by Bucephalus and the bush. Susan had named her mare, 'Bucephalus,' or Bucca, for short, after the legendary horse who belonged to Alexander the Great during the third century BC and was reputed to be afraid of his own shadow.

Susan had found Bucephalus in a knacker's yard, pacing backwards around the muddy enclosure. Her owner had gotten rid of her claiming she was impossible to handle and a danger to her children. Susan had watched her reverse motion around the yard, noticing her reaction when she veered towards the sun. Quietly sidling up to her and whispering the name she'd decided to call her, swung her head away from the shadow horse following her, gripped her lead, rode her once around the corral and out the gate.

They had been inseparable since that day, although "Bucca" as she became affectionately named, was still a little shy of shadows. When she was not accompanying Susan, the mare roamed free about the Daily's property, and had spent some time in the company of one tree, on a grassy knoll, above the creek, on the 'back forty acres' of the farm.

CHAPTER 22
Believe in Love

Susan reined the mare in among the avenue of boulders that still stood marking Sap's transit down the slope, the day she was transported to the mill. The hollow that remained was now a welcoming grassy nest, soft with clover and shaded by a cohort of young xanthorrhoea, the luxuriant grass trees with their fuzzy seed spears, impaling the deep blue sky.

It had been one of those warm, clear, late winter days, and Susan could not resist the temptation to dismount and lie back in this natural cradle. Closing her eyes to the sunlight sprinkling down through the fronds, she drifted gently into a doze as Bucca grazed nearby.

Through her partially lidded eyes, she imagined she saw two perfect clouds hovering above her, not shifting with the breeze that was stirring leaves at the edge of the forest, neither dispersing into vapour nor combining as clouds will. Like a pair of pale giant eyes, they hung there.

As Susan watched between lashes, the clouds thinned and became fine lines which looped about each other, and incredulous as it seemed to her, became script, cursive, jointed script.

Susan opened her eyes, seeking the aircraft that was trailing the writing, but there were none, no sound of engines, no hum of modern technology, in fact no sound at all. Only the light breeze among the leaves, and the swish of teased grasses.

Motionless, despite the soft breeze; above her, a handwritten note on an edgeless blue page, were written the words:

'Believe in Love'

Susan was mystified. Wonder filled the mind that so recently overflowed with doubt. Sitting bolt upright in her grassy nest, gazing wide-eyed up at the sky, where the words remained, Susan began to believe. Not a figment of her imagination, neither a hallucination nor a dream. Awake, dreamer, and see the world as it is and as it could be.

As one in a dream, she drew breath, remembered to breathe again, deeper this time, stronger. She felt in control at last, and the words remained above her. Another breath in, and Susan thought she saw the clouds that formed the words shiver a little. Another breath and they definitely trembled and oscillated from side to side, resembling a negative response from someone. Am I not ready? Her inner dialogue wondered.

'Ready for what?' she answered herself.

Still, she breathed. In and out, one breath following the other, deeper than before, Susan sucked breath in between her teeth. The heavenly script unmistakably shifted, closer to the earth, closer to Susan, where she now stood in the small crater, gazing upwards in amazement. Her disbelief was translating towards conversion, on the path to conviction.

The writing quivered slightly, with each breath Susan drew. Dropping lower and closer to her at every inhalation, the words loomed larger in her vision, until she could identify the water vapour that made up the cloud, if indeed, water vapour was what it was.

Susan could see thousands if not millions of what she first thought were droplets of water condensing, but could now see were tiny beings jostling each other for space, that made up the thinning white lines.

Miniscule translucent pearls trailing gossamer butterfly wings crowded together, hovering before her eyes. So close now Susan could make out faces, eyes, and small expressions of interest and curiosity.

Another indrawn breath and the tiny beings trailed down fractionally, like a tornado's tail, swirling in a spiral towards her. She could now make out individuals leading the throng, and their expression became one of purpose.

Evocative of Kamikaze pilots diving down to crash their craft into allied shipping during World War II, the wisps seemed suicidal in their focus.

Susan was frozen in place, her mouth hanging open in surprise as the squadron centred their attention on that gaping orifice. Swooping as one they entered the cave that was her mouth. Susan immediately tasted cool fresh water and mint, with a hint of eucalyptus, It was a revelation as the tornado's tail washed into her mouth, past her teeth, sluicing the length of her tongue and down her throat.

'Oh,' was all she could utter as the last of the cloud slid down her oesophagus and into her stomach. 'Oh my God,' she gasped, as the flavours of the forest saturated her body from the inside out. If it is true that "we are what we eat" then Susan had devoured albeit involuntarily, the guardians Gaia had placed in Sap's company years before, to wait, suspended above the site She grew on, until the time arrived that they were called upon.

There are worlds existing beyond our ears and eyes, beyond our three-dimensional awareness. Ancient texts referred to these spirits, beyond and on the edge of our senses, as Deva, alluding to 'heavenly, divine, anything of excellence.' It was these Deva that Susan now felt entering her bloodstream.

Osmosing through her stomach wall to race spinning and whirling amongst her red and white blood cells, the Deva began surfing platelets, passing through capillaries, over and through blood vessels, via heart, lungs, liver, and brain. Susan felt them as pleasant tingles exciting all her inner organs, spreading rapidly out to her greatest organ, her skin, which was goose-bumping in response.

The ocean had entered the drop. Susan's anti-bodies saw these beings as allies. Her white blood cells identified them as friends, belonging here in Susan's body. As they were. These beings were as much Susan as her thoughts and emotions, and occupied as much space. Space being relative on the plane of existence these beings occupied.

Within seconds they were one with Susan's body, existing within every neuron and atom, residing in every space and taking up none. Susan was fully aware of their existence, as they were of her awareness.

She felt everything; she felt alive as she had never felt before, as if a veil had been lifted. She opened her eyes for what seemed the first time in her life and saw the world as it really was. A rainbow over a distant ridge was no longer simply an arch of seven colours, it occupied the entire sky. In its stead, there were thousands of shades of colours she had never known existed.

Susan sensed a throbbing beneath her feet, a pulse, a rhythm beating from the heart of the planet she stood upon. Her own heart echoed the throb confirming the oneness she now felt with the Earth. Her senses explored within, following the beating heart rhythm.

The pulsing of her blood led her through those vessels, visualising the benevolent beings in concert with her inner organs. Susan intuitively recognised the healing potential of these bodies alive within her. The expanded perception of both them, and the person she had become, could see endless possibilities in every direction.

Standing there in the small depression at the brow of the ridge, her senses expanding in every dimension, Susan finally realised that what her father experienced on his first contact with Sap, was our due.

This is the consciousness humanity is born with, that we lose, generation by generation. Our expanded spirit becomes eroded by disuse, small-mindedness, ego, and selfishness. She could now see how human beings had become like the narcissus lily of legend, gazing at the wonder of themselves in the pond, at the exclusion of all else.

She could barely wait to tell her father ... but she understood that he already knew. Susan felt all the spirits shift within her. A fierce determination fuelled her with an exciting and renewed purpose in this life.

She must write this experience down on paper, document the new reality and let the world know humanity was no longer stumbling in the dark. She felt a soft nudge at the small of her back easing her forward and understood that Bucca was a part of her new expanded consciousness, and was impatient to take her on the next step of the path.

So, it was that the girl and her mare rode along the edge of the forest, dangling their toes in the pool of awakening. It oozed from the greenness about them and the blue sky above them. They recognised that they shared this space just as righteously as the trees, the birds, and the breeze.

CHAPTER 23

n the garden at home Rosie and Tom harvested honey from the hives sheltered by the mango tree, planted when Susan was born twenty-odd years before. Quietly humming a tune the bees knew well enough to join in on, and enjoying the sunshine on their skin, the pair toiled happily on what was an integral part of their rejuvenation of the land. The bees pollinated the native fruits and flowers that grew all around them, which in turn advanced the message of co-operation with the land.

As they gathered the honey and started back to the shed, another sound eased into their world. Not quite as melodic, but decidedly mechanical. The tap, tap, tapping steel and unmistakable exhaust note of James Pringle's four-wheel drive drifted down the driveway, suggesting Sap was once again manoeuvring through their world.

On the tray of James' land cruiser was strapped the golden teardrop desk Sap and James had collaborated on for months, while Sally, Sap, and Salvatore, fashioned the magic fiddle. Sap's presence was felt everywhere by now, and slowly spreading across the world, but here, where she was born and felled, her company was felt more immediately.

Dust was still settling at the front of the house, as James bounded down the back steps off the porch, to hail the Dailys as they tottered along the neatly mowed path from the hives carrying pails of rich, creamy fresh honey.

'Tom. Rose. Beautiful day. Here Rosie, I'll carry that,' he said, reaching for the heavy looking container she was having trouble hefting. 'Where are we heading? Ah, the shed of course.'

In step with the pair, James strode side by side with them down the track, lugging the surprisingly heavy stainless steel bucket. He ducked his head to clear the low beam over the shed door, and once inside, hoisted his pail up onto the long central bench, stopping to breathe in the cool dimness. Reaching over, he took the weight of Tom's bucket as the older man shuffled through the door and stacked it next to the first.

Rows of cream porcelain five litre jugs lined the shelves to either side, tidy as you like.

'Had to come over. On a mission, you know! Heard Susie's been inspired, we figured she needed the desk. Gotta keep the momentum when the youngns' get keen.' He smiled. 'Sal and Bec are like evangelists on the trail of a conversion: glad to do what the fiddle asks ... So, I've bought the desk over, might need a hand bringing it in to the house, though.'

The readily recognised "clip clop" of Bucca's hooves could be heard on the pavers outside the honey shed, hinting that Susan was back from her ride. Rosie stepped from the dim, coolness of the honey shed into the light.

Blinking, she removed her spectacles to clean them on her skirt, when she realised the light was originating from her baby.

Susan was literally glowing. Her hazel eyes shone like soft caramel and beech leaves, and her hair shimmered like wheat sheaves in the sun. Rosie recognised the luminosity immediately because she had seen it before, in her husband.

Tom had returned from his introduction to the tree on that day almost ten years ago, with the same light shining from every pore.

Susan leapt from Bucca's back into the waiting arms of her parents.

'Dad, Mum, I can feel it running through me.' She was pacing, restless. 'Dad, I know how it was for you now. The tree, the forest, the wood and water, it's inside me, alive and speaking to me.' She turned to face them, determined. Her voice quivered with barely restrained excitement. 'I have to get it down on paper, I have to tell the world.' She stopped to breathe. 'Uncle James, I thought I saw your truck pull in. I have a message for Bec, she'll just love it. It's about healing, and Sap, and everything we've learned from the tree.' Words tumbled from her lips with excitement.

James stepped forward, held Susan close. 'I know, love, I know,' he said. 'You'll have to be quick, though, she'll be packing.' Still cradling Susan with an arm, and with wet eyes, he turned to Tom and Rosie. 'Rebecca volunteered last week for Doctors Without borders. "Medicines san frontiers", I believe they call the organisation. She has been accepted.' He paused, stifling his trembling voice. Calming his raging emotions, he almost whispered, 'She leaves for the Middle East, Monday morning, seven am flight. Egypt first, then Baghdad,' then very quietly, he mouthed the words, *Syria, she's going to Syria*.

Susan had known Rebecca was impatient to make a difference in the world, but was still stunned at the suddenness of her decision.

Tom and Rosie moved to the side of their friend and neighbour. Tom reached out and rested his hand on James' shoulder, sharing his strength. Rosie simply held him as a mother does.

'How's Mai and Sally holding up?' was all Rosie could say, looking up at him.

'Sally understands and believes Bec can make a difference, as do we all.' He released a held breath. 'Mai, not so much.' He looked at the ground for reassurance, found none, looked up at the trees. 'She's lived through a war, has Mai. She knows what happens in war. Terrible things ... unspeakable things. She still has nightmares about Vietnam, although, I must say, since this tree came into our lives, the nightmares have eased.'

He smiled, a little distant, a little indulgent, 'Sally is excited for her. I'm sure if she was old enough she would go too.'

'She's young,' Rosie said. 'She doesn't understand the horror, the dreadfulness of war. We see it every evening on the news, this Syrian thing ...' Rosie could not mouth the words. 'Young people,' she said, raising her hand to her mouth to smother what would come out, 'Children,' she moaned. 'Children forced to kill.' Rosie stood straight and firm, 'It's ungodly!' she exclaimed. 'It is a war against God, and ... Rebecca will be there?' she queried. 'Oh, James! You couldn't stop her? Oh, I'm sorry James, I know you would have done everything you could.' She paused ... clutching at straws. 'What about her leg, surely with her disability they will not take her!'

James shook his head. 'They considered her athletic record from school, and despite the disability – and she wouldn't let that would stop her – she was accepted for her incredible abilities. The fact that she's graduated everything with honours and distinctions, I guess, simply made her irresistible to the medical team. That and her other talents.'

They knew he was referring to her alternative healing techniques, learned from Sap and tribal healers, shaman, witchdoctors, and practitioners all around the world, under the guidance of Gaia.

Susan, standing close to James, sensing his pride and his pain, in his voice and his manner, really felt for the man, his family, and her family. Rebecca, her Bec, would know the beings she experienced on her ride, the beings presently bounding around inside her, and telling her soul, about the Bec they knew, and the respect the Deva had for her.

Susan gleaned from the buzzing in her head that she had to do something. While she could still hear James and her parents speaking next to her, she saw seeing pictures form behind her eyes, pictures of Rebecca, the Tree, and Sally; a movie, really, screening on the back of her eyelids. There was Simon, dressed in blood-stained scrubs, standing among row upon row of sand covered, dirty brown tents, stretching out endlessly on a dusty, beige plain.

Voices, clamouring for attention, rattled in her ears. 'Write, Susan, Write. Write what you see, tell the world what you feel, open your mind and allow us to be alive on the page.'

Susan understood who these voices belonged to, as within her, a thousand beings cried out, wanting to live, to be in the world these humans shared.

She realised they wanted to not only 'be' in the world, but to change the world. Somehow through her writing them down, they could become real.

'Susan? Susan?' the voices intruded from the outside. 'Susan, it's me, Dad. Susan? Hello? Oh, you don't have to tell me, you were listening to those forest voices. Oh, yes, I know how they can flood your head with stuff. You have to distil them, they're from the forest, so, they're all seeking the light. First one to the light grows, that's why we need to work together. Gaia expects you to exercise your mental discipline. That is our human role in this story. Your mind hears, then organises the din, so clarity prevails. People understand clarity.'

Tom cupped his daughter's hands in his own rugged farmer's hands, examined the delicate fingers dwarfed by his own. Looking up at her from under bushy brows, he declared, 'These hands have work to do. You and I both know what Gaia needs now. It is what will help Rebecca most, where she is going.' He glanced across to James, standing by the door, his arm draped around Rosie's shoulders.

James smiled for the first time today. 'I've bought over something to help you along. This woman's voice told me to bring the desk to Susan, she'll know what to do next. It was a voice I couldn't refuse, oh yes, and it wasn't Mai.'

Susan came alive at the thought of the desk waiting on the tray of James' truck. The need to express everything that had happened to her lately, everything the little voices clamoured for, grew, as the urge to get it down on paper became more pressing.

'Can we bring it in, Uncle James? Now? Please?'

'Oh, I don't see why not. I can see you're chafing at the bit, Gaia was right. But, then again, she is incapable of being wrong; that's Goddesses for you.'

CHAPTER 24

The Golden desk floated elegantly a hand span above the deck of James' Toyota four-wheel drive. Where the feet should have met the wooden surface of the vehicle, air shimmered. Although the desk was strapped down with James' usual thoroughness, the ropes could not contain the restlessness of a writing dais designed to change the world. A living, writing being, at that.

As the group rounded the verandah and began descending the broad front steps, the thick nylon ropes began to unravel. Snakelike, they slithered against each other, reversing out of loops, and writhing out of James' super secure truckers' knots, to fall on the ground beside the dusty wheels, coiled and still.

'Well ... I ... never!' exclaimed Rosie. Although she had half expected some 'magic 'to crop up, after everything she had heard about this Tree's abilities, she was still gob-smacked when the desk started to float across the tailgate of the truck and hover before them, as if awaiting directions.

The two men raced to the vehicle, attempting to catch the falling desk before it smashed to splinters on the dirt driveway. They needn't have bothered, and they both knew better.

Even as James skidded to a halt at the tow bar with Tom almost crashing into him from behind, they realised they weren't needed. As sweet as you like, the desk leg extended itself over the tailgate. Delicate toes were followed by a shapely ankle as a woman's well-formed calf stepped down to the dusty ground. Rosie was beside herself with what seemed like hysteria that grew into laughter. Peel upon peel of unrestrained humour poured out of the woman.

Tom and James stood back wondering, glancing at the woman next to them, almost doubled over with mirth, and the woman forming from the desk that flowed out of the rear of James' truck.

Liquid, was how James would describe the motion later, when asked to relate the tale. The teardrop desk, as it exited the flatbed, poured over the tailgate, stepping to the ground, flowing into form, as the stateliest, striking, and regal figure of a woman the four had ever laid eyes on.

Long honey brown hair cascaded over quite broad shoulders, framing an open face, with high cheekbones and soft glowing ochre skin, which flowed and blended with the hair, like the grain in exotic species of wood, one could not tell where one began and the other ended. A short straight nose was balanced above a smiling full mouth, slightly turned up at the corners as if enjoying the joke she had played with these humans.

Sparkling emerald green eyes looked out of the exquisite face directed at them, as they stood, agog. Rosie could not contain herself any longer and stepped forward to embrace the stranger, as the very best of friends that had never met.

'Oh, my love, I've been waiting so long to meet you. Welcome to our home. Oh dear,' she corrected herself, 'It's actually all your home, now, isn't it?'

The figure spoke, 'You know me?' Then again, 'You Know me!'

Rosie, as diminutive as she was, looked up at this gorgeous figure. 'Of course, I know you. You've been in my dreams for night after night, for years now.' Coyly, she added, 'In my husband's, Tom's, dreams as well.'

'Sap, I believe you know Tom and my daughter Susan. And of course you're intimately acquainted with James.'

'I do know you all.' She paused, as if remembering. 'And yes, I am Sap. I am also the mother Gaia. As Annie, I have been also, wife and mother of the Mannings, Trevor and Simon. This is my first sojourn in human form, as Sap. I have chosen appropriately, yes?'

Rosie gracefully stood on her tiptoes and draped her crocheted shawl across Sap's naked shoulders. 'Of course, my dear, of course. It's just a quirk of humans, that we like to wear clothing, attire ourselves in fabric ... you see?'

Of course, the human condition of shame had never taken root in Sap's heartwood. She had allowed souls to utilise her essence to manifest in the human world, so Gaia, and Annie, and even the tables Trevor and Simon communicated with, their "Organic Skype", were channelled by Sap. This was part of Gaia's plan to bring the two alienated parties, both children of nature, together.

Rosie guided Sap past the two stunned males, still standing agape at this miraculous, barely clothed female now conversing with them, over to where Susan stood, amazement growing to admiration transforming her features.

'You ... You're Sap, the – the Tree, sorry – um – desk – Oh ... Hi!' Susan was still coming to terms with visible tangible nature spirits.

with those emerald, green eyes, probed Susan, psyche and spirit, body, and bone.

'Susan, I sense you have my guardians within you.'

Sap was at eye level with the young woman, and those eyes held her in their gaze. 'These beings looked over me as I grew in the forest, they were with me when this one ... Tom, brought me into your human world. I am here, now.'

Susan felt the Devas within her crowding her speech centre, the Broca's area of her brain, shouting suggestions, questions, and pressing issues all relating to their task together.

Tom moved over to his daughter, and with his arm around her shoulder, nodded with respect to Sap, and close to her ear, reminded Susan to filter the clamouring voices.

'Listen, darling, and when you understand what they want, speak. Sap will know what is meant, she speaks their language. you have to trust that both the spirits within, and the Tree before you, meet through you. He turned her slightly towards himself, gathered her close and whispered, 'We are conduits, channels for the forces of nature. Go with it, you'll know what to do.'

'Love,' Susan spoke, 'love is what we need to sow in this garden.'

Sap nodded, and moved closer to the human woman. 'This is true,' She lifted her hands and examined her fingers, bending and extending them curiously, then wove them among Susan's fine pink fingers until they faced each other as one. 'We will weave together the human and the green world, we will make a world for all to share, for none to rule, we will be one nature, one world, all will be renewed.'

The voices in Susan's head were silent. Love, that purest, and most elusive element on earth, that precious gem we all seek, found its way into this gathering of souls and expanded into tangible reality.

This beautiful, golden, wooden woman, and the farmer's daughter, flesh, and bone, were weaving a marriage, an accord that would yield fruit that knew no borders. No racial divide, geographical divide or ocean would restrict the inevitable expansion of affection for this world we share.

Like a tidal wave, a tsunami of change was beginning to sweep around the planet. It would begin in small things, a child planting a tree, a warrior putting down his arms to carry an adversary to safety, a politician voting to supply aid to an ailing country, a move towards a more conscious, and empathetic world.

With hands still woven together, Susan led Sap to her study, where Sap resumed her form as the golden teardrop desk, beneath the open window with its view of the magnificent Richmond Valley, and the mountains beyond. From a drawer that appeared in Sap's thigh, Susan withdrew a ream of Mai, Rebecca, and Sally's handmade paper, and placed it on the desk. From another drawer, Susan produced an elegantly polished, uniquely twisted twig, Sap's of course, into which was inserted a graphite rod, tapered at the tip.

Susan raised the oddly fashioned pencil and gazed out over the countryside.

The sun was setting beyond a jagged Mt Warning. The dark range of mountains to the west fractured the light into a succession of broad shafts reaching down the valley, carving up the approaching dusk, causing shadows to creep through the open window and project themselves along the walls, marking the minutes to nightfall, as she touched the graphite to the paper. Susan thought of her friend, Rebecca, bound for a war zone. She thought of Sally and her enchanted fiddle, and of Simon, last seen in her reflections, wandering among the dusty canvas tents, on a windswept plain, God knows where.

As the carbon tip left its mark upon the paper, a ripple distorted the very fabric of space and time. The former reality, hills, trees, rivers, and oceans; buildings, cities, towns, and the people themselves, all warped and contorted.

Everything was changed so subtly, below the level of consciousness, but rearranging attitudes, empathies, sympathies and allegiances toward each other and the Planet Earth. From Space, the change was recorded by delicate instrumentation on the various satellites and probes orbiting the planet.

Observers on the International Space Station saw the ripple cross their field of vision, later describing it as if a veil had been lifted, resulting in a clarity, a sharpening of focus on the planet, revealing a new world, seen by new eyes.

The dozen or so scientists on board documented witnessing a unique beauty that, 'Touched us to the very soul.' Unaware that they themselves had been also affected by the ripple of raised awareness sweeping across the world and reaching out among the stars.

CHAPTER 25
To the Task at Hand

Baghdad airport was chaos on steroids, as Rebecca stepped from the air-conditioned cabin of the A330 airbus. The heat and dust hit her immediately, causing her to stagger and reach for the handrail at the head of the landing steps. Other passengers on more urgent business pushed past her, ignoring such niceties as personal space or secure footing. No-one seemed to want to delay their exit and linger, even momentarily, for a sight of this legendary city.

The *Thousand and One Nights*, paled when one considered self-preservation in an exposed situation. Sniper fire and rocket attack were often the welcome travellers received on disembarking aircraft here.

As her focus cleared and the flight receded into an unpleasant memory, Rebecca slowly grasped the immensity and confusion of a country that has seen centuries, if not millennia, of conflict, and is immersed in yet another struggle to free herself of oppression and neglect. The crusaders this time, instead of travelling with horses and camels, wagons and wooden catapults, rode in helicopter gunships bristling with weaponry.

The dust was everywhere, whipped into eddies and whirlwinds by a hundred flying and grounded machines, taking off and settling, circling control towers and hovering high above the bedlam, as watching sentinels.

Mother Nature seemed a stranger here.

A few intrepid blades of grass grew in joints in the concrete pavement, a series of sad shrubs struggled to survive in disordered lines, and besides the rows of inevitable date palms, rock and dust were the dominant landform.

Wrapping her head in the recommended scarf and adjusting her sunglasses, Bec slowly descended the steps to the runway. She crossed the expanse of dusty concrete alone, her senses alert to the whisper of the natural world beyond the terminal, among the mudbricks and oases the city was built around. By the time she reached the building, her companion travellers, scurrying for safety and shade, were already within the comfortable air-conditioned arrivals lounge.

She entered through the sliding glass doors and felt the coolness wrap around her, felt her eyes adjust to the artificial light beamed down from the vaulted and domed ceiling by thousands of tiny led globes, strung across the roof, like stars in the firmament of some huge mosque.

The din of thousands of people speaking a multitude of languages suddenly assaulted her ears. Arabic, French, and English signs directed her to the luggage carousel circling lazily along the back wall of the terminal.

As people milled around retrieving their belongings, Rebecca stood back, marvelling at the variety and dress of the travellers, and surprised that she did not see more soldiers amongst the throng, then realised they would arrive at the many military airfields dotted about this troubled land.

The beauty of the written Arabic language intrigued her, calligraphic and elegant, and only barely decipherable to Bec; this was one of the very first written and spoken languages on Earth. This was indeed an ancient land.

Having picked up her traveller's kit of simple soft duffle bag and light shoulder satchel, Rebecca continued on to the exit where she expected she would meet up with the someone from Medicines Sans Frontiers, not busy saving lives. She was approached at the exit doors by several men in traditional garb offering taxi rides into the city, whom she politely refused.

'But Madam,' they all objected in excellent English, 'we can show you all the sights of this magnificent city.'

Another pushed forward. 'I know very good hotel, safe and comfortable, you come with me, yes?'

'Thank you very much, but no, I'm meeting someone. Thank you.' She used her stern, most assertive voice, but they were persistent.

'If they do not come, what will you do?'

'It is dangerous for woman to be alone here.'

'You come with me now, good clean taxi, I take good care of you.'

This assertion worried her more than their inability to take 'No!' for an answer. Eventually, they wandered off seeking more fruitful fields among the crowd of foreigners waiting at the gate.

It was almost dusk when an ancient, dust covered Mercedes displaying the red cross and red crescent flags, pulled into the pick-up zone outside the airport. A woman emerged wearing baggy green scrubs and a once white T-shirt with the logo of Medicines Sans Frontiers across the front, and Doctors Without Borders printed across the back.

She seemed to recognise Rebecca immediately, and wryly snorted,

'Welcome to hell, kid. Here throw your bags in the back, the boot doesn't work, lock's blown off.' She indicated the shrapnel-riddled trunk of the once regal Mercedes, jumped quickly back in the driver's seat, as Bec, taking her cue to move fast, jumped in the front seat next to her.

'I'm Helen, by the way,' the woman said, stretching out her hand to Bec. 'I look after the newbies. I guess you're Rebecca,' She said slamming the Mercedes into gear. 'It'll be great to have someone with your skills on the ground here.'

Helen floored the throttle before Bec had pulled the door closed, and steered the accelerating car into the stream of traffic, pouring into the city. 'Pays to move fast here, honey. Slow's a target, for sure. You don't say much, do you, hon? Stop me if I'm wrong, you *are* Rebecca Pringle?'

Bec was gazing out the window at the ancient world, jammed against the modern. The piles of rubble on the streets. High fortified walls, minarets, and lines of armoured vehicles with American and United Nations markings, filed slowly past, as she answered, 'Bec ... you can call me, Bec.' She could feel Sap calling to her, but from which direction? There were so many strong emotions at play here.

The very air was thick with fear, and the distrust and blatant hatred seeping from the land itself after thousands of years of occupation and oppression clouded her impressions.

She had to be still, go within. Difficult when she had newly arrived, and her first obligation was to establish relationships with her medical colleagues, build trust and perhaps friendships. Sap will be where she will be needed, when she will be needed, Bec simply had to wait.

Helen drove at a breakneck pace, despite the heavy traffic and absence of road rules. Vehicles veered towards them from either side of the road, almost scraping the mudbrick walls that hemmed the cars, trucks, and motorbikes in, causing her to swerve and weave the Mercedes through almost impossible gaps in the dusty procession, all the while giving Bec a running commentary on life in Baghdad, her home in Arizona, the 'Frickin' Middle East, and Baghdad's Imam Ali Hospital, where she was stationed in the newly established mental health unit.

'Know anything about mental health, Bec? Speak any Arabic? Doesn't matter, you'll soon pick it up.' As an afterthought, she added, 'If you hang around long enough.' Rebecca could barely squeeze a response in before Helen was off at a tangent. 'Frickin' Military take our money, to pay off militants that sometimes fight for the government, mostly fight among themselves, tribal jealousies, old scores to settle. It's survival of the fittest here, honey.'

Money sent in from around the world aimed at us, has to pass through the ministry of health, where it ends up is anyone's guess. Really pisses me off.'

'Angry,' said Sap.

Angry, thought Rebecca. 'I speak a little Arabic,' she said in reply to Helen's earlier question. 'Learnt it from a friend, back home.'

'You'll need it!' Helen yelled back over the roaring engine. 'Hope your friend got it right, there's a hundred different dialects.'

Rebecca returned to gazing out the window at the crowds, and the passing walls of mudbrick, ancient foundations supporting new buildings.

'The mud earth of ancient Mesopotamia and water from the Tigris river trodden by mostly Semitic and Assyrian slaves and fashioned into bricks over five thousand years ago, lie beneath this modern city.' Rebecca listened as Sap gave her a history lesson on the origins of Baghdad. 'Built on the suffering of slaves and sacrifice to warrior gods. Fear and oppression are ground into the very fabric of this city. Long, long ago great forests of cedar, juniper pine and oak grew here between these two mighty rivers. The wood that constructed the famous ark of Noah, grew here.' And as they crossed the Jisr al Jumh bridge over the Tigris river, Sap, and Rebecca sighed as one. 'And the great flood of biblical history once covered this land where we now negotiate the streets, between mudbrick houses.'

Helen's shrill American voice sliced into Bec's inner dialogue, 'You okay back there, Hon? Only a couple of blocks away now, be there in time for dinner ... If we don't all get blown to kingdom come, that is,' Helen cackled cynically.

Bec thought Helen's tone was a little too hysterical for her liking.

Another twenty minutes of blaring horns, indifferent traffic rules, and American expletives, the Mercedes swerved into a narrow backstreet and without slowing down slipped into an even narrower walled lane between tall concrete buildings and stopped before a heavily armed gatepost, and an imposing razor-wire topped steel entry gate.

While the armed guard examined their papers, Rebecca noted the machine guns trained on their car from the two watch towers. Looking up into the dark recesses of the 57mm barrels, Bec heard Sap whisper within her mind, 'Earth gives ore to iron, tree gives carbon to steel, bound to wood, flowers and air spit death to humankind.'

It sounded like an obscure Japanese haiku.

I'm sorry, Sap, you'll have to spell it out for me, Bec thought. Although brimming with fear, Rebecca nevertheless stilled her busy mind, to focus on the movie Sap was playing for her. She saw the vast man-made holes, kilometres across, where heavy machinery mined the iron ore, from which, these weapons were made.

Sap showed her the fiery smoking smelters where the carbon from primordial forests was added to the molten bubbling ore, to make steel, then the forges where the steel was rolled, formed, and machined, and bound to wooden stocks, creating the weapons Rebecca was looking at now.

'All from Earth and tree, are these weapons made.'

The vision only lasted a second and Helen was turning to her, saying,

'You right, kid? Scared ya, did they, with their big guns? This place'd be a shit-fight, if these guys didn't watch everyone that came through the gates.'

The gates swung open, allowing them into the grounds of the Imam Ali Hospital as Helen continued her tirade. 'The Taliban hate us fixing the people they're trying to displace. Worse still, they hate that we're popular with the common people. The kids love us ... 'course they would! We make 'em better. The bastards hate that the children want to be doctors and nurses. Think it's above their station, or something ... should stay angry peasants, with the arse out of their pants ... an' do what they're told by the clerics!' She spat out of the open window, 'Bullshit!'

The car swerved around several outbuildings and stopped alongside a row of equally dusty and banged-about vans and four-wheel drives.

'This is us, honey. Grab your stuff, I'll show you around.'

With Sap unobtrusively riding within her mind, Rebecca sensed the layers of emotion emanating from the hospital. Above all was fear. Fear of death, fear of life, fear of happiness, fear of fear itself; it was a veritable soup of sorrow.

The next dominant level was principally pain and suffering. It was everywhere in the building, amongst the patients primarily, but pain existed in the bricks and mortar of the hospital itself. The final level, Rebecca realised, was surprisingly a sense of relief, of sanctuary and safety, here where people were cared for, and their lives were counted as valuable, existed a prevailing sense of love.

These emotions ebbed and flowed throughout her tour of the hospital, interspersed with Helen's black humour. Bec saw this part of her guide as her protection against the horror and injustice Helen saw daily, of war perpetrated by their own people on their own people. This was Helen's armour against insanity.

The wards in Imam Ali Hospital did not exist as such. There were wards, and corridors and meeting halls, offices and admission rooms, operating theatres, laundries, and shower rooms, all full to overflowing, with patients of all ages.

They lay on makeshift beds, bunks, benches, and floors, many with horrific injuries. All with injuries caused by projectile trauma, from guns and bombs and buildings collapsing on them, and there were the mental patients, whose world was collapsing on them, or out from underneath them.

Very few had any blankets, most of them were children. Without parents, without clothes, some without arms or legs, sometimes both, all with that pleading in their eyes, if indeed, they still had both eyes. That plea that says, *Why me? ... I am a child.*

The innocence and anguish that screamed from these children spoke louder than their cries of pain. Rebecca and Sap absorbed it all in silence.

Rebecca saw the enormity of the tragedy in the Middle East with fresh eyes, while the ancient eyes within her mind, of Gaia, Sap, and the green world, observed this tragedy over millennia. Ever since Cain killed Abel, fresh out of Eden, and before, trouble in paradise, the story of the snake, the woman, the man, the God.

Sap gently nudged Bec's mind back to the observer, saving the drowning soul from the stormy seas of emotion welling up in her heart.

'Heal where you can. These are my children, they come from the earth and one day will return. In the time they are here, the spirit grows, as the spirit grows so does the consciousness of the world, on every level of existence. Even suffering as terrible as this has a place. It is a fire that tempers the Soul. This war is not removed, nor separate from the war within the natural world. This is a visible sign of scarcity in the world, of a humanity out of tune and out of touch with nature!'

The words of her father rang true in Rebecca's memory, James had said to her once, 'We're like fleas fighting over who owns the dog.'

Bec was absorbing this dialogue on one level, while the healer in her triaged the ragged remnant of humanity in front of her. Helen's abrasive tenor cut through the moans and crying, 'Over here, kiddo. Let's get you roosted then rostered, but first, coffee.'

In what passed as a cafeteria in the bowels of the building, where the last scraps of paint from the walls littered the floor, and a couple of fans turned lazily above them, Helen bought Rebecca up to speed on the hospitals operation, the ongoing medical supply crisis, and the model of wound care applied in ninety percent of cases presented.

'Patch 'em up, see that they can walk, give 'em antibiotics, and let 'em go. Oh yeah, and feed 'em.'

Rebecca was still digesting the couscous and beans, washed down with strong coffee, as she threw her gear on a low bunk in the dormitory the nurses shared on the upper levels of the hospital.

Dusty light streamed in through a window at the north end of the long room. Dusk was falling fast on her first day in Iraq. To Rebecca, it seemed like even the light and darkness were in conflict here.

The call to prayer rang out from the towering minarets dotted around this ancient city. It's sparse beauty complimenting the fiery sunset she could see washing over the desert.

Sap was still, within her, but in the silence that followed the last echoes of the song, Rebecca's thoughts began to churn, over and over. She sat on the bunk examining her motives for being here. Was she here to heal the planet? Or was she really seeking her lost love? It had been so long since she had any intimation that Simon might have followed a similar course. Was this her real purpose, her destiny?

Thoughts came and piled one upon the other. Perhaps she was simply missing her family. What would Sally be doing? Probably playing that magical fiddle.

Bec knew her Dad would be busy on the farm with the haymaking at this time of year, and Mai would be turning out the pencils and paper, if she could drag Sally away from her passion. She rummaged about in her pack for her mobile, deciding to call her sister, and let her folks know she arrived and was okay.

Now it was dark, staff at the hospital were changing shifts, bringing a cohort of exhausted and cheerless, ostensibly numb, nurses into what had been Rebecca's quiet space. She could see their day reflected in their eyes, and wondered how long a nurse lasted here before they burned out.

She made a few introductions to close neighbours, interested enough to make the effort, and was surprised at the diversity of languages she recognised here in this one room.

With Sap's help, Bec could speak any language with fluency and so struck up a conversation with a couple of interns about her own age, in German and French, until weariness overcame them and catching up was left to the next day.

She made her way between the beds and out to the balcony with the phone, some place she could speak with her family without disturbing anyone, dialled the Australian code and then her home number.

Looking out across the city, the sense of isolation and foreignness sank home. As her eyes misted she heard the ring tones connecting her with loved ones.

It was 21:30 hours in Baghdad and 12:30 pm in Fernyvale, Australia. James and Mai were out on the verandah with lunch on the table when the phone rang.

CHAPTER 26

The phone was barely on the second ring when Mai sprinted through the screen door into the kitchen. 'Sally?' she quizzed the handset, 'Sally, is that you?'

'Mum ... Mum it's Bec. I'm calling from Baghdad.'

'Bec?' came the puzzled reply. 'My Bec?' By now James was at her side, Mai, although a little hesitant, continued. 'My Rebecca ... Oh my dear, my dear ...'

'Mum, what's going on?' Bec's senses were jangling disturbingly.

James gently reached over and rescued the handset from Mai's shaking hand.

'Bec, it's Dad. Um, Mum's been expecting a call from Sally. Sorry she seems a little distant. How are you? How's Baghdad? Have you started work yet?'

She had really wanted to speak with Mai and knew when her father took the phone something was not right. 'No, I just arrived today, and it's been hectic. Only had a chance to walk through the hospital, and meet some interns and nurses, and get set up in the quarters. It's after nine at night here. How are you guys?' and before he had a chance to reply she added, 'Where's Sally?'

There was a moment's thoughtful silence before he said, 'Sally's gone. We don't really know where, but it's a bit of a long story. We're okay, but Mum's a bit worried about her. You see, we had a great harvest and with Sally's help and that wondrous fiddle … I've never seen anything like it, to be truthful.'

Rebecca squatted on her heels, listening to her father, who seemed so far away at that moment. 'Go on.'

'Well, you've seen some of the power that that violin has.' She heard him draw a deep breath, as he continued, 'In Sally's hands, it performs miracles…true to God, miracles. The wheat and barley crops were so heavy, we were wondering how we'd get it in before the rains came.

You know how it can be, Bec. Flat out for weeks if the weather holds, but if it doesn't … well, we already owe the bank for last year's planting, and they've been making noises about foreclosing. You know banks, honey! They've got us by the short and curlies!'

Rebecca had always been home to help with the header or driving the trucks or the tractor, this year she'd figured Sally would be there.

'Oh Dad, the banks are always making noises, how would taking the farm get them their money? They're not stupid, a working farm is worth more than just the land, surely?'

James was not so sure. 'Don't know if that's how their shareholders see it. Anyway, I was telling you about your sister. She saved us, you know.' It was a statement, a clear affirmation of fact. From her Dad, The man that had held the tiller of practicality throughout her life, who would never ask for a handout, or admit he was in difficulty on the farm. Rebecca could hear the humility in his voice.

'Yes,' he was saying, 'Sally saved our bacon, her and that amazing fiddle!'

'Um...Dad, sorry to interrupt you, but could you put Mum on for bit? I'd just like to tell her I love her, and miss her, then you can tell me what happened with Sal.'

'Oh, yes, sorry honey, I get a little caught up, you know me. By the way, you know I love you dearly too ... and we miss you. Here's your mum.' He handed the receiver to Mai.

'Rebecca, my daughter. Love to hear you. Your father, he takes over, he a control-freak, yes?' Bec loved the banter between her Mum and Dad, and wished she was home with them at this moment.

'I love you too, Mum, I really miss you. Hey, what is happening with Sally, where is she?'

There was a pause as Mai stifled a sob. 'Sally go, no argument, no sorry, no say where, she just go. Her and the Italian man, Salvatore. We were just watching the news on TV, you know. It show people running, drowning, blown up with bombs, refugees everywhere, thousands of people, Sally cry. She get upset, then out of the blue she say, "enough!" She say no more this happen. Your sister, she very strong, you know.'

'Last thing she say, "I fix this mess." She say, "love you, Mama, I be back when this mess is fix", that's all.' Mai moaned softly. 'My beautiful daughters, gone.'

James eased the receiver out of Mai's hand as she sat down, head in her hands, shoulders heaving with fresh grief, small whimpers escaping between her fingers.

'Bec, I'm back. As you can hear, your Mum's crushed, but given time and both girls back in her arms, I'm sure she'll be okay. I'm still here.' Bec heard her Dads' stoicism, and the tenderness of his love in his words. Your mother really respected your decision to go overseas and help, but Sally leaving has hurt her, it was totally unexpected, like she said, "Out of the blue." We haven't heard a word since that night. That was a week ago, yesterday. All she took was a backpack and that violin.'

James stopped for breath, 'Luckily, Salvatore went with her. He told me as they headed out, he'd take care of her. I trust him, he's a good man, and he's certainly seen a bit of the world, whether he's four hundred years old or not, he gives me confidence, puts my heart at ease.'

As much as she loved hearing familiar voices, Bec was tired, and now a little concerned about her sister. 'Dad, tell me about the harvest before my battery gives out.'

'Oh yeah, the harvest. Like I said, the wheat was looking great, the weather was our only worry – you know what it's like in January here, forty degrees one day, flooding rain the next.

'Well, we drove the machinery out to the front twenty acres, watching the clouds roll in. We'd headed about an acre, when the sky clouded over, and the day got real dark, had to turn the headlights on the combine and the tractor. Then the wind came up, and lightning started belting the ground all around us, freaked us all out, we had to run to the barn for shelter. But not our Sally.

'Can't harvest in the rain, as you know, and you can't harvest soon after, 'til the wheat dries out, well it looked like it was going to flog down, and flatten the lot. I could see the farm gone; thought we'd lose everything this time.

'Well the next thing I saw was Sally, out in the field. To tell the truth, I heard her first, thought it was the wind howling through the wheat and the fence wire. Never heard such a sound, eerie, wailing stuff. I yelled out to her, loud as I could, 'get out of there, you'll be struck by lightning! I was really scared for her, you know, Bec. But if she heard me she never showed it.

'I don't think she heard anything other than that weird fiddle screaming and the wind. The thunder and lightning crashing all around her, I can still see her hair streaming behind her, rain hitting her face, and her arms raised, holding that fiddle, with water pouring off it everywhere, and the sound you wouldn't believe.

James was re-living the day, felt the rain and the fear. 'Bec, Sally was amazing. You and I both know Sap, we know the power behind her, we've seen her miracles ... I mean with the desk, and the light, and everything, but this was something else.'

Bec had retrieved a pillow from her bed and wrapped her arms about her, and despite the dropping temperature, she was enthralled. 'Go on, Dad, what else?'

'What else ... well, the storm sort of gathered overhead, and started turning, slowly at first, then faster, and faster, keeping time with the fiddle, until, heck! We could see Sally dancing in the field, skipping and whirling, and the storm sort of followed her, the music she played got more intense, more powerful, if you know what I mean, until she reached this crescendo, again and again. Well the storm just seemed to gather itself together, spinning. It formed this upside-down tornado, lightning, and all, disappeared up into its own funnel, gone.'

Rebecca could hear her father breathing heavily on the line, after re-living the drama of that day. 'And then she left, two days later ... Oh, we got the wheat in with Tom and Trevor's help. Couldn't have done it without them, but Sally and Salvatore were gone. We got home late that night, Sal had gone to bed, exhausted. I looked into her room, and there she was, still in her wet clothes, on the bed, holding that violin close, like a lover.'

Rebecca heard the warning beeps of an exhausted mobile phone, and wondered if it was what it had just channelled or really a flat battery. Images were flying through her mind of Sally, the storm, her parents.... tomorrow...

She really needed to sleep. She signed off, telling James she'd call the next day, and not to worry, Sally would return. She was sure of that. Told him both their daughters loved them dearly, missed their Mum and Dad, and that the girls would be back in their arms by Christmas. He seemed happy and relieved by that news. She knew her Mum was going to have a very lonely winter.

Back in Fernyvale, James gathered Mai in his arms, held her close for a long time. He looked down at her now sleeping face, peaceful and at rest, and although it was just past midday he gently carried her down the hall to their bedroom.

They would wait for their daughters' return, while life around them continued, and the farm and each other, were taken care of.

CHAPTER 27

The wool, the warp, the weft,
and the weaver

Susan was astounded at what the pencil had written upon the twenty or so pages stacked neatly at the side of the desk. Astounded, because she could not remember consciously writing this narrative now before her. In fact, she knew she had not actually considered each phrase, sentence, or word, nor had she stitched them together to create this story. Oh, she had held the pencil, but truly, she had only been along for the ride. Susan remembered watching the story unfold beneath her busy hands.

Yes, she remembered the storm, remembered her dad heading out to help James harvest his fields of wheat. She even heard the singing of Sap's violin and understood the language it sang to the storm to make it collapse in on itself. What she was puzzled about was how she could see all this, as well as Rebecca, Baghdad, the hospital, and the desert...while she sat at the remarkable desk, at home in the study, and write about it.

As her mind became still again, her puzzled thoughts were

answered by the multitude of Devas in her physical universe, otherwise known as her body. The magical inner crowd jostling to connect with Susan's unconscious mind, was as inexplicable as it was unpronounceable. But the formula was her as she was them, the pattern and the rug, the wool, the warp, the weft, and the weaver.

Now Susan was still, she again picked up the pencil and continued...

Sally and Salvatore packed their few belongings swiftly, knowing that a quick cut is less painful. To prolong the parting with her parents would be distressing for all, to say the least.

They left in the depths of the night, with no particular destination in mind, only the conviction that Gaia would guide them, and that their purpose was for the greater good.

The night was clear, and star-filled, and as they walked, Salvatore described the constellations to Sally, along with all the ancient inflections and meanings beneath the mythical tales applied to them. There were lessons for humanity to learn, up there on the blackboard of the universe, and stories emblazoned across the heavens for those who had the key.

Salvatore accompanied his tales with music, played on a small fife-like flute, which he produced from an inside pocket of his voluminous topcoat.

He told stories of the Indigenous Dreamtime, gleaned from previous visits to these shores, long before the white man came. Stories he learned from the Elders, as they sat around campfires. Stories crafted over many thousands of years, designed to impart wisdom to the young men and women of the tribe.

He explained how he had travelled, much as he did now, on Gaia's whim and direction, to investigate the mystery of the didgeridoo, or yidaki; how it came about, and how the circular breathing technique came about, and why it was taboo for women to play it. As he told his tale, the tiny fife produced the deep resonant and sonorous tones of the didge, and Sally was captivated and delighted when the song of the Kookaburra and the frogs at night came alive through the small instrument.

Salvatore explained pointedly to Sally that the voices emanating from an instrument, really originate in the player's mind. She learned that the instrument, whether a didgeridoo or a violin, was simply a channel for the musician to express their thoughts.

The more the player was in touch with the divine, or the universe, the more inspired they were, and the more creative their music became, as they were drinking from a much deeper well.

The country travelled swiftly beneath their feet, engrossed as they were with the endless sky above them and the songs and stories coursing through their veins. Time seemed irrelevant as the pair strode through extensive forests of eucalypts, their map of stars glimpsed only occasionally from beneath towering trunks and limbs.

Sally was walking with her tribe, over mountain and valley, through wetlands and deserts, crossing wave after wave of soft sand and rocky gullies. She noticed Salvatore seemed to glide across the terrain, and when she ventured to look down at her own feet they were shrouded in mist; she could have been striding metres above the ground for all she knew. There was no sensation of actual contact with the earth. She never stumbled on loose rocks or sank to her knees in mud, until the moment she realised her feet were getting wet, and that rippling waves were slapping against her legs.

She opened her eyes to a great expanse of ocean before her, and a gigantic golden moon, sinking slowly in the west, beaming rippling reflections across the water back to the white sandy shore where she and Salvatore stood.

The vast Indian Ocean lay before them, and Sally realised they had crossed the great Australian continent on foot, overnight. Salvatore smiled when he saw the puzzled look on Sally's face.

'How ... did we ... ?'

'The ancient songlines are still alive.' He said reverently, 'The people walked them and sang them for fifty thousand years, they are part of this land.'

They stood there, on that white sandy beach, with the iron red dunes of the Kimberly coast rolling endlessly out to either side of them, standing where people had stood and played and sung since time out of mind, and wondered where the people were now?

Of the original custodians of the land and the mystical songlines, energy grids that criss-crosses the entire planet, very few that remembered were left, even fewer who still knew the songs and the Dreaming and kept them alive.

Sally and Sal knew their journey didn't end here, but where to now?

CHAPTER 28

Holding back the flow

The blood from the severed femoral artery splattered across Simon's glasses, blinding him. Wiping it away smeared his vision pink, but at least he could still see. The clamp attempting to staunch the wound found no purchase among the shattered meat of the thigh belonging to the luckily comatose girl.

There was no leg left to work with, this was a red, macerated coalface, leaking vital fluids, and Simon's team were working feverishly to save a life.

Yana, is twelve, she likes modern music, going to the cinema, and ice cream. She and her friends had been playing football among the rubble of their homes, using gaps in the ruins as goals. They lived in the district of Ramouse, a few kilometres from the centre of the Syrian city of Aleppo. The city had been bombed by a consortium of countries, and passed back and forth between the East and the West for the past three years. Most of what remained was crumbling.

Among the destruction and crumbling buildings was the occasional unexploded bomb, live, but not detonated. A slight tap on an already unstable fuse, on a bomb like this, such as the impact of a well-placed football kicked by a group of children into the ruins of a house...

Yana had no idea what happened next, where A'ishah, Aaban, Mohammed, and Eshal disappeared to. One minute they'd all been laughing and playing, then her ears were ringing and her world turned red.

Only fifty metres away, Ahmed and Daud were scavenging among the ruins for clothing and valuables they could trade for food, when they heard the explosion. Dust and rubble still rained down in the narrow alley as they turned the corner, loot on their minds. Yana was the only child they found alive. Even if they could recognise the few small dust-buried mounds as human, amongst the concrete and fragments of building, neither Ahmed nor Daud were heroes. It was enough that they bring this one child to a hospital.

As he swept Yana into his arms, Ahmed was reminded of his own daughter, Ara, gassed by Al Assad's militia three years before.

Her blood was soaking his leg as it gushed from beneath her dress. Ahmed had seen conflict most of his life, and had seen injuries like this before.

'Daud, quickly, wrap your scarf around her leg, tight as you can. We must stop the bleeding.'

Daud did as he was told, as Ahmed, holding Yana close, wrapped his arms around the reddening scarf packed firmly against her wound. An hour later they all staggered into the Medicines san frontiers first aid station.

Simon was attempting to see through the red mist smearing his glasses, trying to staunch the blood leaking past the clamp. The child was malnourished, so the blood pressure was low, possibly saving her from pumping out and bleeding to death or haemorrhagic shock, although the wound was severe, and she was a small child.

In the darkened study of the Daily's home, back in Australia, at the desk lit by a single writing lamp, Susan wiped the tears away that streamed down her cheeks. She wanted to stop writing, stop the pain and horror she saw evolving on the page, but her hand and the pencil she held, continued making their mark.

She was both observer and creator in this tragic play unfolding on the page before her. The story was insistent, it must be told. The fingers held on while the pencil continued.

Simon worked on another level, in situations like this. All his training, simulations and experience had led him here, to this ruined country, these damaged people, and the horror of this never-ending battle, between brothers, cousins, uncles.

Families and tribes that had held enmity for thousands of years, saw generation after each surviving generation, dragging out this same dark drama, inflicting the suffering of their ancestors upon their own children.

In a dark corner of the emergency tent, seeking refuge from the searing desert heat, a solitary solifuge, or camel spider, had crept under the canvas floor. Ostensibly searching for food, the spider found itself between the constantly moving boots of the medical staff and the stationary legs of the operating table. Self-preservation prompted the spider – which is not a true spider, but a creature more closely related to the scorpion – to clamber up a leg of the operating table.

No-one noticed it there until the head and thorax managed to scramble onto the table between Simon's fully occupied hands.

Attempting to staunch the still partially gushing wound, Simon was in no position to halt the spider's progress. Reaching cautiously forward, the spider stretched its front legs, feeling for the warmth of the open wound and smelling the fresh blood.

'Bloody hell!' yelled Simon, 'Someone get this thing out of here!'

The three medical staff in the tent were immersed in the one hundred and one essential jobs offering urgent life support for the patient; anyone abandoning their station would put the entire operation at risk. No-one was going to remove the spider.

The assisting nurse, holding a kidney dish full of syringes and blood-soaked swabs, brusquely uttered, 'Brush it aside, they're big, but harmless.'

In the space of the conversation, the insect, which was the size of a large hand, sprang upon the bloody stump of Yana's thigh and drove its mandibles into the soft flesh either side of the weakly pumping artery, bought them together in a shell mashing gnash, and just as suddenly, the bleeding stopped.

Simon stepped back, considering first the sealed wound, then quizzically eyeing the huge insect. The jaws still held the closed artery, but the spider made no attempt to devour flesh, or even rend the wound open. It seemed content to assist the repairing of the damaged tissue. It then, under Simon's astounded gaze, commenced to stitch the stump closed and weave the damaged fragments of skin over each other, leaving a clean, staunched, and already healing stump where Yana once had a leg.

Given the miraculous journey Simon had navigated to be here. The amazing coalition of nature spirits, angels, and ghosts, who had assisted him through medical school; enlistment in Medicine Sans Frontiers, as well as his journey through the centre of the planet, he should not have been surprised when the solifuge, the spider's correct name, looked up at him with the two, tiny black eyes on its back … and made a connection.

They say the eyes are the windows to the soul, and these windows opened to the soul of the world. Gaia and his mother, both breathed through these onyx beads, welcoming Simon to the marvellous means Nature herself placed at the healer's disposal in this new world of co-operation with humanity.

Yana was placed under close observation in the recovery ward, a long tent of about twenty metres, towards the edge of the compound, intravenous fluids replenishing the blood she had lost. By evening of that day, she was sitting up, eating dhal and speaking excitedly to her new friends Ahmed and Daud, who happened to drop by enquiring about, 'The little girl from Ramouse.'

Each day for a week, the two men would return to the aid station seeking news about the child, until they were both satisfied she would live. They then discussed how difficult life would be for a one-legged girl in a war zone. Perhaps this was not their concern, perhaps they could get on with survival themselves, until they looked each other in the eye and decided, no! This could not be. Accepting that they were both opportunistic lowlifes, seeking existence and profit where profit should not be found, the two friends decided to do something good.

Ahmed and Daud were the go-to guys in Southern Aleppo. Whatever you wanted, the pair could get, either through scavenging, bargaining or outright theft. They could fix things: cars, radios, motorbikes. Fix things: make someone causing trouble to disappear. They had connections, high and low.

It seemed the low connections were the most useful. There were many people, now that Syria was fractured, who wished to cause trouble. Some wanted to squeeze the poor people, the homeless, and the desperate, for the last of their belongings in exchange for passage into Turkey, Lebanon, or Jordan. Nobody wanted to enter Iraq, except some people intent on causing trouble.

Sure, Ahmed and Daud would freely admit they had contributed their own share of strife, but only to those who deserved strife to visit. They had smuggled people, but would never admit to people smuggling. They called it reuniting families, and saving children. Without their aid, many children would be lost to Daiesh, or the vindictive and vicious government forces, or simply used and discarded for their childhood by desperados, or one of the many militia groups.

Yana did not know how lucky she really was, although she would be forever grateful to the two for saving her life. Both men had loose affiliations with the terrorist group, known as Al Qaeda, when it suited them.

Opportunities arose occasionally, when Al Qaeda outsourced reconnaissance and information gathering on the movement of opposition forces to so-called free agents. This was Ahmed and Daud's purpose on the day they found Yana, as well as some opportunistic scavenging, to enhance profitability for their mission.

A month after Yana's clash with the improvised explosive device, when she was able to hobble about the compound with the aid of a crutch, Ahmed turned up to see her with a proposition.

He knew somebody, who knew somebody, who could assist Yana to flee Syria, and because she had no family alive, he and Daud would adopt her. There was no ulterior motive behind the proposition. They were sick of the war, Yana was sick, why stay? there must be everywhere better than staying here. Yana thought for a moment, then said, yes!

They both knew she needed rest and time to heal properly. They also knew a long sea journey was a death sentence for a disabled child, let alone a twelve-year-old girl. The pair decided to travel with Yana, when the time was right, to visit Ahmed's sisters in Turkey, where they prayed she would be safe.

CHAPTER 29

While Yana mended, and the men were limited for now within war-torn Syria, the two continued their specious compassionate profiteering. Neither man had overtly smuggled people seriously, but they knew of men that did this for a living. Men that may or may not profit from such a venture, but were willing and able to assist someone and someone's family to flee a warzone, or even a country, if the situation called for it.

Sometimes the family had the money to pay, and pay willingly, to save them and their loved one's lives – who wouldn't? Sometimes the people fleeing had no money, no home to return to, and a swag of small children in tow. Often, they were the last living remnants of an entire neighbourhood that had been obliterated. On these occasions, those much-maligned men might waive their fee on compassionate grounds.

Such a person was Daud's second cousin on his mother's side, Mahmoud Khalil. Some called him "people smuggler", and cursed him, others thanked him, and called him "hero", and "saviour". Mahmoud had worked for many years saving hundreds of children and families left destitute by the many wars in the region and had made enough money to buy his own boat. This boat was long, broad in the beam, and swift, but also very old.

He had named the boat Nashirah which comes from the Arabic *sa'd nashirah* for 'the lucky one' or 'bearer of good news.' Nashirah had been built in the late seventies in Oman, using traditional boat building techniques that had served Arab mariners for a thousand years. Most of her ribs were left as the tree trunks and branches came, and only trimmed at their junctions with the planks of the boat.

Gaia was strong within the timbers of this vessel, especially as her purpose was to save lives and spare peaceful folk from the ravages of war and terror, much as Noah's ark had done millennia before. Some refitting in recent years had kept her reasonably seaworthy, but she had seen many journeys, saving many lives.

For navigation, Mahmoud relied on an old marine navman, bought for a bargain at a market in Abu Dhabi. This used and weathered device had been reliable for the shorter journeys, carrying people to Karachi, or Mumbai in India, or sometimes Banda Aceh in Indonesia.

Mahmoud had picked up some passengers his cousin Daud had delivered who were in great need. Hungry from a furtive, five-day truck journey, through dangerous border crossings, with children on their back, and few belongings, they sought safety in the form of Nashirah.

They had managed to scrabble together twenty thousand Syrian pounds for the journey, which Mahmoud calculated would barely pay for the fuel both ways, but they were desperate, and he was a compassionate man.

Leaving when they did, in late January, the boat had been caught by the first of the tropical monsoons that ripped through the Northern Indian Ocean at that time of year, and was swept far to the south.

After forty days and nights at sea, driven by monsoon winds and waves, and almost out of water and food, Ali, the small, wiry Iranian lookout, perched on the bow of Nashirah shouted, 'Land! Allah be praised, it is land!'

Mahmoud had expected to see swampy forests and the green tropical coastline of Indonesia, but instead looked out towards low ochre coloured dunes and a barren expanse of red cliffs. He, his crew, and the eighty-six passengers below decks were lost and truly marooned, Allah knew where! Little did Mahmoud know it was Allah and Gaia that had navigated his boat to this precise spot.

Salvatore and Sally had set up camp amongst the dunes under a small copse of stunted bloodwood trees, and were awaiting Gaia's next move. It was now late February, and the heat was oppressive, luckily, a small freshwater stream trickled down the beach and flowed into the sea next to where the pair had rested after their vast overnight journey across the continent.

Mahmoud had spotted the same stream through his binoculars and decided to bring the migrants on shore while he searched his maps and his mobile for some reference.

The sound of almost a hundred people landing, splashing through the shallows, and shouting to each other, woke the pair curled up beneath the trees.

Salvatore, being the veteran of these kinds of encounters, rose to greet the new arrivals.

'Hello ... Hello,' he attempted in English. '*Bonjour*,' this time in French, with mixed success. Some people responded in English, some in French and some in Arabic. 'Where are we?' was common in all the languages.

Salvatore spoke in all three tongues, respectively, answering their many questions, but he could not tell them where they would go from here to seek safety. Mahmoud, feeling responsible, eventually climbed down from Nashirah's cabin and waded across the shallows toward the strangers, looking for answers to the big questions going through his mind, foremost being: 'Have you any food?' and 'do you have transport?'

Mahmoud figured civilisation must be somewhere close by, judging from the flamboyant clothes the welcoming party wore. Mahmoud knew nothing about Australia and particularly the west of the country, where distances between settlements are vast and one could easily die attempting to reach one without reliable transport.

'We will camp here,' he decided, loud enough for all to hear. 'And tomorrow we will find a city and food.'

The crew of six waded back to Nashirah, to unload the little food that was left from the journey, while Salvatore and Sally showed the exhausted travellers some sheltered spots behind the dunes, and where you could safely fill canteens and buckets with fresh water. Soon, a crackling fire was raging; people began to relax, stretching out their bodies in the soft sand and quietly wondering amongst themselves what tomorrow might bring.

CHAPTER 30

t was almost dusk, and the shadows of the stunted bloodwoods and boabs rippled east across the rows of spinifex covered dunes, towards the escarpment, twenty kilometres away. A couple of young men and children gathered fishing gear brought along to catch fresh fish while they were at sea, and sauntered down to the mouth of the small creek to try their luck. The Sun floated for a moment on the western rim of ocean and sank slowly in a rippling river of golden lava.

The creek had cut its way from the gorges and waterfalls at the edge of the distant cliffs, gouging a channel through the ancient landscape to empty into the vast Indian Ocean. In its wake, in deep pools and shady oasis, towered over by giant pandanus, and enormous fan palms, sheltered fat barramundi, mangrove jack and colossal saltwater crocodiles.

The children were excited to be off the boat and eager to join the adults on the fishing expedition. They were proud to contribute to feeding the group as well, which had become their travelling family.

Two of the young men in the group, Baadir, and Saalim, and one of the young women, Ghalia, set their lines where the creek opened out into the sea. Three of the older girls, Rabah, Gamal and Wadi, took the small group of children upstream, hopping from rock to rock, and balancing along fallen logs, washed downstream in the floods of the wet season.

They made their way cautiously in the failing light until Gamal rounded a low rock shelf and spotted a large pool ahead that looked easy to reach. Easing their way down, and clinging to clumps of native lemongrass, they reached the pool scarcely before darkness fell. Wadi produced a stolen zippo cigarette lighter and by its flickering glow they gathered enough wood and dried grass to start a substantial fire.

As the flames caught and the light flooded the ravine, the sounds of the night began to pop and rattle, cough, and slither around them, reminding them all they were in an alien landscape, very, very far from their home, if that, indeed, still existed.

They immediately recognised the pop and croak of frogs, but the other sliding and rattling noises made them nervous. It was too dark to make their way back to the boat by now, besides the others would probably be looking for them. The best idea was to wait.

'Well,' Gamal broke the silence of the group, 'Well, while we're here, we may as well fish?' Who has bait?' She looked at Wadi.

'Don't look at me, I thought we'd pick up some worms along the way! But it got dark too quickly.'

'I have some bread,' Chirped in Baasim, the youngest child in the group, 'It works on the bream, I caught some from the side of the boat.' He handed over some scraps of flat bread he had in his pocket. 'Here, try this.'

Gamal and Saalif, the tallest boy in the company gathered all the fishing gear they had brought, and laid it out in front of the fire. 'Okay, we have line and hooks; we can use small stones as weights and sticks as floats.'

By the time the fire caught and crackled into life, Saalif had fashioned some serviceable fishing lines and lures, and the children were vying for fisherman's duties. It was decided that contrary to tradition, and seeing how they were the pioneers of a new generation, the fishing would be evenly divided between the girls and the boys. Four sets of line, hooks and bread/bait were distributed, and the small party crept to the water's edge, oblivious of the pairs of bright eyes reflecting the firelight back to them, stealthily watching them, waiting for the King Crocodile to say, 'Eat'.

The King Crocodile or Alpha male is top of the reptile tree in Northern Australia. He keeps the other male crocodiles in his 'Kingdom' in check and has a sizable harem of females up and down the Kimberly coast.

This evening, the King was cruising along the sand bars, heading South with intentions of visiting some females living in a large pool only a short wade in from the coast. Ahead of him was a strange foreign object, floating in the deeper water and reeking of humanity. The hull of this vessel, hung enticingly above him, its tree trunk keel sagging in the saltwater.

Instinctively, he rasped his ridged back and tail along the full length of the keel of Nashirah, scraping off parasites, and relieving a pernicious itch he had developed swimming through the oil fields of the Timor Sea.

Like fingers strumming the strings of a harp, the plates on the King's back rippled the length of Nashirah's keel. Six long and muscled metres of scale and bone, a third as long as the keel, set off a rasping, grinding beat. Each ridge and plate, hammered the ancient wood, resonating through the boat, and all the way to the shore, where the immigrants and the two wanderers were camped.

Distant, rapidly beating drums, a segmented roaring, scraping scale, rattled its way between the dunes, amplified by the night and the water to become a primordial rhythm.

The noise travelled up the freshwater stream to the pond where the children were fishing, reaching the ears of six female crocodiles, barely submerged, with their eyes bulging the surface watching, waiting.

Crocodiles have extraordinary hearing. The survival of their babies, buried in deep mounds of earth, near the banks of rivers, depend on it. Tiny calls and the sounds of prey are part of the finely attuned communication abilities they possess. The females immediately recognised the sound pattern in the water as that of the King, and spun around in response, swinging the great tails and sweeping fish up from the depths of the pool and scattering them across the rock platform.

Saalif and Gamal felt themselves dragged back from the edge, grasped by Wadi and Rabah as they all scrambled backwards up the slippery rock face.

Living in a war zone certainly sharpens reactions. The children watched in horror as the tails of the big crocs swept downstream away from them, wondering what had frightened them away.

In the silence following the retreat of the crocodiles, the children, although too frightened to go near the water's edge, gingerly collected their flapping windfall of fish.

Besides the gentle slapping of water on rock, and the constant rattle of frogs, an odd sound came drifting on the evening breeze up the shallow ravine. Saalif heard it first, perhaps being the tallest, with his ears in the breeze, but then Gamal and Wadi, and the others heard it. A violin playing a sweetly haunting melody to a primitive rumbling beat.

The meld of the two tore at the soul, and brought tears to the children's eyes. The drumming was intense, and there was something not human about it, the beat was irregular and rasping while the violin soared above, then dived below, weaving, eerie, sweet, hypnotic.

The five children, bags laden with fish, slowly made their way back to camp by the light of Wadi's stolen lighter, being careful to stick to the high ground, well away from the stream.

As they clambered over the last sand dune behind the beach, the strange music drifted up towards them from the camp. A large fire was crackling, with the silhouettes of figures moving back and forth across it's light, it looked like they were dancing. In a ring, away from the fire, like some exotic necklace, lay seven very large crocodiles, watching the proceedings with the flames reflected in their eyes, each crocodile emitting that rasping, clicking thumping rhythm.

Tails beating sand, bellies rumbling and crocodile voice underpinning the uncontainable soaring and swelling of the violin. Between the fire figures and the crocodiles stood the violinist, swaying in ecstasy, between worlds.

Sally and Sap, flesh, and wood, were inside the crocodile's world, ancient creatures that they were, they understood the rhythms of the Earth, the sounds, and pitches, that were the first means of communication.

It was understood in the most primitive way that this "music" was Gaia speaking. The small object the human held spoke to the King.

'Oh, King of the Crocodiles, do not see these humans as food. They do my bidding. The child with the music and the old man travel to the war in the North to bring peace. They travel to bring the world together, to cleanse your oceans and fill your rivers. We travel with them to open the eyes of humans everywhere, to see a world shared by all creatures, both great and small to fulfil their destiny. The others flee from the war in the North, their children are dying, and their land is ravaged and burned, they seek sanctuary here on these shores.'

Gaia spoke through Sap, with the authority of the All-Mother, Queen of the World, Heart of the Earth, and could not be denied. She commanded the King, 'You will deliver the others to a safe haven here on the shores of this country, and you will deliver the child and the old man to the land they seek.'

She then wove an image the crocodiles would understand, of Nashirah offering her ribbed keel to the plates and scales of the giant reptiles allowing them to contribute to the healing of the planet we all share.

Susan lifted the pencil from the page, amazed at what she had just written, even more mystified because she had seen it, not simply imagined, but actually witnessed the events she had dutifully written down. The page floated to the side of the desk and gently rested on top of the growing pile beneath the lamp.

Another page appeared beneath the raised pencil, ready for the next magical event. Susan wondered for a moment if she was chronicling events as they occurred, or was she creating them? It was then she realised all this was not about her, it was the tree, Sap ... the desk, the paper, the violin. The humans were simply a conduit for the magic to manifest here in this world.

The pencil began to move again, and Susan was drawn into another adventure, without ever leaving her room.

At dawn the following day, Mahmoud, his crew, and the refugees plus two, clambered aboard Nashirah. The old boat groaned and settled as three crocodiles a side lifted her weight upon their backs. With the King beneath the bow, the tree trunk keel resting on his broad back, the great tail sheared the water from side to side, sending white plumes of foaming sea water bubbling in her wake as Nashirah leapt forward under the reptilian propulsion.

She swept along the channel, sand bars slipping by on either side, until they reached deepwater, where the King shifted his weight to the port side and vessel began to head North by Northeast, towards the town of Broome.

Broome is a small town of about fifteen thousand people, closer to Southeast Asia, than it is to most of Australia's population. Over the years, the town has seen the arrival of seventeenth century explorers, Chinese smugglers, Japanese pearl divers, Japanese dive bombers in the second world war, and more recently, hordes of tourists visiting the magnificent sights of the Kimberly escarpment and rivers.

The traditional owners of the land are the Yawuru people, who have walked the land for over forty thousand years. It was to a settlement of these people the King crocodile, his entourage, and Nashirah, now steered.

The Yawuru had sheltered the hungry and the desperate washed in from the sea beyond living memory, and such a desperate group, arriving on the backs of their totem, could not be denied sanctuary.

Jamuny, grandfather, had heard the crocodiles coming. His Grandfather spoke to the crocodiles and the barramundi. A saltwater man going way back, long ago he had taught his sons and daughters to listen to the sea. The wind would bring them stories, and the sea would occasionally bring them gifts.

He told them the gifts the sea brought always carried responsibility, they could accept the gifts or not, But it was a special blessing from the great spirit if the gifts were accepted, along with all they bestowed.

The Sea and the wind told Jamuny about the group of refugees heading North. He listened to the Crocodiles each evening among the mangroves, talking about the music and the magic that walked with these people, and how the King said they are to be helped.

Jamuny and his grandchildren waited on the beach, watching Nashirah round the point and head in towards the shallows. Sally, Salvatore, Mahmoud, and a crowd of children, pressed against the bow handrail, eager to see the shore and stare at the small group of aborigines waiting for them.

The crocodiles were invisible beneath the hull of Nashirah, but Jamuny knew they were there, and cautioned his people not to enter the water. No point in tempting fate, he reasoned. Nashirah swung in through the deeper channel and moved slowly along the shore until she came to rest against a bleached and rock pooled, sandstone shelf, stretching out to sea from among the mangroves.

Jamuny tossed a couple of big barramundi he'd caught that morning into the water, expressing gratitude to the King and his harem. The ladder was thrown over the side and children began to climb down. After a momentary thrash and churn of the lapping waves, the crocodiles were gone.

After brief introductions were made, and before he could answer the multitude of questions the children began to ask, Jamuny hurried the group up the beach, to some shelters thrown together beneath the towering palms. 'Quickly, now, we got to get you people hidden before the Border Force patrol boat comes by. They'll catch you and put you in a camp, where you stay for years and years, until they send you home, or someplace worse.'

This frightened the refugees enough to sprint for the shelters, dragging the littlest children with them. Armed men had herded them before in Iraq and Syria, and it never ended well. Once the crowd was safely beneath the trees, Jamuny told them the plan.

'You are our cousins, come in from the desert. You don't speak English.' He frowned at them pointedly. 'So don't say nothing to any white fellas, until you know you can trust 'em. We gonna say you all staying with us, for the time being. The Aunties have lined up families you can stay with. They'll tell the Department of Indigenous affairs their cousins are staying here, and the Department will give you papers to say you are all Yawuru people.' He stopped and looked at the bedraggled group of men, women, and children, smiled at them and said, 'Welcome to Country. We will have a celebration when all is settled, a corroboree, with Yidaki, you know, Didgeridoo, and sticks, and lots of food, and we will dance under the moon. But now, while the tide is high, my friend Mahmoud, his crew, and his boat, have further work to do.'

Jamuny stepped forward, parting the group until he stood before the two ambassadors for Gaia. 'I see you, Sally and Salvatore, the Great Spirit smiles on you.' He paused for a moment, as if to sniff the air, then looked directly at the bag Sally carried over her shoulder, to house Sap. 'And the Great Spirit you carry in that bag.' He walked over to a table loaded high with full potato sacks, 'We have fish and sweet potato, damper and tea here for your journey. We must go now, or you'll miss the tide and catch the Border Force boat,' he added, 'And that would be uncomfortable for everyone.'

Sally, Salvatore, Mahmoud, and his crew hefted the bags of food and within the hour, Nashirah was ploughing her way across the shallow bar out to the open sea. Mahmoud's ancient navman directed them North by North-west ,destination Oman, from there into the Gulf, then Iraq. He wondered why these two wanted to go there. He loved his country but knew it was hell, especially for westerners, even with magic powers. He had grown fond of the two, and quietly hoped their magic was stronger than bullets and bombs.

They picked up the Crocodile King and his harem twenty minutes later, felt the boat lift into hydrofoil mode; the Crocodiles were going to visit their cousins in their ancient breeding grounds of Mesopotamia.

The vast Indian Ocean is home to many dangerous creatures, but the worst of them are the pirates, attacking any boat regardless of size or nationality, for riches and ransom. As Nashirah was entering the Gulf of Oman, cruising on Crocodile propulsion she was accosted by a motley crew of raggedly dangerous looking, armed men, hailing Mahmoud, and the crew with a loudspeaker, and firing their guns in the air. Apparently, they hadn't seen the powerhouses writhing beneath the hull, driving the old boat forward.

Sally, hidden below deck, heard the gunfire and the shouting and drew Sap and the bow from her bag, closed her eyes and dragged the bow across the steel strings. The hair that Susan's Bucca donated, rippled over the wound strings stirring Sap awake and She began to hum softly, her note rose higher and higher until it became inaudible to human ears, akin to a dog whistle, or a crocodile hatchling in danger.

Sally and Sap held the note for several seconds, then drove the bow home in a grinding, howling sweep of horsehair and dust. Nashirah suddenly stopped moving forward, momentum driving her bow down into the sea.

Waves swept across the front deck, as she rocked on her abandoned keel, until she came to rest, swinging gently in the water. The pirates were as surprised with the speed Nashirah halted, as was Mahmoud. The wake that had trailed the boat, generated by the thrashing tails driving her forward, now parted from Nashirah, and headed for the pirates.

Their leader, a scrawny bandit called Sty, saw the wake heading towards them, and at first thought this old scow had fired torpedos at them. He screamed at the others to throttle the two outboard motors, and spin their boat in an evasive action, just as he recognised the eyes and jaws plunging through the water towards them.

Twin Yamaha outboards roared to life as the rest of the pirates saw what he saw, and almost standing on its end the pirate boat, half the length of Nashirah, sped into the distance, towards the coast of Somalia or Oman, with seven hungry crocodiles in hot pursuit. If the pirates made it home alive, they might make a good living from this tale.

CHAPTER 31

Once they were in the Gulf of Oman, Sally and Salvatore dressed like local fishermen to avoid scrutiny. They spent most of the time below decks as Nashirah ploughed North towards the Persian Gulf and Iraq. With time on their hands, the two turned their attention and curiosity to Nashirah, the boat herself.

Below decks, her raw timber and mode of construction fascinated them. Whole tree trunks had been laid horizontally along the keel with branches still attached serving as ribs curving upwards on either side to reach through the deck and act as bulwarks tied to the handrail which ran around the entire boat. Everything was held together by rough dowels cut from the same timber, and bound with coarse rope that looked old and frayed enough to have been used to build the pyramids.

Nashirah certainly had the character and characteristics of an ark. Salvatore showed Sally the age rings of the timber where she had been cut and together they judged the history and region of her build. Sally played Sap while they were below decks, quietly conversing with Gaia and the wooden spirit she held in her arms, while the ribs and keel groaned along, punctuating, and seeming to answer the vibrating, singing instrument.

They had been at sea for over two months, and their food was running low, when Mahmoud's head appeared at the hatch.

'We are passing through the Straits of Hormuz. We must be very careful, everyone is watching...' He paused, then added, 'Everyone is watching everyone.' He placed his finger to his lips.

Salvatore spoke softly to Sally after hearing this news. 'We need to see how the others are faring. It will do no good to wander the Middle East blindly.'

He walked to the side of the hull where the planking was relatively even and smooth, wiped away years of built up dirt, and stared intently at the whorls and ripples in the grain of the wood. Beckoning Sally to his side, he picked up her hand and placed it palm down on the cleaned area of planking, across from his own.

Sally felt the rough-hewn timber under her skin, felt splinters where the timber was still raw in places, and felt the subtle give and take of the hull in response to the lapping of the sea outside.

Salvatore whispered, 'Reach out with your mind, reach out with your senses to the soul of the wood, to the heart of the tree that she was, and see what the trees see.' He seemed lost in the grooves and patterns, as he murmured, 'Yes ... Yes ... there ... there ... there we are.'

Sally felt the plank give way ever so gently, felt her hand reach into nothing. But it was a warm nothing. Now she felt sunshine on her fingers, and a gentle breeze bristled the tiny hairs that grew along the back of her hand. As she opened her eyes, the brightness of the light surprised her. There in front of her where the plank had been, a brilliant sun shone over an expansive city surrounding a sluggishly winding river, traffic crowded the streets, and here and there columns of smoke rose into the already hazy air, from buildings crumbling back to the mud they were made of.

Sally knew unquestionably, this city was Baghdad, Iraq. Sally and Salvatore gazed down on the city from high above, seeing what the trees see when they drink the rainwater. Clouds change form, carrying news in their vapour, they flow through the cedars and palms and fruit trees growing in the city, trees that are ever watchful, and always listening.

Sap and Gaia guided the two travellers, as their view ranged across the Tigris and Euphrates delta, the ancient cradle of civilisation. From the first place to farm crops and domesticate animals, from the city that over a thousand years ago was called the Centre of the World, Baghdad had certainly fallen from grace.

Constant conflict and brutal wars had seen the city itself turn inward, build protective walls, and abandon her pursuits of scientific and cultural excellence. Baghdad, through the twentieth century, was at the centre of the growth of global super-powers and super wars that carved up the Middle East, to feed the world's insatiable hunger for oil.

Sally could feel the energy of over seven million souls radiating from the city, all striving to live their lives in some kind of normal way, while death by rocket, bomb or bullets stalked them constantly as they visited the market or the mosque.

Strangely, Sally didn't feel fear, simply resignation, as if the violence of the city had designated the gene pool. This was customary, this was Baghdad. With a sense of trepidation, Sally focused her thoughts on her sister, Rebecca.

She knew Bec had been working with Medicine Sans Frontiers in Baghdad city, and that her base was Baghdad's Imam Ali Hospital. Her focus led her to the open square, behind the hospital, where a fountain bubbled peacefully amidst a formal planting of orange and lemon trees, surrounded by tall date palms.

Sally and Salvatore searched the square for some indication that her sister was there, but the square was empty apart from a few small dust devils twirling fallen leaves lazily across the open space.

The date palms whispered, 'She is gone.'

The orange tree, heavy with her yield said, 'The golden-haired Australian who came each day to taste my fruit, was taken beneath my branches one evening as she ate.'

'I saw,' said the Date Palm. 'My fronds and fruit watch over all that happens here in the garden.

It was evening, as the girl, known as "the healer", rested by the fountain eating some fruit, when men wearing cloth over their faces, came from the shadows, wrapped her in a burnouse, thrust their loud sticks into her flesh, and carried her away, towards the setting sun. She made no noise, but struggled wildly, until they beat her body many times, and she stopped.'

Sally and Salvatore looked at each other, at a loss. They'd known it wasn't going to be easy to find Rebecca, but now, this terrible news threw all their plans to the wind.

Luckily, the wind was listening. She carried the exchange back and forth, from the boat at the top of the Persian Gulf to the trees of Baghdad, who passed the information on to Salvatore.

He asked the Date Palm in plain language, 'When was this?'

The Date Palm replied, 'This happened before dark, when the shadows are longest. Before the moon grows her horns.'

'The new Moon!' whispered Sal. 'Three days ago.'

Sally didn't even query how he knew what phase of the Moon was passing. She had seen amazing things since beginning this adventure, and knew Gaia and the forces of Earth were with them; but she was young, and despair still gnawed at her heart when obstacles like this appeared. Before Sally met Salvatore, before her father met Sap, being human meant being anchored to the old reality, a reality that did not recognise the magic in the world and the real power of love.

Sally felt the reassuring comfort of strings and wood under her fingers. With Sap in her hands, all things were possible. She felt Rebecca was still alive, and would have felt the vacuum if Rebecca was not. About to play or be played, Sally's fingers poised above the strings, in position to strike a chord, when the vision through the gaping hull shifted.

A windswept, desolate plain came into view, flat and dust-blown, fading to grey at the foot of distant hills. What she first thought were sand dunes stretching across the plain and covering the floor of the valley, she now recognised as tents.

Barely perceptible beneath the layer of tawny dust, she could make out the faint blue lettering of UNHCR, the United Nations Refugee organisation, and an ocean of canvas, flapping tiredly in a sea of dust. The view swept over crowds of tattered humanity scrabbling for water and food thrown from the back of trucks.

The scene closed in on a series of tents with big red crosses and red crescents on them, the lettering MSF setting them aside as medical service centres. Sally and Salvatore's hearts lifted as they recognised the Medicines Sans Frontiers logo across the tents.

Rebecca! they thought simultaneously.

There was a long queue of battered people waiting outside the Red Cross tents. Women and men, children, and babies in their mothers or father's arms, on stretchers, on crutches, sitting on the stumps of lost limbs, some gazing into space emptily, in shock, bomb blasted, but alive.

Shattered lives, lining up to be repaired, sewn back together by the miracle workers inside the tent.

The queue shuffled forward as the flap of the tent opened, and one of the miracle workers stepped into the midday sun, shaded his eyes, and looked beyond the frayed line seeking something distant, perhaps hope or inspiration.

Obviously weary, he focused again on the wounded and broken people trusting in him, triaging as he walked its length, picking the immediate critical cases from the acute and distressed who would have to wait.

'Simon,' whispered the wind. Some way along the line, he stopped and looked around, as if he'd heard someone call his name. Shaking his head, he continued. 'Simon,' the wind called again. Two bodies along, he stopped. Again the hand came up to the eyes as he searched the area.

Simon had heard his mother call amongst the ropes and the canvas of the tents before, and he had responded, speaking to his dead mother using the fabric, like scrying to the other world. Annie would appear, singing in the twisted hemp, or appearing in the coarse fabric, in memorable perfection, like a Madonna or Mona Lisa, sharing some wisdom or news with her son, keeping in touch, though her body was long gone.

This time she called his attention to the viewers on Nashirah, three hundred kilometres away. It had been almost thirteen years since Sally had seen Simon, and she was shocked at how time and the desert had seasoned the boy she remembered and completed the man before her.

A full, sandy coloured beard highlighted the bright blue eyes looking out from beneath brows matching the beard. He had grown tall and lanky, with that relaxed strength Sally remembered in his father. She saw Trevor's strength in him, and despite the setting, a gentleness reminiscent of Annie.

'Simon!' Sally called aloud.

'Simon,' his mother whispered, 'look to the South, use the sight Gaia gave you.'

Simon had to disentangle himself from the pleading voices coming from the queue of damaged humanity surrounding him, remove himself from the constant slapping of windswept canvas and the whining of the wind, to the silence of inner space, where he could hear his own heartbeat and the rushing of blood around his eardrums ... deep inside the silence, where the soul could hear.

Two waving antenna ruffled the flap of his breast pocket. First one, then another spiny leg hitched over the once white cotton. A pair of onyx eyes followed, saw that all was safe, and the desert solifuge nimbly clambered up to Simon's shoulder, and perched next to his ear. His partner in surgery, from Simon's first operational placement, had travelled with him ever since. His own personal Jiminy Cricket.

The spider gently nudged Simon's ear, garnering his attention, then angled her head as if she was hearing something herself. She then expelled some fluid from a tube hidden behind her jaws into his ear canal. A wet and sticky goo rapidly dammed the canal, forming another eardrum at the entrance to the auditory canal, and suddenly he could hear voices calling his name. Several voices, in fact.

One was weeping, and obviously suffering, the other was calling his name from some space above, in the wind and the dust.

'Simon, it's Sally. My voice is being carried on the wind. If you can hear me, show me some sign, indicate that you can hear me.'

He looked up and around and waved. 'Yes!' he shouted to the

wind, his voice echoing inside his skull. 'Yes, I hear you.' Startling, odd looks from the humanity around him.

Sally ordered her thoughts, so she would get the story across without confusion, then spoke clearly to the man she'd once regarded as her big brother.

'Simon, listen carefully. I am almost in Iraq with Salvatore. We have important work to do, just us. But, you must know, Rebecca is also in Iraq or Syria, we don't know exactly where.' Sally choked down the emotion threatening to crack her composure. 'Rebecca was taken from Baghdad by insurgents, we guess only a day or two ago ... we don't know where they're headed. We're aboard a boat in the Gulf, and we were trying to get up to Baghdad.' Sally paused, 'But now we don't know where to go ...' Sally's composure broke down ... she sobbed, 'We've lost her, and we need...we need to find her ... When we started a year ago, this was one war. We, Salvatore and I, thought Bec would be easy to find ... but now? Now, everybody is fighting everybody. It's gone mad, crazy, stupid!'

Her voice collapsed in a series of racking sobs.

Simon stood with his head tilted to one side, listening, the camel spider still perched on his shoulder, antenna exploring the breeze. He needed to reassure Sally but was reeling from the unexpected contact with the people he'd grown up with after so long an absence, and the devastating news they carried.

He started tentatively. 'Sally...? It's been so long. Umm. First, tell me, what is Rebecca doing in Iraq? How long has she been here? Simon asked the dust and the wind, while memories of a much younger Sally and Rebecca swept over him.

Sallys' voice rattled along with the taut, drumming tent ropes, 'She's been in Baghdad for months now, working with MSF in the city. She was probably hoping to track you down, I think.' Where are you?'

'I'm in doctors without borders camp at Ar-raqqah, in the North. I'm a doctor now. Can you believe it? We're not far from the Syrian border, a few K's from the Euphrates dam.

Tell me more about Bec, why is she over here?' He wanted to hear that his former girlfriend, the woman he still dreamed of and loved, the one he had abandoned in panic and distress all that time ago, had come across the world to a war zone to tell him she loved him and couldn't exist without him, and that now she has been abducted.

Simon had never felt so utterly useless, as guilt and dread vied for prominence amongst his churning emotions.

Sally spoke again, as clearly as if she were standing next to him, 'Bec studied medicine too, and she's really good at it. She came over here to help with the injured and sick, she's working with the Doctors Without Borders as well ...' – another deep shuddering sob – 'before she was ... taken. She also had planned to find you. She still loves you; you must know that ... she ... still ... loves ... you, she never stopped. How will we find her now? Where do we even start looking?'

Even from her distant position in the hold of Nashirah, Sally could see the corners of Simon's mouth twitch in a crooked half smile. 'We have friends, Sal, friends we didn't know we had, far and wide across the land. They'll find Bec, I'm sure of it.' She saw him glance down the line of sad and injured people patiently waiting as the doctor spoke to the sky.

'Look, Sally, I really have to go, I've still got some urgent surgery here, stuff that can't wait, but rest assured, I'm already searching for Bec.

You two be careful in Baghdad, it's a bloody dangerous city. If you need to find me again, use the same channel!'

Sally trusted Simon, always had; even when her fantasies took flight. She had to admit she was occasionally a little jealous of her big sister, but loved them both unequivocally.

Gee, he was practically her big brother after all. She said yes, she'll find him, anywhere in the world, and with that he was gone.

Simon was amazed but not surprised at the ease with which the camel spider had assisted his communication with Sally. As simple as a phone call through a new model of co-operation with the natural world, old paradigms were already shifting.

He and several other medical personnel got to work triaging the ever-lengthening queue, knowing it was going to be a very long night. As it always was when an offensive began. Irrespective of who was right or wrong, what country or what faction they represented, it was always the weak and powerless that paid the price, with injured and homeless refugees fleeing their homes, leaving friends and family often buried beneath the homes they shared.

Dawn was breaking the following day by the time Simon and his team had a chance to rest and grab a bite to eat. He walked down to the well that was their water supply, where the solar pump was silently pouring a constant trickle of clear water into a small reservoir which the whole camp shared.

Splashing the cool water over his head and neck, Simon considered the number of stories of baptism in the desert. Water, everyone needs water, including the good and the bad, defenders and attackers, victims, and insurgents. He knew now what he needed to do to find Rebecca.

CHAPTER 32

Simon looked down at his reflection in the small pool, and became still. The trickling feed sent ripples across his features, distorting, and rearranging his face until he was unrecognisable even to himself. He silently watched the tiny waves arrange themselves first into Rebecca's hair, which was much shorter now than he remembered and gave her an elfin look. Her eyes seemed larger, and her face thinner.

She was as beautiful as he remembered, and his heart swelled with the missing of her and the love that had grown even without him tending it. Almost whispering her name, he reached down to the surface of the water to touch the face he had not seen for many years, but stopped short, for fear he would break the spell.

'Bec, my love,' he breathed across the reflection 'Hold on, I'm coming.'

The eyes in the well turned and caught his own, and despite being within the water, he saw them fill with liquid of their own.

Rebecca Pringle was no longer. Travelling with the Isis fighters, she was treated as less than human, the goats had more value to them. Chained to the vehicles at night, released only to fetch water or cook butchered pieces of goat on the open fire at the brief and infrequent stops.

Ridiculed and cruelly tormented, not only by the men, but by the armed and zealous Isis women fighters, Bec was wearing down. She was kicked and beaten to within a wisp of her life, repeatedly, spat on by children and leered at by the young recruits who had joined them from all corners of the world.

She had been dragged from northern Iraq and was now three quarters of their way across Syria. At the moment they rested amongst stunning ancient ruins that the jihadists named, 'Tadmur,' and some of the western recruits named, 'Palmyra.'

Rebecca had completed her apprenticeship in the mystic art of shamanism with Gaia and Sap using her astral body, and had visited sacred places all over the Earth and was trained and adept at sensing and using the power the ancients had tapped in such places.

Palmyra was pulsing with such power and only she could feel it. For more than three thousand years, this junction of Earth's energy grid had been a focus point for many flourishing civilisations. Situated on the great silk road between the West and the East it was a fertile crossroads where both dangerous ideas, and both mundane and precious goods were traded, eventually finding their way over the Caucasus Mountains to the Steppes, or the frozen wilds of the far Northern Kingdoms.

The militia group that had kidnapped her had joined a larger and well-armed contingent sent to demolish ancient historical sites and shrines like Palmyra and had already planted improvised explosives beneath statues and strategic monuments that had stood here for millennia.

Rebecca, collapsed in a heap beneath the meagre shade afforded by a row of shattered marble columns, stared up at an almost empty sky, but for the hypnotic circling of a pair of hawks. Wings spread wide, controlled yet motionless on the wind, the two birds spiralled higher and higher, until they became almost lost in the ocean of pale blue.

She felt a moment of vertigo, where she felt she was looking down on the pair, to the extent that when they entered the blue, she saw the concentric rings where they had splashed into ... whatever ... The rings grew wider, and the sky darker ... like the water in a well.

Rebecca peered down a tunnel, and at the bottom where the light entered, a pair of eyes stared back at her. Familiar eyes, blue eyes from her youth; lover's eyes ... Simon?

With that thought came the confirmation. 'Bec,' he said. Clear as the liquid through which she saw him, came the words, 'Bec ... Hold on ... I'm coming ... ' Then as soon as he had appeared, his words and image rippled and muddied, then he was gone.

The sky was empty, and the heat returned with a vengeance. Rebecca's heart was buoyant now with faith and trust and hope, those foundations which keep our spirits high. She was back from the edge of despair; help was on the way.

Back in Australia, on the Daily's farm, Susan felt the surface of the desk move, a ripple swelled and rolled across the grain; the grain flowed, glacier like towards its own edge.

Then the desk began to quake. Shaking from side to side, She began to swell and undulate like a magnificent wooden snake. Sap began to transform.

Susan had been diligently sitting at the desk for hours each day documenting Sally and Salvatores' mission to save the world. She had almost forgotten this was a living, sentient being.

Rising cautiously and pushing back the chair, She backed away, to stand against the wall, watching as the desk she was sitting at only moments before, became animated; legs hammering the floor, the form undulating, as Sap returned to the feminine spirit she had arrived as.

She was literally channelling everything she saw, as Sap's emissary and Sap, the tree, saw all that was occurring in her world. Every connection affecting those she loved and had woven their way into the story, resonated with the tree, like messages down a piece of string or vibrations across an invisible web.

Today had begun as a narrative of Rebecca and Simon's reunification through the medium of the well. Now it seemed like Sap wanted to become more physically involved. She knew Rebecca was in a hazardous and totally unpredictable situation. The tree must act, so Gaia steps in.

Desk legs became shapely woman's calves and ankles, still the golden brown and grain of timber, but alive and languidly stretching and limbering out, flexing all the way up the thigh, developing hips and pelvis. The desktop swelled as breasts and abdomen grew, and at last her head appeared, beautiful as ever with piercing green eyes and cascading golden hair. Sap had returned to her human form, eager to help.

She turned towards Susan, her green eyes flashing, intense, purposeful.

'You must continue to write. Much depends on it.' She stepped close to Susan, bodies almost touching. Sap cupped Susan's cheek with gentle reassurance, gazed deep into her heart and kissed her on the lips. 'I must go,' was all she said. With that, and with Susan standing agape at the door, Sap dissolved over and into the floorboards, and disappeared from Susans sight.

CHAPTER 33

Cells divided into molecules, which then became atoms, and smaller still particles of Sap became stars in the inner cosmos of our planet Earth. She was everywhere at once, soaking into the oceans, the air, and the land. All that swam, flew, crawled, and walked had Sap in their veins. Every growing thing on the planet had Sap in its structure.

Nashirah was tangled among the acres of reeds choking the Euphrates river, and there was little her crew could do to free her. Mahmoud and the few crew members left, along with Sally and Salvatore, had been attempting to drag the ancient ship through the ocean of reeds, hauling on rough hemp ropes that cut their hands when dry and burned through them when wet. Sally found herself half-wishing the crocodiles would return, and on second thought, was glad they didn't.

Sap, as violin, had laid dormant beside her for weeks now. Sally still slept with her friend in her arms, but could not bring herself to play. She had bad nights and worse nights, tossing and turning in her bunk, thinking what might become of her sister at the so-called jihadists' hands. Sap lay silent, waiting for Sally to caress the strings and awaken her body.

The desert heat through the days and nights did not bother her, tempered as it was with the regular evening breeze, rattling the reeds and bringing a breath of humidity and coolness to the stifling atmosphere in the hold of the old hulk. Steady heat with a hint of humidity will not destroy a violin as much as dampness, with its slow rotting style and glue dissolution, unravelling many a fine instrument.

But Sap was more than a fine instrument, she had a distinct purpose in Sally's hands and although patient, itched to sing and sound aloud her song of reckoning.

Outside the hull, papyrus and cattails rustled with the arrival of Sap's other forms, coming from deep within the planet. Incarnations, now manifesting in many, many, more organic forms, from the puddles of stagnant water that was the Euphrates and across the expansive reed beds, to within the hull of the boat.

The violin soaked in the magical fibres of her other soul, blending through the world, the prophecy, her destiny, the unification of instrument, desk, paper and scribe, the story was coming alive; this is what she was born for!

Salvatore stretched his hands out, palms down, and swept them over the reed beds that held them fast. Sweeping from side to side in a dance, the green stems joined him. Rattling to each other, waving their bulrush heads, the papyrus partnering cattails, bowing one to the other, then shimmying and rocking in one sinuous motion.

He laughed aloud with the joy of the motion. He knew Sap had come; he felt her rise in the water, low as it was, but felt her most in the vibrant living organisms all around him, moving as one.

Sally climbed up on the deck of Nashirah to see the reeds all sweeping the side of the boat with a rhythm and an oceanic swish, almost processional, beginning to lift and carry the old boat forward. Rocking end to end at first, then lumbering forward with a groan of ancient timbers, Nashirah shuddered and lifted above the sea of green, to then heave, bow down amongst the reeds, to rise again, almost imperceptibly moving forward.

Salvatore joined Sally on deck, both leaning over the railing to watch the hull sweep through and over the reed beds. The motion had woken Mahmoud and the crew, who joined them at the gunwale to see this miracle firsthand.

As they gained speed, Mahmoud was the first to query, 'From here, where do we go?'

Salvatore gestured across the expanse of rhythmically bowing stems carrying them North, and shouted over the rustling and the rising breeze, 'Wherever She takes us! We travel in the arms of the Goddess, now. She has a plan; she moves us like pieces on the gaming board.'

On the farm in Australia, Susan watched all this unfold across, or rather through, what used to be a polished wooden floor, that used to support a desk that she used to write at daily. Instead of solid rows of spotted gum flooring, there was now a large, puddle shaped transparent window on that part of Syria.

Another part of her heard the outside screen door open and the familiar clump, clump, of her dad's boots making their way down the hall.

'Susan ... Susan ... are you busy? Sorry to interrup—' As Tom rounded the open doorway and saw the moving images in the floor, he stopped, mid-stride and mid-sentence.

'Oh my! Oh my God! What th – How?' Susan saw the realisation dawn in her father's eyes, 'Sap is there. Isn't She?' he whispered.

Her father knew Sap was there, she had a task to complete, they all did.

Tom hovered above the void; unaware he was teetering at the edge. Susan brought her father back to the present abruptly, dragging him away from the edge of the gaping cavity before them.

'Sap has taken human form once more and she's gone to help Bec and Sally.'

Susan was really the only one who was up to speed on the incredible happenings half a world away. Some evenings, she would share what the pencil had written, what Sap had written, about her other incarnations, personas ... bits. Susan still found it difficult to reconcile that Sap was many independent and autonomous beings carrying out Gaia's plan for the balancing of roles on the planet, yet still the one tree, one being.

Although split into, pencil ... desk ... paper and violin, plus however many other influences she imbued, like Nashirah, the boat, the reeds beneath her, even the fruit trees in the square in Baghdad, Sap flowed in many directions, like the passage of spirit through matter.

Susan and Tom, now with Rosie just in from the garden – weed seeds in her hair, and knees crusted with soil – all gazed down into the gaping hole in the floor of the study. Still not sure it was a hole, the family kept well back, peering over the edge, if it was an edge, into what could be a large, splatter shaped window on what was happening in real time, in a real place, far away.

At the same time, on the other side of the valley James and Mai Pringle were staring mesmerised by the yawning hole that had formed suddenly in the centre of the mighty slab table on their verandah. The last time they had seen both their daughters together was at this same table.

That gathering with Salvatore, Trevor Manning and Simon, Tom, Rosie, and Susan, was a lifetime away for James and Mai-li.

Now they saw their eldest daughter in a vision, at the bottom of what looked like a well, formed in the middle of two mighty pine slabs.

The two never questioned the reality of the vision. They had both seen enough miracles since the tree's arrival in their lives, to recognise another when they saw it.

Both knew this was Sap's doing, for at the very edges of the abyss they could see the faces of their neighbours, the Dailys, also peering in, concerned faces in the frame, and wondered if it was the same for them.

The scene for all of them was the same: there was Rebecca, thin and dirty, hair cut savagely short. Her eyes appeared overly large in her delicate face. A dark bruise spread across one side of her cheek to above one eye, and her nose had been broken and was pushed to the side. But her eyes burned with fury, deep-set and dark, cauldrons brewing venom.

Mai cried out, pained to see her daughter like this.

From across the world Rebecca heard. 'Mum?' she whispered. 'Mum ... is that you?'

'Bec ... my lovely girl, what have they done to you?' James gathered Mai in his arms for fear she would fling herself into the void.

Rebecca could hear her mother's distress in her voice, but could only breathe an answer to the stones she lay on. 'I know what I'm doing, Mum.' They saw her look around furtively, and when she could see no-one could hear, she said, 'They will not damage me anymore. I am a bargaining chip for them.' She knew this medium, and had used it before ... all Sap's family were connected.

Rebecca understood that Simon and Sally could probably also see her, here in Palmyra among the ruins.

'You, woman! Who you talk to?' came a voice from outside their view.

A heavy boot came out of nowhere and caught Rebecca in the ribs. She doubled up, gasping, looked up at the shadowy figure standing over her and said, 'God ... I'm talking to God!'

The blow never arrived. Rebecca had raised an arm to protect herself from the descending rifle butt, but after several seconds of no impact she lowered her arm and saw the young man, a boy, really; dirty, with the beginnings of the requisite beard, wide-eyed, staring beyond where she lay.

He left her where she was and scrambled back to the trucks in panic. Managing to twist her body around the column, and claw her way upright, Rebecca squinted into the lowering sun, and saw the most amazing sight she had ever seen.

CHAPTER 34

t was an ancient ship – a felucca, Bec recalled from her scanty research into the Middle East and its customs – cresting sand dunes and sweeping down the steep rippled sides on a deep green carpet of wet, undulating seaweed tangled with reeds and bulrushes. The vegetative mass constantly appeared beneath the bow and rushing by under the keel, squeezing streams of water before and behind her, allowing the ship to skim across sand and gibber rocks, a literal ship of the desert.

Nashirah was rapidly approaching Palmyra from the west, out of the setting sun, and heading straight towards the row of columns sheltering Rebecca. At the bow of the vessel, riding high on the foredeck, was Sally, hair flowing behind her in the wind, brandishing Sap's fiddle, bow held high like a sabre at the charge, ready to strike a note. Behind her, Salvatore Fiorelli, cape thrown back, with the red satin lining flashing in the light of the dying sun, with some small object held to his lips, sending metallic flashes across the arena.

Shouts were going up among the militia. Several groups were attempting to manoeuvre large field artillery pieces into position, while others ran with ammunition belts towards trucks loaded with heavy machine guns.

Panic ensued, as Nashirah bore down on the surprised group. No-one was watching Rebecca as she climbed to her feet, staggering towards the ancient gate of the sun, the very gate Alexander of Macedonia had passed through two and a half millennia before. Crouching in the small patch of shade offered by the great stones, Rebecca had a moment to breathe again. The adrenalin rush that had propelled her toward cover subsided, and she had time to examine her shelter.

The ancient stones were well designed to fit together without cement or clay packing, and the chisel marks so clean and concise they could have been executed yesterday.

Rebecca discovered the small crumbling niches between the ground and the foundation stones were packed tightly with improvised explosives set to detonate, the fuses a blatant give-away, trailing out amongst the dust and rocks.

She was beyond caution as she clawed at the crevices packed with the deadly mass, a highly volatile explosive, made on-the-cheap from fertiliser and bleach. Levering herself into a position beneath a pile of crumbled masonry, she wedged her shoulder against the ancient marble, managing to shift it fractionally, rattling stones and mortar loose.

Sweating now, afraid someone would spot her, Rebecca redoubled her efforts. Her fingers pried open a small crack in the masonry, enough to just squeeze her hand in and grasp the tightly crammed package, before it collapsed again, crushing her hand around the explosive.

She could hear the crackling of small arms fire, and the whoosh of a rocket propelled grenade being fired somewhere to her right, when the salt sweat in her hand ignited the peroxide in the explosive.

All she saw was the light, as the flash of ignition took her arm and shoulder apart. The explosion threw Rebecca out from under the lion arch, hurling her body against an ancient stone wall. With her wound pumping a macabre mural across the bleached rocks, she sank to the ground limp as a rag doll, finally coming to a rest in a grotesque sitting position, staring back at the crumbling monument.

Mai-li, seeing her daughter thrown aside by the explosion, screamed, shrill, pained, torn by distance and helplessness. 'Noooo ... No!' Her fingers dug deep into James' arm as she held on in desperation. Still they could not tear their eyes away from the disaster unfolding before them.

The volatile nature of the explosives crudely used by the group meant that when one was triggered a chain reaction ensued, causing one bomb after another to detonate across the ruins, raining debris and destruction down on friend and foe alike.

Sally, riding at the bow of Nashirah, was focused wholly on the armaments now firing at her, missed the blast that caught her sister, and armed only with Sap, steeled herself for battle. Salvatore drew the small fife from his cloak pocket, and brought it to his lips.

What began as a lively trill rapidly swelled to a tsunami of notes cascading forth against the shells and bullets flying and whistling towards them. As each projectile hit the wave, it shattered or spun off in a whining ricochet back to its source. The trill intensified and lowered to a threatening growl; a feral didgeridoo, matching the explosions, blasts, and eruptions, flaring up all around them.

Amid this onslaught, Sally caught sight of her sister, slumped, and sagged against the cobbled wall, seemingly lifeless. Through her half-closed eyes, Rebecca watched her life seep to the ground and soak into the sand. She could not move, there was no pain, only the breeze teasing her hair across her face, and the warm sun.

A trickle of water made its way across the hot sand and mingled with her blood. The water was clear, washing the red blood into the earth, washing her life away, cleansing and cooling. It formed a little delta among the grains of sand, and still it came on, a stream now flowing from the mouth of a lion that once stood at a gate.

Rebecca thought she could smell the water, sweet and clean as it formed a pool at her side. She was slipping away fast; she could feel the world fading and the nurse in her sensed she was perhaps hallucinating from lack of blood when a golden figure rose from the pool next to her.

A woman, strikingly beautiful, with golden skin draining liquid, materialised from the now substantial body of water gathering around her feet and legs.

The water and the woman were one at the base, as she ascended above the pond, a goddess rising, or an angel come to take Rebecca to heaven.

Chaos reigned, buildings tumbled and the ground shook. Rebecca felt none of it; what remained of her focus was on the angel as it reached down into what was now becoming a small lake and drew forth a hand and wrist, an obviously *human* hand and wrist. Wristwatch and shirtsleeves emerged, shoulder and head.

Rebecca was almost gone, but managed a ragged gasp when Simon rose from the surface. Still in his Medicines Sans Frontiers scrubs, wet and radiant, he turned towards her, dragging himself across the water's surface.

He was her first and only love, a ghost from beyond the grave. Rebecca was sure it was her grave and she the ghost. She could even feel his hands, his lips on hers, his words calling her name. Vaguely, she heard a battle being fought somewhere nearby. Explosions and gunfire, seemed to her dying ears, like percussion beneath some strange music, flute, and violin, sailing above the deep drumming of heavy artillery.

Rebecca was floating just beneath the surface of a great ocean. She could smell water and seaweed. She could feel Simons hands and mouth near hers, but she was far, far, away.

In the moment that he touched her, at the very atom of touch, a warm river of what the ancients called chi flowed from his body into hers. Heart and mind, through the conduit of his arm and through his gently reaching finger, it spread in concentric waves, from the back of her hand where he had made contact, spreading in ripples of pain then pleasure across her body.

Rebecca, although losing consciousness in this world, was slipping into Simon's and Sap's world. A parallel existence where all things were possible. The circle of energy required completion, grounding, acknowledgement. He had felt it too and longed to touch her again, but frightened of loss, of never beginning, of never was, he pulled away, stopped, breathing.

As the tides in the great oceans are slaves to the Moon, Simon was drawn back towards her. She was his beach, his rocky headland, his shore, home.

He wanted to crash onto her, smash himself into a million pieces and spray across her wet and draining body. She saw shards of light splashing in all dimensions as he touched her, face and hands met and entangled.

Simon was afraid he was too late, she was dead, past all revival. Sobbing with regret and grief, he took her in his arms and gently cradled her head and shoulder, oblivious of the blood still weakly pumping against his face.

His mouth met hers at a soft angle, rising. Bec was sand and shell and pearls, and all beach-found precious gems. She soaked in the salty scent of him, was drawn and drowned in the seas of his eyes. More than passion and desire, this was Thea and Gaia, planets caught in each other's gravity, inescapable. Indisputable. Simon was the rising tide, Rebecca the sparkling beach, invited to saturation. Her wish was fulfilled with the sweep of his liquid body across her. She was covered and accepting, drawing in every particle of him.

She was broken and whole, neither dead nor alive. There was no pain where she was, only being, and being part of the lover she had been missing all these years made her complete.... the missing piece of her had returned. She could feel Sap blending blood, water, and silica from the sand, making bone and flesh, weaving her arm and upper body back together, but the physical did not touch her. It was Simon returned, she focused on, and with the passion fuelled by absence, his presence touched depths of her she had never explored.

He foamed and roared with her tumbling, sighing, sand voice beneath him, and she was above him, singing as he sank further into and through her silken body. Rebecca wrapped herself around him, whispering softly into his neck, as the soundtrack swelled behind them.

Explosions were again audible, small arms fire crackled in the air, and the nearby whining of bullets brought the pair abruptly back to this world. The pumping blood was once again within the skin, made whole. The arm and shoulder wound were no longer; Rebecca was back from the brink.

This world was white noise and sunburned, dust-blown chaos.

Rebecca opened her eyes to a skewed view of rubble, and an unlikely pond of clear water bubbling about her feet. The aquifer, which the founders of Palmyra had built over, had found an exit again through the giant jaws of the lions of the gate. Moreover, the water was pumping up in a fountain about their feet.

Simon attempted to drag her under cover as the water rose around them. Sap was nowhere to be seen.

Mai and James, Tom and Rosie had all seen Rebecca shattered by the explosion, through the hole in their reality. Susan had felt the demand by the paper to notate and was sitting on the floor by the gaping vision feverishly writing down what she saw, her tears blotching the delicate paper as she wrote.

In the vision, they had all seen Rebecca hurled against the wall, body torn and shattered, while the water began pumping and pooling around her from the lion's mouth. When Sap and Simon arose from the water, Mai fell to her knees and whispered a soft prayer of hope.

When Rebecca and Simon sank beneath the rising pond, their hopes thinned from surrender and resignation to hopelessness. Their daughter was gone from this world.

Rebecca had passed from this world, albeit temporarily, as she was also passing through another, altogether different, healing world. A world of blood and sand, decomposed ancient coral reefs, beaches, and the bleached and crushed remnants of civilisations, tribes and adventurous nomads that had all passed this way outwards to colonise the rest of the globe. So, there was no lack of resources with which to rebuild a body, and Sap used them all.

When Mai and James saw their daughter re-emerge from the bloodied pond, whole and wrapped in Simon's arms, back into the swirling melee that was the confrontation of Nashirah and the insurgents, they thought, From the frying pan into the fire!

The opening in both the Pringle's table and the floor of the Daily's study, gave a panoramic view of the desert, the ruins, and the protagonists, distorted by dust and perspective. They looked down at an oblique angle at the action, a clouds view, with the wind behind them.

Sally rode high on the old ship's prow, legs planted wide, stabilising her on the wildly bucking vessel, her bow sawing, intent on rescue and revenge, as her eyes ranged across the scene searching for glimpses of her sister. Salvatore played feverishly busy trills, deflecting fire from his young protégé, while disarming others with deep hornlike blasts bellowing from the tiny instrument, a lion roaring from a Chihuahua's jaws.

CHAPTER 35

There has been war raging across the entire planet, from Africa, through Europe, the Middle East and North and South America, across Asia, and throughout small Island nations, for countless eons. Wars between the rich and poor, the haves and the have-nots, the powerful and the dispossessed, war between Humanity and Nature at the heart of all disputes.

This altercation was the spearhead, the juncture of them all, and what occurred here would be the catalyst that would change everything.

The Isis fighters mostly believed they were the warriors of Islam, fighting to create a better world; whereas they were simply another minority being squeezed by a world in which they were persona, not grata. The oil beneath their feet and the wealth beneath the sand would never be theirs, but they were paying for it with their lives.

As children, all they had known was conflict, war, and invasion by foreign powers. Palmyra had been a crossroads under contention for millennia. Although parents love their children and shower them with affection the world over, it was rare and fortunate for children here in the Middle East to see both parents survive as they grew into their adulthood.

Bought up in the midst of ancient enmities, used as pawns in the monopoly games of power; love, compassion and understanding were not common currency in a land where survival of the strongest was paramount.

They were furious combatants, and well-armed by both the Russians and the Americans, although the bullets bombarding Nashirah knew no nationality. The old ship was taking the brunt of the damage. Barely seaworthy before, she was now crumbling beneath Sally and Salvatore's feet. Mahmoud had long ago abandoned ship. Woodchips exploded around them as machine-gun fire desiccated the ancient vessel.

Shards embedded themselves in sand and skin alike, as their faithful craft crumbled to inexorable dust, her sleek lines marked by tight cornrows of reed and bulrush, softly dissolving into the sand.

Sally stepped calmly from the prow of the vanishing ship onto the last tangle of the carpet of rapidly decomposing seaweed, then down to the sand with Salvatore hot on her heels. Neither one was certain they would come out of this alive. Sap and Gaia had given no guarantees that they would not be hurt, so they advanced on faith and hope towards a hail of projectiles, armed only with two musical instruments and the power of love.

Behind the weapons, men in black head scarves and sunglasses continued to fire barrage after barrage at the two westerners advancing toward them. Mystified and bewildered by their lack of accuracy, some of the more superstitious tribesmen began muttering about witchcraft and the devil.

Reinforcing this, a tall golden female form began to emerge from beneath the sand, head and shoulders, torso to hips, stark naked and boldly making her way towards them, among the ruins.

Cries of 'God be merciful!' and 'God, save us!' rose among them, as panic began to tighten its grip. The firing became more sporadic as weapons were dropped and men backed away from what they saw as a supernatural foe.

The leaders attempted to rally their force, with calls of 'God is great!' exhorting the now terrified rabble to fight on. To their credit, some resumed the battle, whether for the cause or out of fear, they became the fanatics Isis craved.

The fearsome naked woman was changing form before their eyes, her curvaceous shape began to shred and flap in the wind, what was previously long lustrous honey-coloured hair, gathered itself about her head forming a burnoose. The body thickened and became unmistakeably male, broad at the shoulder, with robes trailing to the ground. The figure looked up at the now silent battle front, the eyes a piercing green below the deep brows. A prominent, fierce hooked nose shadowed a full beard, exaggerating the forward jutting chin. The one they most feared and loved, stood before them.

His booming voice carried by the desert wind, echoed through the now still ruins, 'In who's name do you break this world?' Silence replied. The figure inquired again, impaling the leaders with his stare, louder now, 'IN WHO'S NAME DO YOU BREAK THIS WORLD?'

The leader of the militia, one Osama, gathered enough courage to reply, looked defiantly at his front line and said, 'In God's name, we cleanse the world of non-believers and kill infidels, we do this in His name.' Gathering confidence, he continued, 'There is but one God, and alongside Him we will rule Heaven and Earth.'

The figure before them sighed, a slow, pained expulsion of air. He considered this dogmatic recitation and quietly, almost confidentially asked the man, 'What does this mean? Does this mean there exists separation between Heaven and Earth? Heaven is where we are, Here and Now, if we truly want it! Can you not see? You destroy what is your birthright!'

Osama was about to reply when a shout went up from behind the ruined lion gate,

'I have them! I have the girl and the boy.'

Suddenly, the spell was broken. Shots rang out from the rear of the assemblage, as bullets kicked up dust at the feet of the mysterious individual. Automatic weapons fire riddled the robes, leaving gaping holes through which the desert behind could be seen. Still he stood there, accepting the worst of their fire, not flinching nor falling, but reducing with each salvo until the shredded robes blew away on the wind, no body, no blood, no memory of the existence of a soul having ever stood there.

Osama gathered his brutal reality about him, giving little thought to the seed planted in his brain. He pointed to some men who followed as he scurried over to where the shouts had originated, and found the boy, who had been charged with guarding Rebecca, and although beyond his control, he was instrumental in her recent escape.

Scared and quaking with adrenalin, he pressed a wicked-looking blade against her throat, in a stand-off with Simon, glaring across the gap between them.

While everyone was transfixed with the confrontation with Sap, as the Prophet, the boy had skulked between columns, until he was behind the pair, waiting for his opportunity to pounce. He was proud he was not 'sucked in.'

His name was Ali and he believed in nothing he could not touch. Although he did believe a thousand virgins waited for him on the other side of death. He had the witch in his power, all he had to do was draw the blade back and her throat would open. He grinned viciously over her shoulder at his comrades. Victory would be theirs, and he would earn rewards in paradise. His fingers clasped the handle of the knife tighter, he was sweating, and his grip was failing.

The dagger writhed in his palm, the blade flexed and wrapped itself around his dirt crusted fingers, and began tightening slowly, crushing them. A small, forked tongue slid in and out of what had been a shining blade moments before, two dark eyes focused on Ali's own.

He tried to drop the jambiya, but the grip was too tight. Backing away from the witch and her friend, Ali began to scream.

The tongue flicked over and over at his face, perhaps smelling the fear, the eyes excited by the opening and closing mouth, and the human tongue flapping. The fangs struck, again and again, opening small but deadly puncture wounds at the cheek and lips.

Ali was beside himself with fear, he knew he was dying. All dreams of paradise and virgins had fled, in agony he fell to the dust kicking weakly and gasping for his last breath. No-one moved. Their eyes were on Ali's last feeble attempts to reach his friends, fingers clutched dust, stretching for help that would never come. He died surprisingly quickly, but writhing in agony, a small trickle of foam draining from the corner of his mouth, his eyes fixed on paradise.

The spell was broken, the witch again the target for a hundred weapons. 'Where are the others?' Osama shouted. 'The ones from the felucca.' About to launch a rocket grenade at Rebecca and Simon's position beside the still spreading lake, Osama paused, looking about for the others.

'Let his death be a warning to you all.' Rebecca would be passive no more, her voice cried above the singing bullets around her.

Simon tried to hold her back, but she spun from his grasp and climbed to the top of a monument to a forgotten Assyrian King, began to draw fire from the Isis insurgents. 'You cannot win!' she cried, 'Put down your weapons, we will not hurt you.'

This last statement attracted laughter and howls of derision from the Syrian fighters.

Osama had located Sally and Salvatore, making their way slowly over the rubble beneath the statue Rebecca was perched upon. He redirected his aim and launched the grenade. An almighty burst of flame erupted behind him, and the whistle of a rocket propellant sent the explosive hurtling towards the two.

The grenade fell short, exploding metres in front of them, showering them both with shrapnel and broken statuary, and raising a great cloud of smoke and dust, but alerting them both that Osama had found them. Looking at Sally, Salvatore mouthed, 'No Guarantees.' They may not yet survive this confrontation, but as they both knew, this was the spot Nature had chosen to reinstate her supremacy, and Salvatore and Sally, as well as Rebecca and Simon were expendable.

None of them knew that back home Mai-li, James, Tom, Rosie, and Susan were riveted to the vision revealed to them through the open floor and table, and emotionally invested in their children. To them, no-one was expendable.

Osama discarded the grenade launcher for a more dependable weapon and wrenching a heavy machine-gun from the hands of the man next to him he fitted a new magazine and fired a torrent of bullets at the distant pair, whipping up a flurry of dust and whining metal all about them.

Salvatore, unable to fit the fife to his lips as he dodged flying metal and groped his way through the ruins, dived behind one of the still standing columns, yelling at Sally to take cover herself. The planet would be better served if she was alive. Rebecca continued hurling abuse at Osama's men, creating a diversion, and hopefully weakening their resolve. She felt strong, invulnerable since she had died and been resurrected in the lake. Gaia and Sap were with her, and the universe provided momentum.

CHAPTER 36

Rebecca's words were convincing, persuasive ... her shamanic voice was making men doubt themselves, shaking and eroding their convictions, and her sister was taking the battle to the conclusion all allies of the planet had hoped for.

Sally strode on the breast of the mountain. Walking unhurried amongst the noise and tumult, violin held in one hand, relaxed by her side, as if in a trance, her eyes focused on something otherworldly, while bullets cut the air around her, screaming and ricocheting off rocks and raising dust clouds at her feet.

Slowly she raised the instrument to her chin and lifted the bow. A rocket launched from the floor of an ancient amphitheatre exploded the rubble behind her in a deafening cloud of shrapnel and dust.

She dragged the bow across the 'G' string just so, as Salvatore had instructed. Wrist relaxed, arm horizontal, deliberate, confident, setting her intention. A vibration arose, releasing a note, sonorous and deep, so heart rending and pure, King David himself searched for such a note. A crying, a wounded wailing, keening, sprang from the strings and wood. Vengeful and sad simultaneously, aching with horror and love, that those still with any sensitivity were brought to their knees, their eyes to the heavens.

The Fiddle was alive beneath Sally's fingers. Where the fingers ended, and the string began was blurred. Her vibrato was a dance between the ebony and the air. Sap moved through the instrument, like a restless animal she writhed in Sally's grasp, lifting and arching with the notes.

An extended salvo of machine-gun fire rattled the air to her left, burning holes in space and time. Sally saw the man cavorting with the heavy weapon, attempting to retain his balance on the heaps of rubble below her.

There was no control or real direction in the projectiles he was releasing, except the wish to destroy the source of the soul rending sound shredding his neurons, crippling his hate, and rendering his anger impotent.

As Sally stepped from monolith to monolith, almost gliding down the steep incline, ancient beings rose from the rubble to reinforce her. The prophet and the wood grain woman strode at her side. A queen, garlanded with moss and lichen looking more tree than woman trailing a meadow of flowers, walked with her across the slope.

Sally played as she had never been moved to before, beyond the storm and tempest, notes that rendered the weapons men held useless. The steel barrels resonated with Sap's Ultra-Earthly frequency and reverted to the raw ore they were made of, heavy, unwieldy, and inoperable.

The wooden butt and haft of their weapons grew heavy and developed small buds, which extended to green shoots, which uncannily shot into branches in seconds, dividing and multiplying with leaves and flowers springing from fruitful junctures, until they could be held no longer, nor used as weapons.

Across the ruined city of Palmyra, weapons were being dropped; heavy artillery became intractable, immovable boulders of iron, nickel, and titanium ore, and still Sally played. Sap sang through her wooden soul, and love, as a tangible element, a measurable force, was having a devastating effect on tools of violence and war.

Love as an audible and beyond audible device resonated with the very atoms and sub-atomic structure of machines and minds.

Weapons dropped, and greenery sprouted from their wooden parts, searching for water in the desert sand, and water there was in abundance. The ancient city of Palmyra had been constructed by sophisticated and learned engineers who built the pyramids, the fabled city of Thebes and who had studied Aristotle, and Archimedes, men who charted the stars and recognised them as worlds and suns long, long before telescopes were invented.

Such engineers always utilised local water sources and built near them. Here in Palmyra, water lay in abundance just below the surface, hence, the springing up of the lake and the spring now gushing from the mouths of both lions at the ruined gate.

From the hilts and buts of AK47 assault rifles, and all sorts of exotic weaponry that had a hint of organic material on them, roots extended rapidly down into the sand, hungry for sustenance, which the desert provided and so, as roots fed, towering shrubs and trees began to rise around the opposing human forces.

Rebecca recognised sage, milfoil, lavender, and comfrey, renowned for their healing properties. Flowers and shrubs of every size, sprouted from the rock and sand. Trees erupted from the ground, and shot skyward.

Oaks, sycamores, cypress, and pines, already huge around the trunks, trailing climbing vines forming fruit. Passionfruit and grapes, cucumber, and giant beans, draping towering limbs. Across the ruins and among the dunes and cliffs, an immense carpet of green unfurled across the desert.

The blooming of the desert spread out from Palmyra; Oil was no longer the primary liquid fuelling the war-torn land. Water was being drawn to the surface by roots burrowing through the sand into aquifers not drawn on for a thousand years.

Mahogany, ash and cedar, the trees shot into the air, growing at blinding speed, spreading out from the ruins, greening the dunes, and swallowing the ancient site.

Sally played on and the forest danced in response. Angry fighters became confused and frightened orphans lost in the profusion of greenery, praying for salvation, and receiving redemption in a new world they had never dreamed would be, Paradise, here and now.

Weaponless and leaderless, they ran beneath the towering trees, seeking the sun, blinking above them beyond the shaded depths of the desert woodland. Across the planet, plants, rivers, and mountains responded to Sally's playing and Sap's singing. Shifting balances, and changing courses, opening barriers, and abolishing borders.

Rebecca, arms raised to the heavens, chanted an ancient healing mantra, sending it resonating around the world, soothing the battered souls seeking refuge amongst the trees. A world now tipped beyond the edge of the predicted results of climate change.

Where coastal rivers and gently lapping waves had inexorably crept over beaches and levies, they now flooded lowlands, inundating villages and cities alike. The glaciers and ice shelves of both Arctic and Antarctic split and crashed, thundering into the warm oceans, forcing gigantic waves kilometres high before them. Everything in their path was overwhelmed and what survived above the water was washed clean.

The change spread across the globe. Change is not always welcome from the Human perspective, and in most places, it was devastating. Nuclear power plants built close to ocean shores were swept away, nuclear cores rendered redundant. Radioactive rods disappeared down deep crevasses on the ocean floor and fed into the core of the planet. This was intentional, guided cataclysm, orchestrated by the Earth herself, to save herself.

For the greater benefit of the planet and Her inhabitants, sacrifices were necessary. It became increasingly apparent among the Human population that they were no longer the dominant lifeform, but were on an equal footing withal their co-inhabitants, from Ants to Blue Whales.

Susan, Tom, James, and Rosie, thankfully relieved that their children had triumphed against the terrorist adversary, were dragged from the vision through the floor by the rumbling sound of swelling volumes of water surging up the Fernyvale valley. Through the forests and over cultivated fields the water swept, carrying great trees, rocks and a million tonnes of mud with it, lapping hungrily at hills and slowed only by the flanks of steep mountains. The flood reached its peak some days later, before drawing back upon itself, wallowing gently against projecting fence lines, and settling to the new normal.

Assured that the water would climb no higher, the families dragged themselves away from the new world they surveyed from the verandah, back to the scenes awaiting them through the vista offered via the panoramic floor.

Simon found Osama cowering between the enormous buttress roots of a hundred-metre fig tree in the centre of the forest. On his knees in fear and wonder, he looked up at Simon, expecting reprisal but finding hands reaching down and helping him upright, leading him into the light. Unarmed now, his weapons green and verdant about him, Osama saw no threat in the eyes of this healer, only kindness and, yes, a sense of purpose burning in his eyes. Simon saw the man before him, the warrior he was and the farmer he had been before the war began.

Without fear driving him, Osama was a different man. He had a family he desperately loved back in the city of Homs, and skills he needed to put to use, and now a land at peace in which he could return to the life he loved.

Osama stood and held on to Simon. As the sense of relief washed over him he embraced the man he had, only hours before, attempted to kill. It seemed like a lifetime ago, everything was changed, a new world had erupted around them, it was the paradise he had sought for so long.

Rebecca's song, weaving and intertwining with Sally and Sap's violin, counterpointing Salvatore's flute, became a gentle balm now, to a very different world. Constructing images of light and shade, colour, and tone, awakening in the Human mind the vision of the future.

The musicians played on, their intention and composition carried throughout the world by songbirds, the sighing of great whales in the deep, and the stealthy breath of wind through the forests.

Most wooded areas of the planet coped understandably well with the inundation, and where vast regions had been below sea level like the grand outback of Australia; where the great Artesian basin had seeped to the surface, a prodigious inland sea of fresh water stretched from North to South, East to West, where pelicans and cranes, and waterbirds of every description were already flocking in their millions. The driest continent on Earth had been transformed.

The entire planet had been renovated. The East coast of the United States of America had moved hundreds of kilometres West, Indonesia and South-East Asia had diminished by two-thirds of their land mass, and China had retreated to the great Wall. Europe was a series of islands consolidating into a recognisable landmass only at the foot of the alps.

The great cities of the world had all but disappeared, their populations decimated. Huddled masses of humanity sheltered on elevated islands and mountainsides awaiting rescue that would not eventuate. Gaia took pity on this remnant of Humankind, providing them with calm and clement weather, fruiting trees, ripe grain fields and fish. Humanity would continue, but humbled beyond contrition, it would be dependent upon their co-operation with the Earth.

CHAPTER 37
We Can Change.

n presidential palaces remaining above the waters, governments were in disarray. Without armaments or distinguishable borders, leaders felt impotent and incapable of running their countries. Guidance was necessary to keep populations safe from anarchy and the inherent savagery some human beings are capable of.

But, not all was lost. Small clusters of stand-alone solar and wind powered communities, glittered here and there across the land, shining a light in the darkness.

These communities would show the way forward, providing inspiration for leaders now forced to find a cleaner way.

Fortunately, Gaia had been actively guiding research into green and sustainable technologies for years, engineering the passing of the old paradigm. Leaders arose from community groups, green parties, the scientific community, with support from indigenous populations everywhere who remembered how to survive without depleting the planet, and which technology was important, and which was not.

Most influential in facilitating the great change that was afoot was

Gaia herself. Arising from the wood of cabinet rooms of all nations, from lushly appointed American Redwood benches, Baltic pine to Bamboo conference chambers, she rose with dignity and grace to guide leaders towards cooperating with nature for the benefit of all beings. Occasionally, with Sally, Rebecca, Simon, and Susan by her side.

Legislation empowering nature and humanity equally was enacted, slowing, and eventually stopping runaway global warming and pollution of our planet.

Inequities of food supply, water, and building materials, which some nations had in abundance while others languished, were redistributed around the world by fleets of naval vessels powered by new solar and wind technologies.

The navies, redundant now with the cessation of conflict, rather than turning back refugees and homeless boat people, now transported them to safe havens and sanctuaries in hundreds of welcoming countries. Armies became busy building schools, hospitals, and new universities, gestating new ideas.

Soldiers assisted with the construction of dams, housing and feeding the millions left deprived after centuries of war. New farms flourished, orchards and rice paddies sprang up in previously arid and barren lands.

Governments discovered their countries had full employment, developing sustainable technologies. The natural geothermal sources of the planet were harnessed to provide Gigawatts of clean energy, the solar cell, wind turbine and battery industry bloomed as never before, using materials supplied by Gaia, recycling defunct weaponry, and gutting disused power generation equipment.

To the astronauts aboard the space station orbiting the planet, the greening of the earth seemed, 'Like an artist wielding a broad brush and completing a masterpiece.'

Magic was evident everywhere. Tangible and otherwise, from family homes through communities, including governments and the United Nations. A tidal wave of love for our home, the Earth, and each other blossomed as competition for resources faded into history, and co-operation became herstory.

Days still sweltered under a hot sun, droughts occasionally came and went, rivers continued their yearly flooding, but these elemental climate phases were necessary to maintain balance on the surface. Gaia and scientists worked relentlessly to return oil and gas to their home within the crust of the planet, returning the natural lubrication and suspension for the ever-shifting tectonic plates.

The cycle of earthquakes and cyclones continued as before, but people had moved aside, offering these irresistible forces passage. Where populations existed in their path, humans built accordingly, and had insight from closer observation and communication with the world and her weather.

Humanity no longer considered other worlds as lifeboats for civilisation to escape to. Realising two thirds of the planet is beneath the oceans, humanity went about building habitable settlements on the seabed. Gaia assisted with more astonishing, natural technology. The human being came from the sea, eons ago, and so, in our genes lies the secret of extracting oxygen from seawater.

Gaia, guiding human geneticists, manipulated the human genome to accommodate seabed living, farming and even new era sports to take to the Olympic Games.

Within a generation, the Planet had recovered from the brink of lifelessness.

The tall eucalypts shaded the verandah where Simon and Rebecca sat around the now legendary viewing table, observing the event unfolding in the great hall of the United Nations. They gazed past the edges of the aperture-dissolved grain-whorled wood, into a world of brilliantly diverse and colourful national costumes worn by representatives of almost every nation on Earth.

The occasion was assembled to honour Susan Daily, who's phenomenally best-selling book *If a Tree Falls*, was being celebrated as the catalyst for the greatest change the world had ever seen. The Nobel prize for literature had been combined with the Nobel Peace prize for the first time, and given to the farm girl from Fernyvale.

Rebecca called out to the two small boys playing on the balustrade at the end of the deck, 'Eden and Brendan, come and watch Aunty Susan receive the prize.'

As the Mannings gazed down on the proceedings, they could see gathered at the edges of the void, Tom and Rosie, James, Mai-Li and Sally, and Trevor, holding a woman's hand grown from the very wood of the table, her other wooden arm framing the picture and embracing all the families together as one.

THE END

NFB
NEW FOUND
BOOKS

New Found Books Australia Pty Ltd

www.newfoundbooks.au